Praise for the novels of Leslie Glass

"Nerve-wracking suspense and wry humor…a unique narrative filled with sharp dialogue, quirky characters, and shades of oriental mysticism. Glass brings the Big Apple and its inhabitants to life as only a native New Yorker could, and Manhattanites—as well as mystery aficionados—may well find Woo to be one of the most compelling heroines to grace the genre in years."

—*Publishers Weekly*

"Skillful…compelling…Weaving together divergent cultures and their people is one of Ms. Glass's strengths."

—*Dallas Morning News*

"Glass anatomizes relationships with a light touch on the scalpel."

—*New York Times Book Review*

"Glass writes  l…"

—*Booklist*

"If you haven't yet succumbed to the Woo/Glass one-two punch, The Silent Bride should win you over."

—*Chicago Tribune*

"Fast-paced, gritty."

—*Library Journal*

More Praise for the novels of Leslie Glass

"The plot is clever...and the ending is a genuine surprise. Woo is so appealing a heroine Leslie Glass can keep her going for a long time."

—The Newark Star Ledger

"This series is a winner." *—Mystery News*

"Tough, fast, edgy...a layered and rewarding book."

—Contra Costa Times

"Glass does a masterful job of building suspense, and she's a wizard at creating believable, unforgettable characters."

— Romantic Times

"I'll drop what I'm doing to read Leslie Glass anytime."

—Nevada Barr

"If you're a Thomas Harris fan anxiously awaiting the next installment of the 'Hannibal the Cannibal' series and looking for a new thriller to devour, you'll find it in Burning Time."

—Fort Lauderdale Sun-Sentinel

"A masterful storyteller in the field of psychological suspense."

—Abilene Reporter-News

Other Books by Leslie Glass

The April Woo Series

A Clean Kill

A Killing Gift

The Silent Bride

Tracking Time

Stealing Time

Judging Time

Loving Time

Hanging Time

Burning Time

Stand Alone Novels

For Love and Money

Over His Dead Body

To Do No Harm

Modern Love

Getting Away With It

SLEEPER

LESLIE GLASS

the Peppertree Press
Sarasota, Florida

For information regarding permission,
call 941-922-2662 or contact us at our website:
www.peppertreepublishing.com or write to:
the Peppertree Press, LLC.
Attention: Publisher
1269 First Street, Suite 7
Sarasota, Florida 34236

ISBN: 978-1-936051-63-2
Library of Congress Number: 2009943595

Printed in the U.S.A.

Printed March 2010

For Tom and Marie Belcher

ACKNOWLEDGEMENT

As a Trustee of the New York City Police Foundation for many years, I was privileged to attend Citizen's Police Academy, participate in the Commander For A Day program in many New York City precincts, learn about firearms, serve on the Crime Stoppers Committee, interview officers in many units and learn about police procedure, the development and training of officers and issues of the day. The April Woo series was a direct result of my deep interest in law enforcement and the everyday lives of major case detectives, for whom I have the greatest respect. I loved every minute of my NYPD life and still attend emergency services simulated training events whenever I can.

For *Sleeper*, I spent several months in Portland, Oregon, magnificently and generously hosted by Tom and Marie Belcher, who worked tirelessly to teach me about Portland and the wine country, and who helped me in so many areas of research for this book, including the drug trade, real estate, and banking. Marie is a banking and finance sleuth extraordinaire. She should have been a spy. Tom is the best tour guide ever. I shall always be grateful for the wonderful travels and their encouragement and support.

I also want to thank the Portland Police Department for welcoming me, allowing me to interview officers, do ride-alongs, and be a viewer in TOPOFF 4, the simulated dirty bomb event in October 2007 that showed how a full-scale response to a coordinated attack would work. Over 14,000 participants representing federal, state, territorial, and local agencies were involved in the event. Without the invaluable local experiences over a two-year period, I would not have learned to love Portland or the wild splendor of the Pacific Northwest.

While the Financial Crimes Enforcement Network of the U.S. Treasury (FinCEN) and the Portland PD are real agencies, all the events, characters, and places depicted here are purely fiction. None of the characters are based on real people except for two. Marjorie Peter and Mary Lou Loughlin, who live in Sarasota, Florida, made charitable donations to their favorite charity to become characters in *Sleeper*. They had no idea how long it would take to see their names in print. More about Mary Lou and Marjorie can be found on authorleslieglass.com

PROLOGUE

It is a well-known fact that people disappear in Oregon. It happens in a variety of ways. Some folks don't want anyone to find them and take off into the wild for personal reasons. Others vanish by romantic mistake. The wilderness is like a huge magnet, calling out for exploration just as it did to the early settlers a hundred and fifty years ago. Wild places, however, still pose risks, and no amount of knowledge and expert gear can prevent them from dispatching the unwary, one way or another. Tourists, hikers, even workers on the way home make wrong turns and end up in places where search parties have no clue where to look to find them. They might hike up a mountain on a sunny morning and meet snow or fog too dense to fight through by afternoon. Gone.

They go hunting with provisions for a day or two; and instead of finding deer, they find killer weather. Cars pull off onto deserted logging roads for a better view of Mount Hood, or the volcanoes, and tumble down ravines, crashing out of sight in lava fields where no one ever goes. There are thousands of places where a person could get hurt and never be found. But there are also hazardous places to stumble into right in the middle of farmland. Criminally inclined groups with ideas of their own stake out territories right in the middle of civilization, grow weed, train to fight the establishment, or some personal enemy, smuggle guns and moonshine. In some ways it's still the Wild West and there's no way to know where it's safe to wander, and where a fling in the wild can go bad in a heartbeat.

When Matt Brand and Cheli Abrio left Fiesta Vineyard near Dundee at four p.m. on May 23rd, they had no idea a wrong turn was about to kill them. On the contrary, they were happy, giggly, and high. Matt wasn't quite ready for the hour and a half ride back to Portland on his new Honda Shadow, so he didn't take the paved road down the hill to Route 99. Instead, he turned right onto a dirt path that led to more remote vineyards above, even though it was a bumpy ride. Winter rains had turned the gravel and dirt bed into a washboard that was not an ideal surface for the classic cruiser designed for the open road. A series of hairpin switchbacks further challenged the bike.

For Matt, the bumps and skids only added to the fun. Cheli was a brand new love, a skinny girl with a trusting face, long dark hair and a tattoo of a cat on her left wrist. She was hugging him hard, and hanging on, as the Honda slid through tight turns, barely holding the path. Matt was showing off, taking some of the curves too fast, almost spinning out. He didn't care. He was euphoric with this new girl who was so different from others he'd known. She was game for anything, and he was thinking about that as he pushed the groaning bike higher.

Fields with greening hazelnut trees were on the right side of the worsening track. Vineyards just coming to life dotted the hills to the left. Best of all, there were no fancy buildings to attract tourists as he headed for the crest of the hill. What Matt had in mind was seclusion. He wanted to commemorate the perfect weekend on the first really warm day of spring, and so he was looking for a sheltered bit of hidden field to make love to the hottest girl he knew.

Matt and Cheli were graduate students from Eugene on break, staying in an apartment owned by a friend who was in Italy for a month. One Sunday morning, at a popular Portland coffee bar, they happened to pick up an insert from the Oregonian that somebody had left behind on the next table. It featured the wine country just south of the city where two hundred of Oregon's three hundred and fifty vineyards were located around a few farm towns in Yamhill County. A map detailed the area, pinpointed a cluster of vineyards, and highlighted some worthy local restaurants. Matt's plan for his last adventure started over a latte.

The two lovers made it to Dundee by lunch time. They ate sandwiches in a little place that offered over a hundred varieties of wine. Afterward, they hit the road again and visited five wineries, where they sipped flights that were mostly pinots, the best-known grapes in northern Oregon. There were a few sauvignon blancs, a chardonnay here and there, but Matt and Cheli didn't know the difference. The flights came in red, white, and pink. They were nothing more than dashes of bright liquid in huge crystal glasses. Four or five of them at each stop was hardly enough to get their tongues around, much less intoxicate them. But this was their first time, and they were high from the ambiance of wine country alone. They got the lingo down. The vineyards were where the grapes were grown. The wineries were where the wine was made. They stood at the windows on the floor above "the caves" and stared at the huge stainless steel vats where fermenting occurred.

Each winery had its own special allure, its own history and flavor. Together they held out the promise of more pleasure than just the array of lavish Tuscan-style buildings with stone terraces, tasteful gardens, and chilly, high-ceilinged tasting rooms. The visits promoted wine clubs in which members received monthly offerings of expensive bottles and invitations for special tastings of even more expensive bottles and gourmet pairings with expensive food. Matt and Cheli had no money for $75 bottles of wine, but they stood on the terraces and imagined a future in which they would. He was an engineer and had already received job offers.

The road made a sharp turn just below the summit. The land fell away to a vast field filled with little green bushes of some kind. Matt was disappointed but kept going. He was more interested in the vineyard on the steep hill to his left and was hopeful that the road would switch back somewhere up ahead. He didn't see the eye of a camera in the tree in front of him as the road dipped. As he sped along, he almost didn't see the chain across the driveway ahead, either. It was hanging low, almost touching the ground, but not low enough for him to go over without crashing the bike. He thought he was extremely lucky when he stopped in time. He could have been a lot luckier.

In the trailer at the end of the driveway, George Hamid was

not watching the monitors next to his TV. There were four of
them. Two showed the road, one showed the front of the cabin
where the former owners had lived and Ali did his magic with
the meth. The fourth was trained on the side of the barn where
the nurse tank of anhydrous ammonia was anchored and, at the
moment, a feed hose led into the cabin. George didn't see the
bike pass the first camera. He was busy taming his daymare with
his favorite porn video. George was not in survival mode. Instead, he was engrossed in the story about a guy who'd never had
pussy. Like, never.

He loved the story because he knew a lot of guys back home
who were just like this. When he'd known them, they'd been boys
in school. Now they were faceless soldiers who fought and died
virgins. There were probably millions of them who never saw a
girl naked, much less kissed one. Their not knowing was a sad
deprivation he thought about. It could have been him.

George concentrated on watching each scene of the seduction
over and over. He kept flipping back a dozen, two dozen times,
until every frame was fixed just right in his mind. The guy works
in a warehouse where a pretty girl comes on to him. She takes off
her blouse and lets him look at her. That was a frame. She puts his
hands on her breasts. That was a frame. She kisses him. That was
another frame. Unzips his jeans and takes out his dick, bigger than
any George had seen in real life. Frame. Frame. Frame.

He watched it over and over. He watched the girl's mouth,
watched the guy's face. Sometimes he watched just this much
for two or three hours. Other times he focused on the part when
the girl asks for money after the blow job. Or when she screws
him and asks for money. He likes how the poor slob doesn't
know she's a whore. Even after he's lost his job, all his money is
gone, and he's homeless, the asshole never gets it. Addicted to a
whore. George smoked a joint to take the edge off and thought
the video was hilarious.

The last thing he was prepared for was tourists this early in
the season. He'd had a lot of privacy up there all winter when the
vineyard and the farm were dormant. No one had lived at the

end of this road since the sale over a year ago, and he considered the place his now. The vineyard had once been a hazelnut farm, but the trees had been ripped out to make way for grapes a number of years ago, and the potential for development was what attracted his uncle. A producer bought the grapes for a blend he claimed had hazelnut in the nose. George's uncle had liked that and talked about building a winery, a resort with time shares, and maybe condos, too.

But it was the farm that brought George up here week after week. The nurse tank beside the barn was a bonus that had changed his life. He hadn't been into methamphetamine production before then. There were too many federal bans on purchasing the ingredients. Meth could be made with battery acid, paint thinner, drain cleaner, antifreeze, all kinds of nasty stuff that was cooked up with cold and cough medicine. Quality ingredients like ammonia were almost impossible to get. Federal bans had opened the way for Mexican cartels to take over production in labs in northern California and Mexico, and they distributed up I5 all the way to Canada. Mexican meth was brown and pebbly, but meth made the Nazi way, with ammonia, looked like sugar, clean and healthy as could be. It could be used a lot of different ways, and on the street it got top dollar. George was making the very best meth with the legal fertilizer ammonia on his uncle's farm.

He didn't see the motorcycle stop just short of the chain, or the girl dismount and remove her helmet. He didn't see her shake out her long dark hair and signal to the driver. The real movie started playing next to the fake one, and he missed it. The lovers dumped their helmets and embraced in a swath of sunlight. Then they linked arms and walked toward the chain. The moment they stepped between the poles the buzzer went off in the cabin.

George didn't see any of this, but he heard Ali's scream. It was the piercing sound he'd never wanted to hear, and it made his heart stop. Fear of an accident or a spill, or an explosion, were his constant daymares. He didn't have to be asleep to have them. The hose from the tank to the cabin couldn't be more dangerous in so many ways. If it leaked, just breathing the fumes for a second or two would burn a person's lungs out. Whatever it touched, it froze. The pain and damage to skin and flesh was worse than hydrochloric acid. Then, if it expanded too fast inside the tank or hose, or got too hot when cooking, it exploded. A really big bang with a lot of fire. Whenever a lab went up, the toxic chemicals condemned all the buildings in the area.

If this happened on his uncle's property, George would have a lot more to fear than the Mexican cartel or prison time. He handled his anxiety about the production end of the business by staying out of the cabin and parking his SUV far away so he could escape quickly if he had to. He'd failed chemistry a bunch of times when he first got to the U.S., and didn't have a lot of faith in Ali's safeguards. Shit, he was so frightened by that scream he could not catch his breath. It seemed to take an hour before his next heartbeat came. Finally, it kicked in with a thud, and he gasped for air. Whew, at least he was still alive.

Then he checked the monitors and saw the problem. Two kids were walking down the driveway, paying a little visit. And Ali had come out to meet them with his goggles and mask still on and the hose in his gloved hands. He looked like something out of a horror movie. George wanted to rip the asshole's head off for screaming and scaring the shit out of him like that. He burst out of the trailer, swearing. Now he was in survival mode. Christ! Two stupid kids, looked like tweakers. What was wrong with him?

"Hey, what's going on?"

The biker boy looked from Ali to him. Thin kid, curly hair. Something made George think he might be a Jew. That caused his gut to tighten. The fact that he didn't seem afraid of Ali in the goggles and knitted hat pissed him off even more. The kid didn't know enough to be scared.

"What can we do for you, sonny?" Sonny was what George's uncle called him, and he hated the name more than anything. It was the worst kind of put down as far as he was concerned.

"Nothing at all. Sorry to bother you." The kid shrugged and took one step backward, signaling that he was on his way out.

But before the kid moved any further, George could see his eyes take a quick tour of the yard. He followed what he now was sure were Jew eyes as the kid registered the cabin with blacked out windows, the rusted trailer with blacked out windows, the garbage bags everywhere. A meth lab was a dirty place, pretty much unmistakable if you knew what you were looking at. There was also the odor. Despite the fresh spring air and new growth in the field, the cooking chemicals smelled pretty bad. Vomit. Cat piss. Body odor of the worst kind. Yeah, the kid knew where he was. That was not good.

"I think you're looking for something," George said. He prided himself on being cool, being able to talk to people. Right then he wanted to get to the bottom of this. "Somebody tell you to come here?"

"Nope. Followed the road to the end, that's all. We're going."

"Not so fast. Maybe we can help you out."

The girl tossed her hair back. Suddenly he was sure that she was a tweaker. "Who sent you here? What did he say? I won't be mad," George added. He had a bit of an accent, but he didn't think it was coming out now.

"Chill, man. Nobody sent us. Forget it, we're leaving." The kid grabbed the girl's hand and they started walking away. Fast.

George wasn't sure what to do. Let them go, or punch them out? He didn't like the fact that they had come and now they were leaving, both without his permission. Who did they think they were? He felt a rush of paranoia, and didn't want to let them get away. Much as he admired the jihad fighters he supported, he was not much of a fighter himself. He saw this as one his major problems in life. He needed a strong man around him whenever there was trouble. Without one to do it for him, he could not punch anyone out. He had a gun in the trailer, but he didn't think about it soon enough.

And then they were walking away. If they had just stepped over the chain and kept going, it would have been over. But Matt

Brand didn't step over the chain. Something made him sidestep it, maybe to get farther away. He led the girl around the pole on the vineyard side of the driveway. It turned out to be a lethal decision. George had rigged the sides of the driveway with trip wires, and he'd been thinking of getting a bad-tempered dog. The dog would come too late for this pair.

They hit the first trip wire together and both went down hard. Before they knew what happened Ali had that hose as far as it would go from the tank, which was far enough. He didn't say a word. He just started spraying them with the liquid ammonia as if it were a can of Raid on two cockroaches.

George couldn't believe it. That was going too far. It was insane. He leaped up and down, screaming, "Are you fuckin' crazy? Are you crazy?"

Ali didn't stop, and there was nothing George could do. He couldn't even get close to them, couldn't do anything but watch as Ali's victims writhed on the ground, screaming in agony until the ammonia both burned and froze them to death.

This was not the first time George had seen people die. He'd seen his own father shot down in front of him, and car bomb attacks that blew body parts in all directions. But this was the first time he was witness to a kill and felt good about it. Something about the torment the girl suffered before she died turned him on.

1

Spring always brought a surge of visitors to Washington, D.C. In April, it was common for the Cherry Blossom Festival to lure tens of thousands of tourists from around the world to see the pink and white and crimson blooms open and nod and finally blow in clouds across the malls like summer snow. Then the two-week window closed. Crowds thinned, but only briefly. A new window opened when Memorial Day brought three generations of veterans from six wars and a dozen other battle zones where war may not have been official, but U.S. soldiers died nonetheless. Thousands of family members attended every year, and media from all over the world watched and memorialized as commemorations, speeches, photo ops, plaques and medals were handed out, and prayers were offered.

A lot of what happens in Washington is show time all the time. But as the catastrophic events of 2001 had changed the world forever, so, too, the devastating events of 2008 and the election of Barack Obama in November made the spring of 2009 different from any year that preceded it.

For Michael C. Tamlin, Intelligence Specialist in the Financial Crimes Enforcement Network (FinCEN), a department of the U.S. Treasury, the last eight months had been the busiest and most perilous of her career. For six years, her job at the Treasury had been undercover, investigating possible violations of Bush's signature Patriot and Secrecy Acts. An attractive young woman skilled at looking like a cog in some bureaucracy--a nobody of much importance with a name that confused everyone--Michael had traveled through many industries. She'd searched for money trails that led to terrorists and other enemies of the U.S. and for money-laundering members of drug cartels and organized crime that might not directly harm the U.S., but all too often financed war in some remote hot spot. Good at bland and unthreatening, Michael was a valuable agent who could blend in anywhere. She could even sound like a man when she wanted to.

Michael told her family and her boyfriend, and everyone else she met along the way, that she was a bank compliance analyst for the Treasury. And she was secretly pleased when they yawned. As long as people thought she and her job were boring, no one ever suspected what she really did. She explained that an analyst was a special kind of auditor. She never used the words investigation or intelligence in her job description. Even most people in her own office didn't know she often traveled off the radar with back-up from many agencies, and that things could get hairy in the field. Like the military, FBI, DEA, ATF, DHS, and other branches of national law enforcement, FinCEN, too, was a way of life.

Everybody knew the 21st century was getting more and more dangerous. In the first eight years alone, the U.S. had been fighting military wars on many fronts, plus counter-terrorism, illegal immigration, and drugs. They might be different kinds of wars, but they were all wars nonetheless. Not to mention the attempts at reconstruction after hurricanes, tornadoes, floods, and fires, of which there had been many. For FinCEN, private and taxpayer funds went in all directions, and wherever money went it had to be followed.

Then, in the fall of 2008, the economic situation in America got a whole lot worse. Financial markets floundered. Stocks and bonds tumbled and crashed. Treasury rates fell to nearly zero. World markets reacted in kind. In the U.S., markets lost more than 50 percent of their value. The investment giant Bear Sterns was found to have no value and was sold to JP Morgan. Lehman Brothers had no such rescuer and went bankrupt. While the banking and auto industries teetered on the brink, the real estate and credit bubbles burst with bankruptcy resulting everywhere. Spending virtually halted. Hundreds of businesses closed, people lost their jobs and their homes, and the threat of the worst depression in American history loomed. And even then the bleed didn't stop.

Suddenly the richest of the rich needed their assets. And that's when Ponzi schemes of a size and scope that no one could possibly have imagined were revealed. From relatively small-time hustlers to well-known society darlings to huge philanthropic saviors of the arts, some of the biggest crooks in American history started coming out of the closet one by one. Major and Mini Madoffs, they were called. People who had collected their friends' money with no intention of investing it, or ever giving it back, as they had promised.

When the scams like those of Art Nadel and George Theodule, in Florida, and Nicholas Cosmo, in New York, came to light, there were suicides and attempted escapes. Upper-class perpetrators ran away, and undercover agents like Michael Tamlin went after them. As had happened many times before, FBI, Treasury, and local law enforcement agencies worked together. Sometimes uneasily, sometimes well.

For six years, Michael's job had caused her to miss the pleasures of holidays, blooming cherry trees, and many other basic joys of life. She'd missed being among the million revelers on the mall for Obama's inauguration, and had never even caught a glimpse of the new President except on front pages and TV. She was always working and always accepted that as part of the deal. But Tuesday evening, just before Memorial Day weekend 2009, Michael was spinning in the wake of an assignment that had gone badly. Really badly. And she was having trouble coming back.

"Mike! You haven't heard a single word I said." Claude Fleisher, M.D., put down his fork and stared at his girlfriend with the boy's name, who half the time seemed to be on Mars.

She gave him a quick, rueful smile, appealing as she could make it. "No, I heard every word," she protested.

"Then what do you say?" he asked.

She gazed at the half-eaten slab of fish on her plate and tried to remember the question. Okay, so maybe she'd blocked out one or two of the things he'd said. Claude was a pediatric surgeon who tended to go on about complicated procedures on infants and children that were less than fun to hear described in the minutest of details. Too many body parts, of which one or more had to be removed, intestines rearranged, sex organs tampered with. He was hot, gorgeous, and distracted her with his surgeon's hands. But did she always listen?

Oh yes, now she remembered. He'd been telling her that his final year at Hopkins was over and he was returning to Portland. It was a little nugget of information that could bring on catatonia in anyone. If she hadn't been under investigation for the shooting death of a husband and the father of two young children, she might have been able to rally better.

But it was hard to think about her boyfriend's move when her head was back in the Louisiana swamp where Bobbi Lee Rhueland had faked his death in a private plane crash. Michael had been tracking him from the ground. He'd taken off, flown a few miles from the private airport where he kept his plane to a swampy area where he circled around a few times before executing as controlled a crash as he could manage.

His location was no secret since he'd left his car there the day before. Unfortunately for him, he was not the clearest thinker, which is the problem with so many criminals. They think ahead, but not far enough. Bobbi Lee was careful enough to under-fuel his plane. It was light and going slow, so it didn't catch on fire when it came down. He'd planned to be dead, escaped, or if not escaped, then too injured to be blamed for bilking his friends and relatives of $350 million. He had some of the money with him and made it down alive. After that, it didn't go well.

Michael was among the first on the scene. Her goal was to bring Bobbi Lee out of the wreckage alive, if at all possible. When she identified herself as a Treasury Agent, he fired at her and missed. Surprised by the reception, she identified herself again and was reaching for her gun when his second and third shots slammed into her chest and took her down. Only then did she aim and pull the trigger. She'd been wearing her vest. Company rules.

The forensics of the case proved that Michael was definitely down when she fired, but the whole thing was crazy. Killing a Treasury Agent is the same as killing an FBI Agent or a cop; it's not something you're going to walk away from. You might not even make it to the station for an interview. Rhueland's demise was an example of that.

Later, an investigator told Michael that Bobbi Lee must have had a death wish. "He cut his wrists before exiting the plane. Looked like the poor bastard wanted to go one way or another," the investigator said.

It didn't make Michael feel any better. The last thing an agent wants to be is someone's exit strategy. Shooting a guy who'd crashed his plane and slit his wrists was hardly something she could put on her resume, or tell her mom. It felt kind of creepy, and that creepy feeling didn't go away. Michael's name wasn't in the papers, but the investigation would churn on in local jurisdictions for a long time. When a target died, there were a lot of questions and a lot of paperwork, and probably something on her record.

Creepy was something she felt a lot. There might be over 35,000 law enforcement agencies around the country, from the two-man sheriff's office in one-horse towns to the 40,000-person armies of a city like New York, but most people didn't know that the Treasury had secret ops. And they never would. There was a lot about her life that no one could ever know.

She focused. Okay. Sexy boyfriend, whom she might even love, was about to move on. Real life could break your heart. If you happened to have one left. Michael stopped thinking about Bobbi Lee long enough to raise her glass. Claude had ordered champagne for the occasion. It always gave her a headache, but what the hell?

"I say congratulations!" Claude's leaving hurt more than she would admit, and she didn't care much for the West Coast. The Portland to which he was returning was in Oregon, not Maine. Which might have made it a different story altogether. At least she was familiar with Maine.

"Thank you. And I want you to come with me," he said with a smile.

"Ha ha." A genuine laugh slipped out of Michael's mouth and morphed into a nervous giggle. Hope? Thrill? Disbelief?

"No, I mean it," he said earnestly.

"Oh, Claude, I don't know if I could leave Washington.

There's so much going on right now." More than anyone knew.

"Oh, you're going to love it there." Claude went on as if she hadn't spoken. "No pretensions. Better food than here." He waved his hand in sudden contempt at the expensive restaurant where he'd insisted they go.

The gesture reminded Michael how hard it was to get a reservation, even now, in the middle of a recession. She thought for a second and frowned at the possibility that he had known about his appointment for some time, and hadn't bothered to tell her. And now he was disparaging the food even though he'd cleaned his plate.

"But we had a great dinner here."

She was confused. Did he really think food was a good reason to leave a government job from which it was almost impossible to get fired--unless you happened to kill somebody on purpose, which she hadn't. A new question began to spin in her head like clothes in a dryer. Could she possibly be having an inappropriate response to a marriage proposal? Her first ever?

"Uh oh, green eyes. What's the matter?" Claude took a teasing tone.

"You could have given me a hint. When did you apply for the job?" Michael asked slowly.

"Oh, years ago. I always planned to go home when there was an opening at Honeckky Children's Hospital. It's one of the best in the country. You knew that. And you're going to love my family." He rolled his blue eyes up at the potential rapture of that union.

Claude's brother was a cop. His sister was in the FBI. His mother grew mushrooms or something, and they all drank a lot of wine and climbed mountains. Could be nice, Michael thought. She had something in common with the siblings but could never tell them what she did. There you go. She was feeling better. Claude poured some more champagne and refilled his own glass.

"I love you. I know you love me. So let's go out West and get married." He picked up her hand and kissed her fingertips one by one, brushing each with the tip of his tongue. He'd done this before often, but this time it shot the hot promise of a lifetime of great sex right through her. Okay, there was the correct enthusiasm.

She waited for a moment to see if the excitement would last. It did. She loved the blue shirt he was wearing, the tweedy jacket that didn't quite match, the way he was holding the glass of champagne, the look in his eye that said she was The One. Yes! Claude was what she'd been yearning for. Claude was her One, too. Michael's breath caught as she stared at him in surprise. He was actually asking her to marry him. And she actually wanted to.

"I know, I know. It's kind of sudden, but I'm certain this is the right thing for both of us." He hoisted his paper-thin flute a little higher to toast their rosy future.

On cue her eyes misted at her good luck. Something good was finally happening to her. To the real Michael, not the secret Michael. It was beyond, beyond good luck. Claude was a rugged-looking guy with hands that seemed too big to operate on the brains and hearts and tiny colons of preemies. Michael had always been easily turned on by his hands, reassured by the skill they possessed. Now one of them reached into his jacket pocket and pulled out a ring. He'd even thought of a ring. Her heart swelled. She leaned forward to see it. I have to call my mother, she thought.

He held out the ring. "This was my mother's. It was her mother's, an antique."

"Oh, Claude," she said, thrilled that so many mothers were in the moment.

Michael took the ring with reverence. Nothing in the world could have made her happier than having his mother's ring. It was thin rose gold with a rectangular red stone surrounded by tiny seed pearls.

"That's a ruby," Claude said excitedly. "It's a family heirloom. Do you love it?"

"Yes, it's gorgeous." Michael had worked more than one case involving precious stones and antique dealers, diamond brokers, etc. She didn't have to pull out a loop to know that this here heirloom ruby was a piece of glass. But she'd never tell him in a million trillion years. She'd cherish it forever, like his mother and grandmother had. It was the man who was important. She loved the man. Loved his smell, his face, the whole passion thing they had going.

So she decided there and then not to let her rating of his proposal ruin the moment. He was a great guy, but she'd give him about a five on the proposal. That springing Portland on her out of the blue? Not sensitive. Then the not getting down on bended knee? Not traditional. And finally, if he was going to give her a fake, why not give her a splendid fake--a big gorgeous CZ that would fool anyone? Who could blame her if she liked the sparkle of diamonds? She didn't care if they were real or not. Then she really had to stop herself.

What's wrong with me, she thought. I love this guy. He gave me his mother's ring. He doesn't know it's a fake. We're going to get married. Forget about the diamond. Pull up your fucking socks and cry a little.

But crying for joy wasn't that easy for someone who came from New England, where sentiment is as scarce as sand on rocky beaches. Also, she was an intelligence expert whose job was to question everything. She smiled a secret smile instead. She'd scored a real hunk with a sexy French name, a surgeon whose schedule was even more erratic than hers. Michael was small and pretty, had a slender build and watchful hazel eyes that turned green when danger flags went up. They were an un-suspecting hazel now.

"Try it on." He lifted his chin at the ring she held between thumb and index finger.

She slid it on--too big even for her thumb.

"A little surgical tape will fix it for now," Claude said happily. "Looks great on you. What do you say?"

"I hate to leave my job," she murmured. There was so much to do. The country was threatened on many fronts. Everybody was nervous about the economy, about pending fraud cases, vola-tility and instability in so many industries. Violence and war ev-erywhere. Getting married was fine, but it wasn't a good time to bail out and move West.

Claude frowned at her hesitation. "What about all that scrutiny you hate? Your bank accounts and emails are monitored. Every time you go on vacation, they have to know about every contact you've made. Who you talked to--"

"I know. But I have great benefits and health insurance. And I've made a name for myself." She said it slowly, just working the issue through in her mind. The job was her life; she wasn't practiced at being anything else.

Claude made a face. "So what? You can make a different name for yourself." His hand flipped up impatiently, brushing her career away as if it were a bothersome fly.

The gesture felt like a slap. For some reason it reminded Michael of all the women through the ages who'd followed their men to the ends of the world and died there. "You don't understand," she said softly. "It's important work." And Federal; it operated from Washington, and wasn't something you could relocate.

"What I do is more important. I save lives. I'm moving in two months. I want you to be there with me." Claude took her hand again and gave her that deep, earnest stare that always made him seem so incredibly noble. He saved precious babies' lives every day; how many people could do that? His look and touch ignited her.

"Let's go home," she said.

2

Michael didn't say a word on the way home in the car. From time to time she glanced at Claude's manly jaw, his concentration on the road, and she allowed herself to adjust. At thirty-three, she would join the special tribe of women who leave everything they know for love because that has been the way of the world since the beginning of time. Some women make that journey, and Michael was going to be one of them. She focused not on the life she would lose, but what she would gain: a permanent lover, a home, safety from the storms of war. She turned her engagement ring with the red stone around and around on her finger. It was her turn for happiness, and she needed to keep that thought.

"This is great," Claude said several times. "This is the best day of my life." And he patted her hand.

It was hardly poetic, hardly deep and thoughtful, but Michael went for it. At last he parked the car, and they were home--her home, anyway. She opened the door of her apartment, stepped out of her heels, and lost four inches. Claude made a happy stallion noise and picked her up without turning the light on. She wrapped her legs around him as he spun her around, singing, "We're going to the chapel, and we're going to get married."

Claude was a strong man with a nice voice, and Michael trusted him. Her pencil suit skirt was hiked up to her waist. She giggled as he squeezed her bottom. Her arms circled his neck, and they kissed. He was a good kisser, but it wasn't a make-out night. He peeled down her pantyhose as he quick-stepped to the bedroom. He didn't take the time to turn the light on there, either.

"Oh, baby," he groaned. "You're my honey."

"Uh huh," was all she could get out in the frenzy of shedding clothes and tossing many colorful pillows to the floor.

Then they were at each other like never before, using the bed like a jungle gym and ending up on the floor. Really hot and heavy in every position they'd ever tried, and even a few new ones, before coming at the same time with great heaving convulsions. If this was commitment, Michael was for it. After a brief respite, they made love again, slower this time. In the big armchair. It turned out to be a very good night indeed. And then it faded to black in the usual way.

By midnight Claude was gone, on his way back to his home near the hospital where he worked in Baltimore. And Michael had too many thoughts in her head to sleep. She wondered if all women did asset assessments when they decided to marry and change their lives forever. The champagne had given her the predictable headache, and through the dull haze of alcohol-induced misery she did the personal profit and loss statement that would allow her to move on.

Michael had arranged her life just so. She had her own carefully decorated apartment on Columbia Road in D.C.; credit cards that she meticulously paid every month; a brother out West who hated her, but a few really good friends, too. She had her best friend, Marjorie, who was also at FinCEN, and a chilly mother with whom she carefully limited contact. At the top of the list she had Claude, her best friend and lover of nearly four years.

Michael knew the pluses put her way ahead of most people. But sometimes she saw a different picture. She was thirty-three and never been married. A number of times she'd been deeply hurt by family members she'd trusted and loved. She had a boyfriend whose job was to care for other people's children and until now hadn't committed much to her. They still lived in different apartments an hour's drive apart, and met only when Claude's busy schedule allowed. Her life always seemed simple in comparison to his, and that was saying something. She had no idea what he was up to during the many nights they were not together, but Claude's secrecy was not imposed by government regulation like hers, and for that reason it bothered her. It was impossible to reach him, and he wasn't a talker or a sharer when she did. For an undercover agent that was normal. For a regular person, it struck an odd note.

Michael had always controlled her concerns about his reserve. Her motto was to keep assembling the facts of each situation (work or personal life) until clarity emerged. What was truth? What was reality? Tonight Claude had come clear, and so had her defining moment. She would finally take her place as a regular person with a regular civilian job. No more accessorizing with Kevlar. No more guns in her pocket, no more investigating bad guys, no more SWAT teams as backup. No more falsehoods or secrets. And never again would she be somebody's fatal exit strategy.

Michael came to her conclusion sitting at her computer at 1 a.m. Her hand twitched. It touched the wireless mouse. Her computer came to life, reminding her of the many job offers she'd received from headhunters over the years, the most recent one in particular. A few months ago she'd been contacted by a search firm for a bank in Portland. The position of chief compliance officer had no interest for her then, but now she sent the woman an email asking if it was still open.

3

"Sonny, come over here." Frank Hamid called his nephew away from the staff dinner in the back of the restaurant. Four o'clock Tuesday on the dot, he stood midway in the room, wiggling his finger in front of everyone in a familiar way that said, "You are special. You are mine. Jump."

George set his face to obedience and carefully put his napkin down. He followed his uncle to the usual front table, where Hamid waved his hand for service even though the staff was eating. One of the Columbians, who had his mouth full, ran to pour him a scotch. Then the meal went on as before, plates being passed, people chewing, swallowing, but it was quiet back there now. Best moment of the day was ruined again.

Hamid sipped and considered his words. He was forty-five, five years younger than Rhea, George's mother, and George could tell by the way his lips curled around the glass that he was angry.

"Sonny, do you know why I'm upset?" he said.

George shook his head. "No, Uncle. I have done nothing wrong."

He sounded courteous when he said this, but his uncle made a face as if he'd been disrespected, insulted by another bold-faced lie.

"What do I do with a kid like you?" He reached into his pocket for a cigar, changed his mind. He might be furious, but he wouldn't pollute his own place.

"I'm a good man," Hamid said, slowly gearing up. "I own four restaurants, and that's only one of my interests. I work so hard I don't have time to marry. I work for your grandmother, and your mother and your sister. I give you every opportunity."

"Yes, Uncle. We are very grateful."

Hamid waved his hand as if that were nothing. "We're Hamids. That's what we do."

But he had yet to forgive his sister for leaving Portland to marry a Lebanese and raise a son and daughter over there for fifteen years until the jerk got shot dead on the street seven years ago, leaving them destitute. He was still furious that he had to bring them back and take care of them, getting nothing but trouble in return.

"I've raised you like my own son. I gave you my name. Now you have to act like a Hamid." He lifted his palm. End of story. Business was the core of the Hamid family. It was the genetic driving force passed down through generations of traders when the land was part of the Ottoman Empire, when it was Syria, and when it was Lebanon. Business, not politics, was what mattered. The gesture said it all.

Hamid saw the look on his nephew's face. He wasn't a Hamid. "You have no ambition," he said softly.

"I do have ambition, Uncle," George replied.

"For what? Sitting in bars?"

George smiled. "I do more than sitting in bars."

"I already had my first restaurant by the time I was your age. And you're skipping work. I never know where you are. How long do you expect me to put up with this?" Hamid tapped his glass for a refill. He was really mad this time.

It was time to say something. George shifted in his chair. "Oh, you're talking about Sunday. Yeah, I remember. Dal needed the work. He asked me for the shift."

"No, Sonny. You didn't turn up."

"I was going to. I had a flat tire, up in the hills." George put on his easy smile. He had to clean up a situation. Not his fault. He handled it. Ali had made a promise, no more loose cannon. George also made a gesture. It said, chill.

"There's a spare in the car. I never missed work when I was your age," Hamid said.

"I went to check on the lodge. I do it every few weeks, just like you asked me," George said. Deep chill.

"That's too often," he said. "Once every six months is enough unless we have people there. And I thought you went to the farm."

"No, I wasn't at the farm Sunday, Uncle," George said firmly.

"I know where I was."

"You said you were going to the farm."

"Why are you bugging me? I told you I went to the lodge."

"That's a long way to go on a Sunday morning. I never know where you are. You're not doing those drugs again, are you?" Hamid's look went hard, and silently begged him to say no. A grown man begging a kid. Hamid didn't like having to do that. His anger was clear in his face.

"No, I haven't had anything to do with that in a long time. Couple of years now," George said easily. As far as he was concerned, smoking his own home-grown marijuana was not illegal, and definitely not doing drugs. His uncle relaxed a little when he heard the words.

"Okay. I believe you. Listen to me, Sonny. You have everything. Good looks. You're smart. You could do anything you wanted--" The lecture began.

"I'm doing all right," George said. He didn't want to hear any more.

"No. A good-looking boy. You could do better. You could have a business. A man needs a business of his own."

George smiled. If only his uncle knew. He had a business, a good business.

"What's that smirk? I didn't drop out of college. When I was your age, I was running my own restaurant. Not working as a busboy in my dad's."

"I know the story."

"You have no ambition. Isn't there anything you want to do? How about the jet center? I could find something for you there."

George shrugged. "What's wrong with being a busboy?" He gave a friendly nod to the staff in the back, all of them pretending not to listen. Several were very good clients. He did not want to work at the jet port. They weren't his people.

"Look, I've been thinking about this. I want to spend some time with you this summer. We'll play golf, talk. I think we can talk through this. You're like a son to me, okay? I want you to go back to college. Meet a nice girl. Maybe that will light a fire. With an education you could take over."

"Thank you, Uncle," George said. He knew his uncle was blowing more smoke his way.

Hamid finished his drink, looked at his watch. "By the way, where did you get that motorcycle?" he said casually.

"What?" George was startled by the question.

"Did you get your poor mother to buy that for you? She doesn't have that kind of money."

"No, a friend gave it to me," George said quickly.

"What kind of friend gives you gift like that?" He shook his head, not wanting to hear the answer. "I gave you a car. What's wrong with the Toyota?"

"Nothing, Uncle." Except that it was six years old, a piece of crap castoff that not even the manager of the worst restaurant would drive anymore. Truth was, George could buy any car he wanted. But he had to keep a low profile, didn't want to attract attention from the Mexican suppliers. He didn't want the scrutiny from Hamid's people, either.

Hamid touched his hand. "Listen, Sonny. I'll buy you a new car if you take on more responsibility, drop some of those deadbeat friends you hang out with, and show me that you're growing up. What do you say?" Hamid looked hopeful, like a guy who was offering a deal that shouldn't be refused.

But George didn't need a deal. And he didn't like being called Sonny. He wasn't some loser from The Godfather. And his friends weren't deadbeats; they were separatists. There was a difference. They had the kind of ideals that Hamid didn't know a thing about.

"Yeah, sounds great," he said cheerfully. "But I don't need a new car. I'm good, really."

Hamid's teeth came together with a click. He was trying to be a good guy, a role model, a good dad even. He dismissed the boy, and made his own plan. When the weather warmed up, he'd take the kid out to the club, let him mix with better people. George would drop the bums and come around.

4

The headhunter called Michael early the next morning. Her name was Greta Shaeffer, and she had a smoker's gravelly voice.

"I have great news," she said excitedly. "Pacific GreenBank is at the end of their search, but the president has been waffling between the two remaining choices. I know he'd be impressed by your credentials." She barely drew breath before plunging on. "Can I send him your resume ten minutes ago?"

"What's the rush?" Michael asked.

"We have only a tiny window, Michael. They're close to making an offer. I'd like to put you in the mix. What made you change your mind about Portland and banking, anyway?"

"I'm relocating there. I got engaged. Kind of sudden," Michael told her.

A hearty guffaw that ended in a cough blasted through the line. "Well, good deal! This is going to light a fire. I know Caulahan, the president, well, and he's been holding out for someone like you. Runs a straight-up organization and wants to keep it that way."

"Straight up is my middle name."

"It's a perfect fit, Michael. Let me get back to you."

Greta called back before noon. "Okay, got your interview for tomorrow. As luck would have it, the company plane is at National right now. We can fly you out this evening. You'll have to return commercial Friday morning, that okay with you?"

Michael said she preferred it, and marched into her boss's office. She told Max she was marrying Claude and interviewing for a job in Portland tomorrow. She had to do it quick, like ripping a Band Aid off. And the look on his pudgy face said it all.

"Let's see the ring. It better be good," he growled.

Max was not the most polished fellow in the world. He wasn't a health nut or bodybuilder or a spiffy dresser. He was kind of soft in the middle, wore unfashionable glasses, and was in possession of an auditor's mentality. But he was no dummy. His jaw dropped at the engagement ring. "This is a joke. You're kidding," he said. "Right?"

"Actually not. It was his mother's."

"Oh, I'm sorry." Max put a freckled hand over his mouth. "What is this, you trying to show your human side?"

Michael shook her head. He would say that.

Max started flipping the end of his tie up and down. "All right. Is it about Rhueland?" he asked finally.

"No," Michael said. "Claude and I have been together four years. He's moving to Portland. He comes from there."

"Being together four years? That's a reason to marry some guy who gives you a fake ring?"

"I told you. It was his mother's." What did Max know? He lived with a cat.

"Anything we can do to change your mind?" he asked.

"No."

"All right, then. I'm delighted you're going to Portland. Couldn't have chosen a better town for you myself." Max got up to give her a hug. "Live and be well."

"Thanks for the kind words." Michael was hurt. What kind of kiss off was that?

Five hours later Michael was the lone passenger on a large, expensively fitted-out private aircraft with no logo on the side and a red stripe on the tail. The door closed and the jet taxied to the runway, where it sat with dozens of others, stalled by the worst weather in months. Thunder boomed, and the sky cracked open. Sheets of rain slammed the queue of planes patiently waiting for a break. Eventually, it took off in pelting rain, bumped its way up through the clouds to clear sky, and started to race the setting sun across the country.

"Hi, it's going to be kind of bumpy for a while. Would you like to try the chairman's favorite?" Pat, the blond flight attendant, held out a bottle of wine. "We brought it on board for him when he came out yesterday."

"Thanks, I didn't know they made wine in Oregon."

Pat smiled. "It's Oragun."

"Excuse me?"

"You said Ore-gone. Like Gone With the Wind. They'll laugh if you say it like that. And yes, some people say Oregon pinot grapes are the best in the world." She expertly opened the bottle, poured, and presented the glass.

Michael peered at the deep garnet splash in her glass and swirled it around. She preferred the clear liquids: gin, vodka, sake, tequila, but drank some to be polite.

Pat waited patiently for her reaction, holding the bottle carefully with the label showing as if it actually mattered what Michael thought of it.

"Very nice," she said. After all the corporate abuses of taxpayer dollars on perks and compensation for executives, she couldn't help wondering about the fancy jet with no logo and the chairman's wine. "What about the plane, is it owned by the bank?" she asked.

"Not anymore. They sold out to a leasing company a few years ago. It was good timing. Dozens of these aircraft are on the market now. Nobody's buying. The bank still uses it occasionally. Anything else I can get you?"

"No thanks, this is great." Michael settled in. At 3 a.m. her time, the jet landed at PDX. It was foggy with a light rain falling. Michael thanked Pat and the two pilots with crew cuts, picked up the bag with her change of clothes, and deplaned onto the tarmac. A limo was waiting to take her to the Heathman Hotel and a lavish suite, where a welcoming note and a basket of fruit were set out for her.

5

"Miss Tamlin. Good of you to join me on such short notice."
Ashland Upjohn, the silver-haired senior vice president watched
Michael cross the hotel dining room at just after 8 a.m. on Thursday morning, then rose to greet her.

"It's a pleasure." Michael smiled. She had received his request
for a casual breakfast only three minutes earlier. Luckily, it was
eleven her time, and she was already dressed.

Her hair was down, her makeup was minimal, and the round
glasses she often used to look prim and colorless were in her
purse. She was wearing a navy suit with a short jacket, could have
fit in anywhere.

Ashland was tall and thin, a stiff Old World type. He gave
her a nod to sit just as a waiter appeared to hold her chair.

"Well, then. Tell me about yourself. I'd like to get to know
you from a personal perspective."

The slick general counsel had a single slice of smoked salmon
on dark bread and watched Michael eat scrambled eggs and toast.
Michael understood that Ashland didn't want to know anything
personal about her at all. He was just testing to see if she could be
in the room with important people, knew which forks and knives
to use and could chew with her mouth closed. Yes, yes, and yes.

Breakfast finished without a single substantive issue discussed, and they walked across the street to the bank building,
where Ashland's office suite was extremely posh.

He sat at his desk, put on reading glasses and studied Michael's
resume. Then he looked away as if it were of no consequence.

"Let me tell you about us. Pac GreenBank has some 400
branch locations with assets north of $40 billion. The commercial banking group specializes in real estate, construction, and
health care institutions, such as OHSU. The Portland branch
operation is heavily involved in home, commercial and construction lending, as well as having equipment leasing, agricultural

and commercial lending teams."

Michael nodded. OHSU was Oregon Health & Science University, up on "Pill Hill," as it was known to the locals.

"If hired, you would report directly to me. Your total staff count is 22, I believe. They oversee all of the compliance and regulatory functions for the entire organization."

He tapped his fingers. "Your challenge here will be trust. We lost your predecessor to a tragic hunting accident two months back. Allan Farber was universally admired by both peers and superiors. I suspect the compliance organization is going to be somewhat wary of his replacement at first. And of course the TARP program put us under a different microscope. We need to be able to respond. I suspect you have the skills for that component, anyway." He looked at the resume and paused to fiddle with his pen.

"The successful candidate here would be wise to take it easy until he or she gains the trust of the staff," he added after a moment.

Michael wasn't aware of it, but her eyes turned green. TARP was Troubled Asset Relief Program, or bailout money. He didn't ask her anything about herself, just told her what was required.

Later, she and Ashland were on their way to a lunch meeting with the president of the bank, Clifton Caulahan. Ashland had made the introduction and clearly expected to join them for lunch, but Caulahan turned him away.

"Ah, here we are. See you in an hour, Ash."

Caulahan smiled at Michael as Ashland retreated stiffly. "I was Ashland's predecessor as general counsel, you know. I hired him for the job. When I retire, he'll probably be sitting in my chair."

Caulahan waved her into a chair in the private dining room. "I've known Greta for twenty years. She has the highest regard for you."

"That's nice to hear," Michael murmured as she was served a chopped salad and grilled fish with a gray item beside it that she couldn't identify. She studied it for a moment, wondering if it was a caterpillar, a slug, or just decoration that she shouldn't try to eat. She was jolted back to the conversation.

"That's why I wanted to meet you myself in private."

"Thank you, sir," Michael said. "That's very flattering."

"You may well get an excellent job offer in a few days. And I want you to think about how important this is to me personally. I don't have to tell you that all banks have been under scrutiny with the debacle of toxic mortgages," he said, and took a moment to sip his water.

"I'm not going to tell you we haven't had our share, but we feel we have the situation under control."

"Mr. Upjohn told me as much," Michael murmured.

"Well, I'm sure he would. A general counsel is paid to make those assurances. That's his job. I don't want to just hear assurances." He gave her a small smile.

"The board and I want to make sure there isn't anything else we haven't discovered. I will be frank with you. We need someone of your background to head our compliance area, first to audit our accounts to make sure all is well, and then to set up systems to detect any potential future problems. This is the highest priority for me. If you take this position, I will expect you to keep us out of trouble. You have only one loyalty, and that is to the highest level of integrity."

"I understand," Michael said solemnly. She got it. He wanted an independent to investigate his own bank. Good for him.

"By the way, it's a mushroom." Caulahan indicated the thing on her plate. "We Oregonians are very proud of the exotic varieties of mushrooms we have. They grow in our forests, you know. Very primeval. In the summer our tomatoes are legendary, too. Have you tasted our heirlooms? No, well, all of our organic vegetables are extraordinary. We're not the backwater you might think."

"Really," Michael said with some relief. Mushroom. Interesting.

In a half an hour Caulahan checked his watch, thanked Michael for coming such a long way on such short notice, and told her she was due down in HR.

"I look forward to having you on board," he said.

6

Michael hurried to the ladies room to check her cell phone. There were two voicemails and a text message from Claude. She listened to the voicemails, standing up at the sink. Nice marble, she thought. This was hallowed executive private banking territory. It was getting interesting; intrigue was exactly what she liked. She smiled at herself in the mirror.

Claude's message said it was just like her to get engaged and disappear. "Call when you can."

She left a message telling him she was in Portland on an interview. Two other messages were from Marjorie. Both followed the same script.

"Hey, where the hell are you, babe? Max told me you caught a fish? What the hell does that mean? Are you leaving us? Call, I'm freaking out here," were Marjorie's last words both times.

Michael turned off her phone, reapplied her lip gloss, ran a comb through her hair, and went to meet Curtis Smith, the head of Human Resources, a preppy-looking guy about her age. For the next several hours he took her on an extended tour, showed her the offices and explained the long-term health care insurance; 401K savings program with the company matching up to 5 percent; and eligibility for bonuses.

"Do you not have a freeze on bonuses?" she asked.

"Ah, yes. Sorry." He gave her a regretful smile.

"It's all right. I'm not used to them," she said.

"Well good. As part of your orientation, you will also have the benefit of a counselor to help you transition into the corporation, both personally and professionally. You can think of him as a guide or a corporate life coach."

"Sounds interesting," she said, although it didn't really appeal.

Curtis told her she was on the short list and would have a letter or notification shortly. Traveling first class the next morn-

ing, Michael boarded a 7:45 a.m. commercial flight for Washington. She landed at three thirty in the afternoon. She didn't start
making calls until she got home. She'd been off the radar for just
over forty-eight hours and hadn't killed or threatened anyone. It
made a nice change.

7

Monday morning, after a weekend of sunny skies and warm days so soothing and deep they popped the first roses open and confirmed D.C. as a southern locale, Michael's best friend, Marjorie Peter (at work people called them M&M), was even more agitated about Michael's engagement and trip out West than she had been when she first heard about it. Marjorie demanded a meeting outside the office, so the two women walked across the street for paninis in a local restaurant. Michael sat in the window with the sun warming her face and felt the glow of real happiness all the way through her. She was going to be a sunny person from now on. Marjorie launched her attack before the sandwiches arrived.

"Everything about this Oregon thing is so wrong!" she said, raking her short strawberry blond hair that happened to be the exact color as Doris Day's. "I'm not kidding, Mike. This is not on the up and up." She looked really unhappy.

"It's Oragun," Michael said quickly.

"Isn't that what I said?" Marjorie gave her a sharp look. She was a very pretty girl, on a bigger scale than Michael. She had that drop-dead hair, a pearly complexion, not a bad figure for someone who didn't exactly count calories, and no vanity at all. She wore glasses with big red frames, had turned thirty-six on her last birthday, and wasn't going to mind hitting forty. She also wasn't looking for Mr. Right. Her heart had been broken several years back, and she didn't have a high enough opinion of men to try again.

"No, you said Oregone," Michael told her. "That's not the way they say it."

"So what? I got a call while you were on the plane. You understand? You gave me as a reference, right?"

Michael nodded. Of course.

"And you didn't alert me. That's not like you. I could scuttle this."

"You're my friend. You won't." Michael picked up her sand-

wich. Nice melted cheese oozing out. No funny looking mushrooms on the plate.

"Hello, Michael Tamlin, anybody home?"

Michael smiled. "I'm here."

"You didn't authorize that jackass to call me, did you?" Marjorie
gave her another one of her looks, but Michael didn't care.

"I didn't think they'd jump so fast," she finally admitted because Marjorie was right. It was all a little unusual. The bank was
making a real run at her, but it felt nice to be wanted. Max didn't
seem to give a shit. It rankled.

"Don't you think there was something odd about this guy
calling me while you were still traveling?"

"Well, they're in a hurry to fill the position." Michael de-
fended Curtis Smith. It was true he shouldn't have called the
reference without her permission, but she'd already told Max she
was interviewing.

"Max says you're just doing this just to show you're human. I
don't get it." She looked stricken.

"Max told me he thought it was a good thing. He wants me
to go."

"That's not true."

"He said Portland was a perfect choice."

"No! Really? Why would he say that?"

Michael could see the grief in her eyes. They did a lot of
things together--went to the movies, played tennis on weekends
when it was warm, went shopping. They played board games, but
neither would have admitted it to anybody else at the agency for
the world. They didn't want to be known as nerds. They cooked
together and were closer than many sisters.

"Don't be mad," Michael said slowly. People got married. It
wasn't the end of the world. They were friends. It wasn't like a
break-up or a divorce.

"It's kind of like having my best friend die," Marjorie
muttered.

"Come on," Michael murmured. "Don't make me cry."

"I know you're not supposed to tell people you don't approve of their mates, but it's true I don't like your Claude. A lot of ne-glect, among other things, going on there," she said, and added, "I think it's weird."

Michael erupted. "You think he neglects me? Huh. He's a surgeon. Emergencies don't always happen between nine and five on weekdays."

Why did Marjorie have to go and do that? Michael wasn't go-ing to be able to forget it. Weird? She thought he was weird? Well, they all were weird. Max, Marjorie, Michael. Shit, all M words.

"He's controlling and manipulative. And that ring! Who's he kidding? That's not an engagement ring."

Ow. Michael flushed. The ring again.

Marjorie went on without noticing. "I don't have a good feel-ing about this bank offer, either. For what it's worth, I've told you. Now you may never speak to me again." Marjorie reached for the check. "Here, I'll take this. It may be the last one."

The next day Pacific GreenBank sent a letter offering Michael $150,000 a year, plus a $6,000 moving allowance, and a $50,000 bonus once the deal was struck. Michael called immediately to remind Curtis that there was a freeze on all forms of bonus. There was a long, embarrassed silence on the other end of the line be-fore Curtis admitted his mistake and said he would send a new contract right away. It was also weird that Max was the first one to congratulate her. Kind of made her wonder.

8

Claude was also ecstatic at the news. "You pulled off quite a surprise," he said when Michael landed a job in less than a week. "And I have a surprise for you, too. We're going to live on Council Crest, in a house with a white picket fence, three bedrooms, and a hot-tub on the deck." His smile broadened. "Am I not a great guy?"

It took the wind right out of her sails. "When did you find a house?" she asked slowly.

"Oh, I've had my eye on this place for several years. It's been on the market, but the owner hasn't been able to sell it at his price. We'll rent it for a year or so and see if we want to buy. It's a cape house, the kind you grew up in. You're going to love it."

Michael's eyes were green. Was this controlling, or was she just naturally suspicious?

"You don't trust anybody, do you?"

"If you'd had some of my experiences..." she murmured.

"When we're married, you'll have to tell me," he said, pouring wine to celebrate.

"When are we getting married?" she asked. It was the only thing her mother wanted to know.

Claude winked, and that was the end of the discussion. All right, she thought. Keep your eye on the ball.

Michael's last days in D.C. passed very quickly. Marjorie had an engagement party for her, and everybody in the department came. She got a lot of useful gifts, like edible thongs and nipple clamps, as well as greeting cards with sex advice they weren't going to need. A ball and chain. Furry handcuffs. The girls pitched in and got her some nice stuff, too, "for her trousseau." And they all drank a lot. Max seemed unusually cheerful. It hurt.

The night before she left, Michael and Marjorie sat on the floor in her empty living room and ate pizza for the last time.

"I'm going to miss you," Marjorie said, fussing with her extra cheese so she wouldn't cry.

"I'm going to miss you, too," Michael admitted, feeling a little teary herself.

"If you don't like it, you'll come home, won't you?"

Michael looked around at the apartment she'd called home for six years. The living room had a bay window with a southern exposure that gave her a lot of sun. She'd kept purple and pink African violets in a window box there, and they bloomed year around. She made "yes," absolutely she'd come back, motions with her mouth, but wondered why Max had been so eager to let her go.

"Portland," he'd said. "I couldn't have chosen a better town for you myself." It still stung.

"And call me when you have a wedding date. I want to save the day," Marjorie was saying.

Michael smiled. "Me, too."

9

A girl was standing outside when George made his weekly drop at Rio, a club in the west hills. Her skirt was really short and her top was even skimpier. It had rained and the air was cold, but she didn't have a jacket. He was tempted even though she had skinny arms and legs, and the tats gave her away.

"Want to buy me a drink?" she said.

George preferred the better-fed college girls, who never seemed to prefer him. So, he was used paying for it. His customer, Kel, was watching him with a familiar look of contempt that said skags were all the pussy George could get. Made him want to kill someone.

"Maybe later," George said and made the drop. He walked away with over eight grand, and still somehow felt like a loser.

Easy money. That was how it started for George. He wanted to fit in. His Uncle Frank had five cars and traveled on his own jets. He went to Vegas and Miami, South America and the Far East, and had a thousand friends to party with. But the old man never took his nephew on the trips or gave him a good time.

His uncle said a good role model made a kid go to college, get a degree, learn to play golf. Go without cash in his pocket to learn the value of a dollar. His uncle said George couldn't learn the businesses or angle for the deals until he could be in the rooms with the rich people.

"You have to go to school with them, learn how talk to them," his uncle had said.

It never happened. George's friends at college came from the other end of the spectrum. Some of them looked good enough to go to preppy bars. But the ones he really liked were trouble makers, the kind parents cry over. Awkward and unhappy fellows who shave their heads, wear black coats, and carry guns. The only thing they ever dreamed about was blowing up something big and killing a lot of people in the process.

So George defied his uncle and started dealing his first year in college. He learned the value of a dollar. Then he dropped out to help his friends. And his uncle had not forgiven him. His uncle had wanted another front man, someone who could bring in the younger generation, a relative who was just like him. And he punished George every day.

How could George explain that he wanted to serve the cause his own way? He wasn't some crazy jihad follower, who knew nothing about the real world. George came from over there. He knew what struggle and war were all about. He didn't need a classroom to know that war in the Middle East didn't come from some outside oppressor. Killing had always been a way of life there. If there wasn't a reason for it, they made one up. He'd seen this firsthand in Lebanon. And he knew how killing was done.

George believed that some day his uncle would respect him for taking matters in his own hands. But right now his uncle was a pain in the neck. He had noticed the bike, and if he saw it again he would ask George's mother about it.

The thought of more questioning made George mad. He'd felt good on that bike. He'd ridden it for a couple of weeks. He'd left it parked on the street, and nothing happened. That proved that nobody was looking for the losers Ali had killed. Nobody knew they were gone. So George wanted to keep the bike. But once again his uncle wouldn't let him have anything he wanted, even if he got it himself.

George turned left, headed toward Taboule, reviewing the situation. Fact was the two losers on the bike were not the first drug deaths. A few months earlier two suppliers on the east side of the river had been beheaded in their house. Everyone knew Mexicans had done it to discourage local competition. And then six weeks ago one of his original nine friends from college had died of an overdose in his room at home. George knew for a fact his buddy hadn't been a user. He'd been a dealer. Someone had killed him in his own home to serve as a warning and to shame his family. Therefore, it followed that the losers on the bike had known where they were going, and Ali may not have overreacted to the security breach. He may have been perfectly justified.

But two more people were dead, and now George's uncle was making matters worse by asking pointed questions. Why was George going to the lodge so often? What was he doing at the farm? Why did he choose to be a loser when he could run the whole organization some day? Where did he get the bike?

Bottom line: George's life was getting dangerous. He wasn't safe on the outside anymore, merely planning some distant operation that never happened. People wanted to hurt him. He could feel the ground shifting beneath him and it was a change he didn't like. Four years ago the business was a small operation, easy to manage. Now it was a problem he needed to solve. He had agreed to be the undercover guy and let his college brothers front for him in the clubs. The good looking ones made the friends, he grew the weed, then Ali starting making the meth.

But there was more to it than that. George was funding four guys up at the lodge. They were making bombs and preparing for a mission. He didn't want his uncle to know about it, and he was afraid he had enemies who would tell. It wouldn't be Ali. But maybe someone was spying for his uncle. Otherwise, why would anyone in his operation want to hurt him?

George thought of it this way: The sites belonged to his uncle, but the drugs produced on them were his. Without him, there would be no business; there would be no separatist camp, no protest against the fraudulent Presidential election. His uncle might be mad that blacks and women were now running the country, but he and his brothers were the only ones who cared enough to do anything about it. They should think of him as a hero. End of story.

George pulled up in front of Taboule and killed the engine. He was glad to see the snake, Sami, waiting for him without even knowing it.

Sami was leaning against a street light, smoking. Smoking wasn't allowed in the restaurant. When he saw George, he slicked his hair back and gave his rival a sour look.

"What's up? You're not due until tomorrow," Sami said.

"Something's the matter," George told him.

Sami shrugged. "What?"

"You have a grievance against me. I want to know what it is."

Sami shook his head. "I'm on your side. We're all good." Sami looked like he was telling the truth.

"Then I have a gift for you," George said with a smile.

Sami looked surprised. "What kind of gift?"

"A motorcycle, brand new. I got it from my mom, but now she's afraid to let me ride it. Someone told her bikes are dangerous."

"Women can be stupid." Sami laughed. "But your loss, my gain."

"That's right." George nodded solemnly, handed over the keys and told Sami where the bike was parked. Sami had the look of a sheik who'd just been given his due. He could be pretty stupid himself. Sami high-fived George and turned away without saying thank you. That was a sign that he was not telling the truth and made George vow to take the grin right off his arrogant face. He would not let Sami take his place as his uncle's favorite.

10

When Michael arrived in Portland, a heavy mist clung to the valleys. Low clouds hid the mountains, and it looked like rain. She wrestled her luggage into a taxi without help from the driver and gave him the address of Claude's rental.

West Portland was hilly land, rising steeply from the Willamette River through deep and ancient lava-cut ravines. When the taxi entered the woods on Greenway and started the climb up to Council Crest, Michael saw why Claude had chosen this area. Above Pill Hill, the neighborhood was upscale and old, with houses sitting side by side in a wide range of architectural styles. Lush gardens in lovingly worked front yards had already yielded to spring where it was now summer in the East.

The taxi stopped and Michael recognized the house from the photo Claude had showed her. She paid the fare and got out. Then she saw that the building was not a true cape cottage. French doors spread across the front, and there were dormer windows on the second floor. The sky darkened as a middle-aged blonde with a tweed skirt and cable-knit sweater came running out.

"Michael Tamlin? You made it. Yippee."

A fat raindrop hit Michael in the eye. Yippee.

"I'm Charlene Mellon. Welcome." Charlene made it to the driveway the exact moment a monsoon commenced, drenching them both in a second.

"Oops, don't worry. The rain never lasts long here," Charlene shouted. She grabbed a suitcase and ran for the house.

Michael took the other two bags and stumbled after her into the house.

"Here's the real charm," Charlene said, leading the way to the kitchen.

Michael followed her past the renovated kitchen into another room with an immense glass wall that marked a jarring change of style. The starkly modern space jutted out at least twenty feet beyond solid ground.

"Gorgeous, right? When the sun comes out, you'll be able to see Mount Hood. Isn't it a dream?" Charlene gushed. "Excuse me a minute."

Michael ran outside and down the brick walk. Shit, the taxi was gone. She turned toward the garage and found herself in a covered breezeway. She peered into the garage that had been turned into some kind of studio; it didn't even have a door a car could get in. Her precious Acura would have to live outside in the rain.

She leaned against the wall, wishing she could have made her own choice. She turned back to the house and noticed a motorcycle parked next to a hot tub. Claude must have arranged for the delivery of his bike. Next there'd be his hunting rifles on the wall, which reminded her of the unfortunate demise of her predecessor, which reminded her of Bobbi Lee shot dead by her hand in that Louisiana swamp.

She went out into the driveway to investigate further. Just past the garage, a few white-painted posts marked the end of solid ground. A deep ravine fell away beyond it. She sloshed through puddles to the driveway of the next house. From there, she could see that half of her house was supported by stilts. Rain had carved distinct gullies into the hill around the poles and the whole area looked like a mudslide waiting to happen. Thank you, Claude. Thank you very much.

Out came the cell phone. Michael didn't want to be a killjoy before she was even married, but she had to tell Claude this place wasn't for her. His phone rang, but he didn't pick up. Unacceptable. She hurried back inside where Charlene was pacing nervously. Her perky hair had gone flat, and she had a worried look on her face.

"Everything all right?" she asked.

"No. This is not what I expected," Michael told her.

"I don't understand," Charlene said. "I sent you the photos, the virtual tour."

"I saw the MLS," Michael said. A photo of the front of the house with a description, that's all. "I never saw any virtual tour. Nothing I received from your office indicated this place is built on the side of a canyon."

"Ravine," Charlene corrected her with an anxious laugh. "It's perfectly safe. Many houses around here are built this way. It's considered a feature."

"And I was told it would be clean. It's filthy."

"Well, it's broom clean. I could give you the name of a cleaner. I have a list of very good people." Charlene tried to keep an upbeat smile on her face.

"I'm going to have to find something else," Michael said flatly.

"That won't be possible. You signed a lease. Your first rent check was due two weeks ago," Charlene protested.

"I did not sign a lease," Michael corrected her.

"Eighteen months at twenty-eight hundred dollars a month. I have your signature."

"No," Michael said. No.

"If your name is Michael Tamlin, I have your signature on the lease dated last month."

Last month! Michael shook her head in disbelief. Claude had made these arrangements before proposing? He signed her name on a lease without telling her and--little detail--before she even accepted his proposal? It didn't take a Treasury Agent to know that was not just sneaky. It was fraud. Fraud always gave Michael a sick feeling.

"The lease can't be binding without a check," she said automatically.

Charlene shrugged. "I knew you were coming. Your husband and the owner have an agreement. You want to break the lease, it will be a problem."

Michael shivered. Now Claude was her husband. Did she somehow miss the wedding?

"Look, I've got another appointment. I'll come by for the check tomorrow." Charlene quickly handed over the keys and took off without another word.

Michael found herself stranded without a land line, Internet connection, car, or cleaning supplies, and no one local to call for help. She glanced at her ring. Welcome to Portland. Now she had big doubts.

11

Around 6 p.m., Michael watched a woman pedal into the driveway on an old bicycle. It was still cold and misting outside, but the woman was wearing knee-length cargo pants, a T-shirt, and deck shoes without socks. A nylon jacket was tied around her waist, and a heavy-looking backpack hung her from her shoulders. Her black hair was braided down her back, and she wore no make up. On her head was an FBI baseball hat.

Michael was still wearing the black business suit and matching pumps she always traveled in, still waiting for the movers.

"Hey, Michael. I'm Pam."

"Pam! Pam, I'm so glad to see you." Michael couldn't believe that Claude's sister turned up without warning.

"Sorry I couldn't get away sooner. Pete will be here in a minute." Pam headed into the house.

"Pete?"

"Yeah, your first night. We're taking you out to dinner, didn't Claude tell you?"

Ah, no. Another little surprise. "Great," Michael said, following her in. "Great, I'm starved."

"Don't you just love the house?" Pam enthused.

"I get vertigo," Michael admitted. "Some inner ear thing."

Pam stood by the window, gazing out at the canyon and surrounding forest. "Oh, it's gorgeous. Wait 'til you see Mount Hood."

Uh huh. "Isn't this earthquake country?" Michael asked.

"Yep," Pam replied cheerfully, and turned to look her over. "But we don't worry about it."

She obviously didn't worry about rain or pedaling up steep inclines on a bike with fewer than five gears, or calling ahead, either. Michael did have a cell phone, after all, and the number was not a secret. FBI, huh? Pam certainly didn't look like any agent Michael knew. Maybe that's the reason she had to wear the cap. Definitely a nature girl. Hair way too long, and clearly she ate more than the recommended 2,500 calories, maybe thirty-five hundred, four thousand a day, Michael guessed.

"Claude's in surgery. He's working on a hermaphrodite. Poor kid has two sets of wee-wees. He told me to say hi."

Micheal blinked. Claude had time to call his sister from the OR, but not her?

"Two wee-wees?" She tried to imagine that.

Pam walked back into the living room. She was a powerful-looking woman, and Michael couldn't help disliking her right away. "Sorry the place is so dirty."

"Really? It looks fine to me. Here's Pete."

Pam went outside as Pete parked an old pick-up truck in the drive and jumped out. Michael watched him from the window. Another Fleisher in shorts. This one was a shorter and slighter version of his brother. He was about the same size and weight as his sister. He had a tattoo of a jumping fish on his forearm and was wearing sandals without socks. Pam flung an arm around his neck and gave him a gentler hug than the bone crunching one Michael had received. She glanced back at Michael, whispered something in Pete's ear, and laughed. He looked up quickly and caught Michael's eye. She felt a little kick with the connection.

The two came into the house. Pete held out his hand. "Hi, Mikey. Great to finally meet you. I've heard a lot of wonderful things. Claude wasn't exaggerating your beauty."

"Thanks. Likewise." Michael shook the hand and felt another jolt of electricity. She looked at her hand with surprise. What was that?

"She doesn't like heights," Pam said matter of fact, like she had the crabs.

"Really? You like fishing?"

Michael eyed the leaping fish tattoo on his arm. "Your favorite?"

"He ties his own flies," Pam said.

Okay. Michael wasn't at all competitive, but she was sure she could kill the mountain people at Scrabble. Pete glanced around.

"I made a reservation at Paley's. Might as well start with the best. It's in every Portland guidebook. You ready?" Pete glanced at Michael's dead serious suit, high heels, and the matching purse she'd left on the counter. They were going to a good restaurant in shorts and sandals? "Yeah, I'm ready," Michael said, just a touch defensively. She would never go out looking like that.

"Whatever you say." Pam threw her bike in the back of the truck, and they all squeezed into the cab. Michael hoped the moving van would not show up while they were gone and leave because no one was home.

Pete drove to Paley's, and parked the truck. The restaurant was jammed and they had to wait at the bar. Michael drank club soda. At the table, Pam immediately ordered a bottle of wine, and Michael put her hand over her glass when the waiter came to pour. She was working the next day. Pete and Pam exchanged glances.

"I'm starting my new job tomorrow," Michael said.

"Good luck with that."

They raised their glasses, not exactly warm congratulations, but cordial enough. The dinner was excellent, and Pete paid.

Two hours later Pete drove Michael back to Carl Place.

"Great to meet you. Are you okay here alone?" he asked.

"Thanks for a great dinner. I'm fine," she told him and got out.

"Okay, see you." He sat idling in his truck while she wrestled her front door open and went inside. Then he backed out and was gone.

All right, fine. The mover hadn't come. Michael didn't like the house and didn't care much for Claude's siblings, but she'd been in plenty of worse places. She figured they thought she was a pencil-pushing Treasury wuss. Well, fuck them. She found some sweats in her suitcase and put them on. It was going to be a long night.

Two hours later, she heard the sound of a heavy vehicle and thought it was the moving van. She ran out outside to meet them, but it was not the mover. It was Pete, returning with boxes.

"Hey, what's all this?" Michael asked.

He gave her a sly smile. "I thought you could use a bed and some bedding 'til your furniture gets here. You could have asked, you know. Real life is not Pam's thing."

"Or Claude's." Michael shut her mouth. Or mine. I've just made a big mistake, she didn't say.

Pete laughed, dragged the boxes inside and looked around.

"Right here in the living room, there's a basement in this part of the house," Michael told him.

"Why, are you expecting an earthquake?"

"Yes," she admitted, "but I hope not while I'm here."

He laughed. "You're funnier than you look."

"I'm not kidding."

"That's what's funny." He plugged in his blow-up bed and helped her set it against the wall so the pillows wouldn't fall down. Queen sized bed, classic height. Michael felt a seismic jolt when he winked.

"Listen, if you're scared here, you could come home with me. I make great coffee. You like it with frothed milk? Girls usually do."

"Ah, I appreciate the offer, but I don't scare easily." The delivery of the bed was nice, but the clear flirtation was not a plus. And she knew how to froth milk, maybe better than anyone.

"Okay then, nighty-night. Sweet dreams." As Pete left the second time, he dropped on her pillow one of the chocolates he'd taken from the bowl at the restaurant. Then he waved over his shoulder as he left.

Jesus. Claude's unusual family made Michael's look good. Michael crawled into bed stone-cold sober and full of regrets for accepting Claude's proposal so fast. You can't marry someone who isn't straight up, said the little voice in her head. People who went ahead with doubts were sorry later. She was sorry already, so now what? Tell Mr. Caulahan she'd changed her mind and leave Pac GreenBank before even starting the mission he'd hired her for? Go crawling back to Max after he'd let her go so easily? Sleep didn't come for a long time.

12

At 7:30 the next morning, Michael's cell phone rang. She was already dressed and jumped to get it.

"Hi, this is Mary Lou Loughlin. I'm going to be your assistant at the bank. Just checking in to see if you need anything."

"Oh." Michael's voice dropped. She'd hoped it was Claude, finally getting back to her. She wanted to tell him she had some major doubts about their engagement.

"Are you all right?" Mary Lou asked.

"Yes," she said after a slight pause. "I'm fine. It's just that my car didn't get here. I have no transportation."

"Okay, I'll be right over."

"Really? That would be great." Michael gave her the address.

Mary Lou turned up twenty minutes later in a bright red Prius and walked through the French doors without knocking. She was a woman of indeterminate age--could be forty-five, could be fifty-five—with a plump open face, a suit that looked as if it had come off a zebra, bright red dangling earrings, and frizzy hair with a carrot red dye job. Not exactly a corporate type. She carried a notebook with a glossy photo of ballet shoes on the cover.

"Nice to meet you," she said brusquely, as if she didn't really mean it, and handed over a paper bag. "Coffee and chocolate croissant, I hope that's all right."

Michael opened the coffee and almost swooned with gratitude. "Very thoughtful. Thank you. And thank you for coming. I appreciate it."

Mary Lou nodded. "Not a problem. Looks like you could use some help. Cleaner, Internet, phone?"

"Ah, I haven't decided to stay yet," Michael said slowly.

"You heard, then," Mary Lou said flatly. "I wondered why they chose a woman. They didn't tell us until yesterday, you know.

The name Michael...we thought it was a man..."

Michael's eyes turned green. "Why would that make a difference? Do you have something against women?"

Mary Lou clamped her lips together. "I just meant given the situation a man might be better suited."

Michael stared. Was the woman from the Stone Age? Maybe. She had one of those frilly names from the fifties. Given her own, Michael had a thing about names. She'd been studying them since she was a kid. And Mary Lou already bothered her. There were enough M names in her life.

"What situation?" she asked.

Mary Lou took a breath. "I'm sorry. I shouldn't have brought it up on your first day."

"If you're talking about my predecessor, I know about the hunting accident. I'm sure it's been difficult for you."

"When I heard Treasury, I thought maybe..."

Mary Lou stopped suddenly, and Michael raised her eyebrow. "Maybe...what?"

"Someone was coming out to investigate." Mary Lou finally spit it out. "So many banks have gotten in trouble. And when he died that way, it just seemed not right--" she shook her head. "He was an experienced hunter."

"I see." Michael flashed to her lunch with Caulahan and started getting excited. Maybe there was more to his message than an innocent request for transparency.

"That incident would be a local, not a Federal, matter, though," she said. "Are you suggesting Allan's hunting accident might somehow be related to the bank? And not an accident?" Just saying it made her heart beat faster. Compliance officer killed in a hunting incident because...? Homicide and conspiracy were music to her ears.

"I'm sorry." Mary Lou dropped her eyes. "I know you just got here, but when you said you weren't sure you were staying, I just assumed..."

The first thing they teach you in any investigating business--whether law enforcement, or forensic accounting, or plane crashes--is never assume. Already Michael had made a bunch of incorrect assumptions. She'd assumed that her sketchy boyfriend would somehow morph into an excellent husband just because she wished it so.

She'd also assumed that a corporate job would be routine. Now Mary Lou over there assumed something different. She assumed that a pencil-pushing Treasury wuss, who happened to be a woman, would be frightened off by the possible murder of her predecessor. The very opposite was true. If Pac GreenBank was somehow involved in the death of its chief compliance officer, Michael had the reason she needed to stay. If she uncovered something worthwhile, she could return to Washington with dignity. People changed their minds all the time, and dignity was all she required.

"I was talking about the house," she said, sipping the coffee. "I don't really like it, do you?"

"The house?" Startled, Mary Lou looked around. "I think it's a sweet house. If you stay, I'll take care of the cleaning and everything. Say yes."

Michael nodded. Her furniture was on the truck. What did she care where they put it? She'd stayed for months in places a whole lot worse than this.

"Okay, I'm on the job," she said. Any cop knew what that meant. "Do you mind if I call you Loughlin?"

Mary Lou shook her head. "Do you mind if I call you Michael?"

Michael laughed, and her eyes went back to hazel. Right up until the Rhueland case, she'd always believed things happened for a reason. But maybe they still did.

13

The morning was a blur of paperwork and introductions. Apparently the memo hadn't gone out about Michael's gender, so she got the usual reaction from her team. Not pleased. When Loughlin took her into Charlie Dorn's office, the Audit Manager was the least friendly of all. He was a skinny, fussy-looking fellow, with thinning hair and thinner lips, probably forty and definitely startled by his new boss. After a slight and revealing hesitation, he got up to shake her hand.

"You're Michael?"

"Yes, the old story. My father wanted a junior," she said.

"You look pretty junior for the position." He gave her a limp hand and didn't squeeze. "You're certainly a far cry from Allan," he said, deepening the chill even further. "Big shoes to fill, young lady. Big shoes." Charlie took his seat again.

"I'll do my best. I'm certainly going to be relying on your help to get me up to speed," Michael told him. It was clear she was going to have to watch her step.

"Sorry about that. They were close," Mary Lou said, finally leading the way to Michael's office down the hall.

"It's always hard getting a new boss," Michael murmured.

Her new office was smaller than Ashland's, of course, but still very impressive. A conference table and four leather armchairs were placed near the door. On the other end was a large mahogany desk with a credenza behind it. On the credenza was her computer with a flat screen. And there was a big window with the same view of the Willamette River that Ashland had. Mary Lou touched the back of one of the two guest chairs in front of the desk, and Michael guessed that's where she always sat when she met with Allan.

"The computer is hooked into the bank's main frame. When we get your passwords set up and activated, you will have the highest security clearance, total access. I hope you have a good memory. You'll be required to change your password every two weeks."

"Can I get it activated today?" Michael asked.

"Most people have to attend a two-day orientation course on the system in San Francisco, but I have a tutor assigned to you so you don't have to travel. It's on your schedule."

Loughlin handed over the schedule, and Michael read it.

"Very thorough," Michael said. "I'm impressed."

"I've been here twenty-seven years. I've seen a lot of changes. I know what goes on."

"That's good to know." Michael smiled and thought that it was going to be like having her mother run her life.

Loughlin had filled the day and then some. A tour and introductions in the morning. Check, that was done. Lunch at the club with Ashland...in half an hour? She looked up.

"Lunch at the club so soon?"

"He sees it as orientation," Loughlin said.

A staff meeting in the afternoon was followed by her first computer briefing. And Marty Williams came after that.

"Who's this?" She pointed at the five o'clock.

"Marty is your life coach."

"My life coach? I thought you were my life coach."

Loughlin laughed. "No, I'm just support. He's benefit."

"Good. Does he do back rubs?"

Mary Lou laughed again. "I wouldn't say that out loud." Then she checked her watch. "I'll take you downstairs to the car. Mr. Upjohn likes to be there exactly at noon."

Michael had not been given a moment to sit down at her desk, make a single phone call, or even powder her nose. She'd have to talk to Loughlin about such tight scheduling. They were in the elevator and then downstairs in the garage. She saw that her boss, the silver fox, was already waiting in his car in his reserved spot right by the elevator, tapping the steering wheel of his Mercedes with an impatient finger.

Mary Lou nodded. "I'll check on your personal issues while you're at lunch," she said retreating into the elevator.

14

The car traveled through downtown streets Michael had seen only once before, out Barbur Boulevard and finally over the Sellwood Bridge. She was preoccupied, trying to absorb the names, the route, the people at the bank, and the subtext of it all. Ashland read her mind.

"How is it going so far?" he asked.

"Great." Michael did not elaborate. Whatever she said to anybody now, she'd be thinking of what happened to Allan Farber.

Her cell phone vibrated in her jacket pocket, and she reached in to see who it was. Finally, Claude had a moment to talk. Unfortunately, she couldn't take the call. Ashland was parking the car close to the entrance of a sprawling structure from another age. He got out and led the way through the clubhouse to a dining room that was country casual, beautifully appointed, and very old line. He walked in and surveyed the scene. Then he guided Michael through a maze of tables, greeting members as he went. "This is our new VP, Michael Tamlin. We got her from the Treasury," he said, as if she were part of the bank's bail-out package.

It reminded Michael that some banks got the money and hoarded it, instead of using it to stimulate the local economy. She made a mental note to check that out as all over the room, gentlemen jumped to their feet like Jack-in-the-boxes to shake her hand.

"Great addition to the bank."

Michael heard the words "Breath of fresh air."

More than you know, she thought.

Ashland stopped last at a table by the window where two handsome, dark-haired men were having an intense conversation. The older man stopped talking when he saw Ashland, then he looked at Michael and stood like the others.

"Ashland, good to see you. Who is this lovely lady?"

"Frank, you devil. Don't get any ideas. This is Michael Tamlin, our new VP. Michael, I want you to meet Frank Hamid. Frank is one of our important clients, very influential in our community. And, I warn you, quite the ladies' man."

"It's a pleasure," Michael said.

"The pleasure is all mine. This is my nephew, George."

George was already standing. A handsome boy, he shook Michael's hand and murmured, "Nice to meet you."

Hamid nodded at him as if he'd done well, and turned back to Michael. "I know you people specialize. I hope you're in the commercial banking side. Or private banking would be fine, too." His eyes teased. "Can I be a client?"

"No, no, Frank, she doesn't have clients. She's an officer. She comes to us from the Treasury, moved all the way from Washington, D.C. to be with us. And we're very lucky to have her."

"Oh, too bad," Hamid pretended to pout for a moment, then brightened. "But surely you eat."

Michael laughed. She liked this guy. "Regularly."

"Frank has four high-end restaurants in Portland. I'm sure he'll be wanting to feed you a lot more than you'll ever want to eat," Ashland said.

"I'm certainly an eater. What cuisine?"

"Lebanese is our specialty; but we do fusion and seafood as well," Hamid replied.

"How exciting," she said and meant it.

"You have no idea." Ashland put his hand on her arm just a touch possessively and said his goodbyes.

He didn't speak again until they were seated at a table facing the patio and the putting green beyond. "Frank is a great guy, and owns a lot of real estate. He's a developer, into a number of businesses, a terrific client and very creative," he said enthusiastically. "A very important client."

"And quite the charmer," Michael added, still feeling the heat from his smile.

"Look out for that, I don't want to have to worry about you,"

Ashland said primly.

"Not to worry. I can handle myself."

Ashland clapped his hands. "Good. Here's Marty."

A sandy-haired man with a houndstooth sports jacket and khaki trousers cruised toward them. Medium height, compact, and very self-assured, Michael noted. His hair was longer than bankers' and he had an easy way about him. Ashland made the introductions.

"Michael Tamlin, this is Marty Williams. He's our counseling resource for executives. I think you have a meeting set up."

And coming up all too soon. Michael nodded.

"A pleasure. I look forward to working with you," Marty said, giving her a friendly once-over with deep blue eyes as he shook her hand.

"It will be a first for me," Michael said.

"Good, I know it will be a useful experience. Enjoy your lunch," Marty said, and wandered off.

Michael watched him leave. She didn't think there was any way she could enjoy her lunch. She wanted to get back to her office and get to work. Ashland was gracious, but gave out no useful information. She was grateful when the coffee was served and he didn't order dessert.

Frank Hamid stopped at the table on his way out. "I always like to welcome new people," he said, handing Michael his card. "Please call me, and I'll take you to dinner at each one of my restaurants. I'm sure you'll like them all equally. Oh well, you might have a favorite." There was the teasing grin again.

Michael reached for the round glasses she always carried in her purse. It was a reflex action. Was the client coming on to her, or was he just being friendly to the new kid at his bank? She put on the glasses and read the card.

Ashland nodded approvingly at her response.

"You can always reach me on my cell phone," Hamid said in a honey voice.

"That's very nice of you," Michael replied, looking suddenly very governmental.

Hamid's business card had a list of numbers but no restaurant names or business addresses. And he'd added his cell phone number in a tiny, precise handwriting. She put the card in her purse, kept the glasses on and did not offer her hand to say goodbye.

"Good to see you, Frank," Ashland said.

"Always good to see you, Ash." Hamid and his nephew moved on.

Ashland waited until the two were at the door. Then he leaned forward. "Now, tell me about your fiancé. Have you set a wedding date?" he asked.

A painful flush rose to Michael's cheeks at the unexpected question, and she experienced something she hadn't felt in a long time. A cold sweat soaked her armpits. It was like Max back at the Treasury looking doubtfully at her not so very engagement-like ring. Men didn't say things like that to men. She felt uncharacteristically and unexpectedly blindsided by the mention of her personal life. How did he even know she was engaged? She didn't remember mentioning it to anyone.

Back at the bank, it was nearly five on the East Coast when Michael finally connected with Claude. She called him on her cell phone because she didn't know who could listen in on her office phone.

"I had to do an eight-hour procedure yesterday, an interesting case. I'll tell you all about it. And then I had to do an appendectomy at eleven. I didn't get out until late. When I left this morning, it was too early to call. How is it going?" he asked.

Michael was sitting at her new desk with her shoes off, turned away from her open door and looking out the window at the river and faraway mountains, still half-hidden by fog. "I had a nice dinner with Pam and Pete last night. You didn't tell me they were coming."

"You liked them?"

"Oh, they're great. But I have some questions about the house."

"What's wrong with it?" Claude's voice got suddenly defensive.

Mary Lou came to the door and pointed at her watch. Five

minutes to two. Shit, it was almost time for the staff meeting. Michael nodded a thank you.

"You signed my name on the lease. Didn't anyone ever tell you signing someone else's name is illegal?" she said.

"Jesus, don't be a stickler. We're engaged, aren't we?"

"You signed my name last month, before we were engaged."

"I was there. You weren't. What's the big deal?" He sounded angry.

"It's two things I didn't know. What else don't I know?"

Mary Lou was at the door again. Michael nodded at Mary Lou and held up a finger. One minute. Mary Lou disappeared, frowning.

Claude made a noise. "We haven't even started our life together, and already you don't want to compromise. That doesn't bode well for the future."

"I agree with you there." Michael took a breath, but it didn't help. She'd left her job and her home for him, crossed the country with a fake ruby on her finger. If that wasn't compromise, she didn't know what was. Shit! Mary Lou was back. Damn woman was not going to let her be late.

"I have to go," she said.

15

Shaking off the unpleasant exchange with Claude, Michael stepped into a medium-sized conference room where Charlie and the rest of her staff was waiting.

"Let's take a moment to get to know each other. I know you've had your way of doing things, and I've heard from the president on down that Allan Farber was a great boss. I'm sorry to have to replace him under such sad circumstances," she began, looking at each one in turn.

Charlie's thin lips got thinner.

"I'm also sorry that I will not have the benefit of his training in the weeks ahead. You all know that I come from the land of financial analysis and rule-making, not rule-following. I know government think from the inside, but I don't know bank think from the inside. So this is new for me."

Charlie snorted, and she laughed with him. "I'm glad you understand what I mean. I'm going to start by learning your process, see how the bank functions so we can stay out of trouble. That's what I've been hired for." She smiled disarmingly, and poured herself some water from the carafe in front of her.

"Now let me give you a thumbnail description of myself. I grew up and went to college in Boston, and joined the Treasury six years ago. I have two masters' degrees. With FinCEN I have been an intelligence research specialist, a compliance specialist, and a law enforcement liaison specialist, but I've also worked on policy and training. Now you.

"Do you prefer to be called Charlie, or Charles or Chuck?" she asked turning to the auditor, the one who should know everything.

He gave her a rueful smile. "Everyone has always called me Charlie. I don't fight it anymore. I've produced a report of our audit process and schedule for the year." Charlie handed it over.

"Thank you, can't wait to read it." Then she changed the subject. "I know this is hard," she began, "But before we adjourn, I'd like to know how Allan died."

It was as if she'd sent a jolt of electricity through the room. Mary Lou locked eyes with Charlie. "You'll have to tell her. I can't talk about it."

"I know it was a hunting accident, but not the details. It was deer season, right?" Michael prompted.

"No, deer season was over. But Allan was an avid hunter. He'd go after anything. There was a group from the bank that went regularly. Allan liked to invite clients. He had Frank Hamid with him that day," Charlie said. He seemed to want to talk about it.

Michael blinked. Frank Hamid, the good-looking guy from the country club? She made a mental picture of Hamid stalking some poor defenseless animal with a shotgun.

"They were hunting cougar," Charlie added.

"Cougar!" Wasn't that some kind of tiger? "In Oregon?" she said.

"Yeah, we have cougar here. The way I heard it, the party had split into twos. Frank and Allan were together, near a deer stand, when they saw some recent scat."

"What's that? I'm not much of a hunter."

"Droppings. See, cougars are very territorial. They tend to stay in one area, so when they saw the scat they knew a big cat was nearby."

So they tracked prey by following their shit. Same as she did, Michael thought.

"Allan decided to stay in the tree stand while Frank followed a trail out maybe a quarter of a mile, hoping to flush the cougar back to Allan."

Michael jumped ahead and quickly assumed. "Hamid shot him?"

"God, no!" Mary Lou exclaimed.

"No, Hamid saw a good-sized cat take off toward Allan and some minutes later heard a single shot. He thought maybe Allan had been successful, and worked his way back to the stand. When he got there, he found Allan on the ground with his head blown off. The police said he'd fallen out of the stand, and his gun discharged and killed him. Freak thing."

Mary Lou blew her nose. "Those deer stands are terrible rickety things."

"How dreadful for Mr. Hamid," Michael murmured. "He's such a good client of the bank, too. Thank you. I could have looked up the newspaper stories, but I wanted to hear it from you." Okay. She gave Charlie a moment to recover.

"I'd like to complete a thorough self audit quickly so I can see in detail what's working and what's not working in the operation."

He looked uncomfortable. "If you're talking about toxic mortgages, we never dealt as sub-prime lenders, but many of our clients still have found themselves upside down. You'll find defaults."

Michael nodded. "I expected that."

"The housing market is flat, commercial real estate, business loans, the whole enchilada. The bank has certainly been affected by the real estate meltdown. Is that what you want to examine?"

"The mortgage issue is at the top of the list. But we are also interested in all banking practices to assure they meet compliance requirements." Michael didn't mean to sound chilly, but he picked it up.

"We?" he said with a smile.

"All of us, Charlie."

"Is there anything specific that you're concerned about?"

"Nothing specific. But I'd like to see what Allan was working on when he died. And let's keep this angle confidential."

Suspicious Activity Reports were one of the most important functions of bank regulation, and the cornerstone of the Patriot Act. Michael wanted to make sure the bank was filing those reports, watching out for fraud and money laundering, and if Allan Farber had been doing his job.

"Got it," he said.

"Thanks. I appreciate your help."

Mary Lou tapped her watch like a general, giving the sign that Michael's systems tutor would be waiting for her, so she moved on.

By five the computer was up. Michael had email and access to bank information and only five more two-hour lessons to go for learning the system. It wasn't that difficult. She was fast. She figured she could do the rest of it in two hours, maybe less.

16

Michael had one more task to complete before she could stop for the day. Her shoes were off under the desk and she was trying to take a thirty-second break when Marty came in without knocking. As soon as she saw him, she tensed up. She didn't need a life coach.

"Too soon?" he said instantly.

"It's been a long day," she admitted.

"Why don't we just have a cup of coffee, then? Or tea, if you prefer. No company business. Sound okay?"

She glanced at her watch. She didn't really want to leave the office so early on her first day, but she figured he might not be paid if she rejected the hour.

"All right."

"Get your shoes on, and I'll take you into the Pearl District. It's fun, lots of shops where you can spend your money. Then I'll drive you home."

She raised her eyebrows. He already knew she shed her shoes at every opportunity and didn't have a car.

"There are no secrets around here. Mary Lou told me your car won't be here until tomorrow; I have to take you home or call her. Of course, I'll take you myself."

"Well, thanks," Michael murmured.

She couldn't tell if he was just being friendly, or was another flirter. She glanced at his ring finger. He caught her looking and smiled. Then he watched her squirm in her chair, searching for her shoes.

"Got them, let's go." She grabbed her purse.

It would have been impossible to sneak past Mary Lou. Loughlin was like a road hazard you couldn't get around. "I've called the phone company," she said. "Here's your new number. It will be on by midnight. Car and furniture will arrive by noon."

"Thank you, Mary Lou. Good job."

"You too," she said. "Have a nice evening. If you need anything, don't hesitate to call. I can be there in a half shake of a lamb's tail."

Michael hadn't heard that expression since her grandmother died fifteen years ago. Or was it two shakes of a lamb's tail? Could you even half shake a lamb's tail? Marty was looking at her. What?

He drove an old BMW, and every road in Portland seemed to be a work site. It was impossible to get from downtown across town without a dozen detours on narrow one-way roads.

"What's the weird thing about?" she asked pointing out bumper stickers on cars that said: Keep Portland Weird.

"Oh, this is a city of individuals, very liberal. Everybody does his own thing and wants you to know it."

Michael was reminded of Pam wearing shorts and her FBI hat, riding her bike in the rain.

"A lot of protest here, too. Whatever's going on, somebody isn't going to like it," Marty added.

Marty was driving north away from the river. It wasn't going to be that hard to learn the way. Michael saw a homeless man who hadn't had a shave or haircut in many moons, holding a sign that read "Rocket scientist, need beer parts."

"He's my favorite," Marty laughed.

The Pearl District was a little like Greenwich Village in New York. Artisan shops, trendy restaurants, galleries. Marty found a place to park, and they walked back to a restaurant with a huge bar area where he snagged a table in the window. Before sitting down, Michael glanced behind her at all the colorful bottles on the long bar. She longed for a couple of shots of tequila, a martini or two—vodka with blue cheese olives. And maybe a double gin and tonic. One of each.

A petite, dark-haired server with a tiny tattoo of a star above one eyebrow waited expectantly for her order.

"I'll have a hot tea," she said.

"Hey, it's after hours. You can have anything you want," Marty told her.

Yeah, trick offer. "No, I'm good with the tea." Michael's cell phone buzzed in her pocket. She plucked it out. Claude at another inopportune moment.

"No problem. You can take it," Marty offered, and ordered a Diet Coke.

She shook her head and replaced the cell in her pocket. Now, she really needed that drink. She turned to Marty. "Tell me about you," she said.

"I help with the transitions."

"Now, that sounds a little sinister."

He looked surprised. "What does that tell me about you?"

"I don't know, I just flashed to the word cleanup. And when I think cleanup…I don't know."

"Humph." He reached into his own pocket and glanced at his cell phone.

"You can take it," she said with a smile.

He shook his head as the tea and Diet Coke came. Michael waited exactly ten seconds for her tea to brew and then poured.

"So, set me straight."

Marty made himself comfortable. "We want everyone who comes to the bank to stay with us and be successful, so I help people with that. Have you ever had therapy?" He gave her a look with those marble-blue eyes that were really a strong movie star kind of color.

"Ah, no." Lots of reasonably healthy people didn't have therapy, right? The eyes gave him away. Blue eyes could be killer cold.

"I just made you anxious," he said.

"Not at all. Are we in session?"

Marty laughed. "No, but I can see you're worried about this, so let me tell you how it works. In a couple of days I'll give you a baseline review."

"A psychological test?" She'd had plenty of those.

"Sort of. It will consist, in part, of a series of questions that will be utilized in a personality and management style evaluation."

"Fair enough."

"And after that we'll talk about whatever personal issues you may be having with--" he lifted his palms "--any bank employees, anybody at home. I can help you work things through." He smiled. "I know all the players, how things work here. I can get you through anything."

"And you'll write a report on me, of course."

"Oh, it's not that formal," he said easily.

Sounded pretty formal to her. Michael watched a tempting cheese plate with crunchy flat breads and a variety of dried and fresh fruit delivered to the table next door. Oh, baby. She realized she was starving. Ashland was a food restricter. At lunch he'd had the same smoked salmon he'd ordered at breakfast weeks ago. One slice, crème fraiche, and a dinner salad. Michael had ordered the Ceasar salad and regretted the lack of protein now. Give me some mac and cheese, she thought. And three or four drinks.

"Would you like to order?" Marty said.

"No, no, thank you. I had a huge lunch at the club. What about confidentiality?" she asked.

"Anything you say will be held in strict confidence, of course," Marty said. "That's a rule."

Except for those tests, Michael thought.

"Is there any documentation of that rule?"

Marty stared at her. "My. No one's ever asked me that question before."

"Really? I'm surprised it hasn't come up. How do you manage the separation?"

"I'm not sure what you mean."

Michael sipped her tea. He'd driven her here and offered her drinks; he was taking her home, asking questions of her assistant, giving tests, evaluating her. She explained.

"I'm just curious about the process. You test me, fair enough, and share the results, I assume, with HR. I tell you my personal problems and issues with people in the company, and is that... shared as well?"

"Oh, I see what you mean. No, no." His deep blue eyes flickered. "You don't have to worry about that. Do you have an immediate worry you'd like to share with me?"

"No, no." She echoed his words and then shifted the conversation to lighter subjects. Where to go grocery shopping and things like that.

After the meeting, he drove her home and let her out without trying to come in and see the place. "Thanks for the tea and the tour," she said. "I enjoyed it."

"Me, too. I look forward to working with you," Marty replied warmly.

She waved from the door as he backed out of the perilous drive. He fished out his cell phone and was already speed dialing his missed call.

"How did it go?" said the voice on the other end.

"Got to tell you, your Michael Tamlin is very sharp," Marty said. "I like her."

"Well, sharp and likable is what we wanted. Are you confident she's the right person for this job?"

"There's an element of paranoia in her we hadn't counted on. I think careful management will be necessary," Marty said slowly. "I'm not sure."

"Jesus." The line went dead. The contact didn't have to say "Keep me informed." Marty knew his job.

17

After eighteen endless holes of golf and lunch at the club, George smoked a joint and cruised around in his forgettable Toyota. For hours, he smoked and went over every word his uncle had said, muttering responses he couldn't make in person. His uncle got all over him again. He just couldn't take it.

"I'm not a fucking loser, you asshole," he muttered over and over. When George smoked, he sometimes got careless. Just then, an even more careless cyclist cut in front of him and barely avoided hitting him.

"Shit." He smacked the steering wheel in a rage. Nobody looked where they were going.

It was too long a wait for his Taboule drop, and George couldn't calm down. Spending time with his uncle was one long put-down that always set him off. After their last talk he'd given the motorcycle to Sami. That's how it always was. George didn't have a single thing to call his own. He couldn't stop brooding about how he had a whole operation, a million bucks hidden away, and he still couldn't have the things he wanted. And the secret feeling of power didn't help anymore.

He used to enjoy helping people out, supplying them. He could get whatever they needed. But now, more and more often he felt unappreciated because no one knew what a great guy he really was. No one had any idea. He'd gotten swallowed up by his own cover. He especially hated going to the country club, where everybody could hear his uncle's rants about his not getting ahead. He had to listen to the same old stories about the fucking sacrifices his uncle had made for the family. Support for his mother and sister sounded like charity.

"I don't need your fucking charity." George spat out the window. His uncle was punishing him with a shit job to get him to return to school. And it wasn't working. He paid all his own expenses, and gave his mother and sister money on the side. Nobody knew that, and they'd never tell.

There were a lot of things George didn't understand. He wasn't aware that smoking weed had the opposite of a calming effect on him. Weed made some people happy and compliant, but he wasn't one of them. Weed changed the way he thought and reacted. It magnified his grievances and paranoia. Now he was thinking that he'd dropped out of college for his friends, gone to work as a busboy where no one paid much attention to him so he could come and go as he pleased. For their benefit. He was the only one who made a real contribution to the camp where they trained. And he was tired of playing the loser to the entire world. Even his mother thought he was a slug. He had a million dollars stashed away that he couldn't spend. Most people couldn't even count that high.

He drove slowly, half listening to the music, feeling sad, and not daring to hang out with anyone as he waited for the day to be over. His thoughts kept returning to his uncle, who was the core problem of his life. His uncle traveled around the world, visiting his stupid restaurants and business interests, glad-handing clients and associates day and night, always looking for a new deal, a new angle, a new way up to the very top of society. He liked pretty women, and they liked him. But he didn't stick with any of them long enough to settle down.

George wasn't stupid. He noticed that his uncle drank a lot, had a bad temper and a taste for revenge. He was tough. Yet, he appeared to be the perfect guy, sitting in the first row in church every Sunday with his mother and sister and niece beside him. He pledged big bucks to all church projects and charities and anything to do with Middle Eastern food and culture.

It enraged George that his uncle had never even been to the Middle East. He couldn't speak Arabic. His grandparents had never been there, either. All were born in Portland, and were pure Catholics, so pure these days that George's mother never uttered a single word to anyone about their lives in Lebanon. It was a taboo family subject, as if their whole history had been erased the minute they got off the plane. His sister had forgotten everything, too. But George had not forgotten. He was not a Hamid; his father had been a Sunni, closely aligned with Syrian interests. Something, something so secret George knew he was not likely ever to know who had killed him or why.

He brooded about fake and true facts every single day. His uncle didn't know what he was talking about, didn't know shit. That was a true fact. But certain things, unsaid things, were also true. Being underground on the opposition side anywhere in the world could get you shot. True fact. Being out there, a wealthy man, picture in the paper, donating food to the festivals, and cash to Catholic widows, gave you recognition and made you a good guy. Nobody shot a good guy. True fact. Something about that thought prompted another. If his uncle were gone, then he, George, could be the good guy driving fast cars with his picture in the paper. He'd have a better lifestyle and a deeper cover. No more making drops in a crummy car that sober girls wouldn't ride in if their lives depended on it. The bitches were snobs, too.

Time passed. Around six he made his drop at Taboule. He went over there on Tuesdays and Fridays. It was one of his uncle's best restaurants, but a lot of people came to the bar there just to drink. Sometimes it was so crowded it took a half an hour just to get served. That never stopped anyone from hanging out, though. Seven days a week. What George always did was cruise by and stop down the street. Sami would be watching for him and come out to do business.

Today when he drove slowly past the window, he saw the girl from the club at lunch, the one his uncle had thought was so hot. She was sitting at a table in the window. Her legs were crossed and she was leaning forward, smiling at the guy at the table with her. George felt a shock of recognition and almost hit the brakes. Earlier he hadn't thought she was anything special, but now he was surprised to see that his uncle was right. One of her shoes was on the floor under her chair the other one dangled off a toe. She had good legs, but it was her feet that got his attention. There was something very appealing about a girl who would take her shoes off in a restaurant. It made her seem kind of wild. She had small feet and an intelligent face. He remembered that she'd given him a special smile when they met. And now that he'd seen her twice in one day, he knew it was a sign.

In the rearview mirror, he saw Sami running down the street, waving his arms for George to stop. George drove another half block before he pulled into a no-parking place and turned off the music. Sami was the manager of Taboule. He was taller than George, but not as good looking. Sometimes George wondered which was more important, height or looks. George had loved Sami when they were in high school together, but not anymore. Sami was friends with everybody. On his off hours, he went to all the other restaurants and clubs. He knew the menus and clientele, could stay up talking and drinking and never show any signs of wear. Sami was a front man and a good salesman. George was a back man, and he didn't want to be a stabbed-in-the-back man. Sami scowled as he got in and shut the door.

"What the fuck?" he said about having to chase the car two blocks.

"I would have come around," George told him easily.

"I don't have time for this. What's going on?" Sami looked at himself in the mirror and patted his hair back into place just like a girl.

George watched him preen. He was high from the weed, and paranoid. Sami was the one his uncle trusted these days, the favored one. George burned with a deep resentment.

"How are you doing?" he asked.

"Okay." Sami handed over the plastic bag with the Styrofoam boxes they used for take-out from the restaurant.

George pointed at the two pastry boxes on the floor by Sami's feet. They came from a store that made really good mamoul on the other side of town. The pastries had little plastic bags along with the date filling. Sami opened the top box and swore when he saw them.

"Jesus, what's this shit?"

"I gave you the bike, didn't I? This is another gift. Smart, huh?" It was like something George had seen on The Sopranos.

Only on The Sopranos, it was cannolis. Now Sami was going to have to dig around in the mamoul to get at the dope. He'd have sticky fingers. George didn't have a way to get rid of him yet, so he had to amuse himself somehow.

Sami gave him a look. "Don't get crazy on me," he said. "Don't do this again. And you took the bike back after three days, you asshole. What kind of gift is that?"

"You were riding it around my uncle. I told you not to do that," George barked back.

"All right, all right. But what's the big deal? He saw me on it. It's just a bike."

Sami didn't ask where George had gotten the damn bike, or what made it special, just as his mother hadn't asked. And George didn't ask if Sami had sent the biker kids to the farm. They were taken care of, that was all that mattered. Anybody who came up there would not come back. End of story.

Sami didn't say good bye. He jumped out of the SUV and slammed the door, unhappy with the boxes of pastry. George laughed and laughed.

18

Jesse Halen shut the doors for the day on the storefront where the New World Hedge Fund was located in a mall area on First Avenue. First Avenue was four lanes wide with a median and two extra lanes for parking. Lots of traffic moved parallel to the river all day long. It was a good location, close enough to downtown and the financial district to walk, but far enough away to be off the beaten track. There were no surveillance cameras there to record who came and went. Still, many of Jesse's visitors did not come inside.

He stepped out to open sidewalk and glanced up and down. Every day, doing this gave him a little anxiety. Sometimes he was ambushed by Frank Hamid or one of his partners. Jesse would have to get in a car and drive around for a while, terrified he might not get home. It came with the territory. Inside the office he felt safe. Outside, he was vulnerable. Otherwise, life was good. He wore his ample black hair the way Donald Trump only dreamed he could. He was athletic, hadn't put on too much weight, and he was friendly-- the kind of guy any father would love to have his daughter marry.

So Jesse had gotten himself a pretty blonde wife named Cissy and two cute kids, both girly girls. He liked it that way. In his family it was all sucking up and no fighting back. He was so smart he got along fine without a college education. His popularity had carried him a long way. And what made him especially lucky right now was the salary he was paid in an economy that was tanking all around him. Cissy and the girls would never feel any pocketbook pain. He was proud of that.

He could live with the few cracks in the retaining wall of his life. So what if it was uncomfortable being the man in the window at a hedge fund. Less fun was his strong resemblance to the Illinois governor, Rod Blagojevich, who was arrested, among other things, for attempting to sell Obama's Senate seat after he was elected president. Cissy wouldn't stop teasing him about it.

Ha ha. It wasn't so funny to Jesse when everyone in town noted his face was just like the one that had become a symbol of national corruption. The sad fact made him sigh, but that was it.

Jesse liked to say his job at New World was to sit in the front office and watch the rain. It was a good line, and it was the description he planned to give if the shit ever hit the fan, if anyone came after him. I didn't know a thing. And in large part it was true. Frank Hamid was the one who collected the funds from his friends, associates, and his contacts overseas. Hamid was the one who invested the funds as he saw fit. Hamid was the one who decided how much interest would be paid out. Jesse didn't have documentation on any of that.

In fact, Jesse did not know where the funds went after they were deposited. He did not personally follow the money trail. And it did not matter as long as investors got their eight, nine, ten percent year in and year out. It did not matter to anyone involved where the money came from and where it went. New World had certain rules that could not be broken, and because large sums of money came from sources that could never become public knowledge, most investors would never dream of even trying to break the rule of not being able withdraw funds for five years from the date of deposit.

This was not an uncommon requirement for hedge funds. What it meant for New World was that Frank Hamid was in total control. No investor or government agency was checking up. The Lebanese community trusted him. His Italian partners trusted him. And his clients from the Middle East trusted him. The last category trusted him in a different way, because they did not expect to get their money back. Jesse did know that Middle East "clients" were paying Hamid for a service, but Jesse pretended he had no need to know what that service was.

This way, Jesse could honestly consider himself an innocent party. He was a partner in name only. He was a principal who had certain connections and understanding about filings and reporting that he'd learned over the years, and was good at the art of the cover. Very good at it. He was like Art Nadel's Moody or Bernie

Madoff's wife and sons, who had been there every step of the way but weren't likely ever to be prosecuted for the crimes committed. Jesse planned to say that he didn't know anything was funny at New World. That was what the car rides were all about, reinforcement of the code of silence.

Jesse was simply the one who created the reports based on the data Hamid gave him. He was the one who answered the phone and assured legitimate investors that all was well during the stock market plunges and during the following months, when hedge fund after hedge fund crumbled and bankrupted thousands of wealthy and not-so-wealthy clients. Jesse sat in the window and said it could not happen to New World. He read his script well and watched the hard winter rain and first deep snow of twenty years thaw into the summer of a deepening recession, and he didn't believe complete meltdown could happen to them. With the constant stream of revenue coming in from the Middle East, Jesse figured New World would always be able to cover those interest payments. He wasn't a deep thinker. He went home at night, slept well, and thought that whatever happened to the company he was going to be all right. But it didn't turn out to be a good day, after all.

Jesse swore and his shoulders caved a little. Hamid cruised by and jerked his chin. Get in the car.

Hamid had a lot of cars. This was one of the Testa Rosas. Jesse practically had to get on his knees to get into it. Some people loved those low sports cars with the jet engines that roared right into the brain and vibrated worse than a shake machine, but Jesse wasn't one of them. He lowered himself into the capsule and Hamid locked the doors. Jesse didn't like that special feature, either. Everything done for a purpose. Hamid drove for twenty excruciating minutes without saying a single word. And Jesse wasn't allowed to speak unless spoken to. So unnerving it made him want to scream. He was ready to pluck his eyeballs out and swallow them when Hamid finally relented.

"Pac GreenBank hired someone for Allan's job," he said, as if they'd been conversing for an hour.

"Really? Anything we have to worry about?" Jesse asked.

Hamid laughed. "No, she's very pretty. There are other ways of dealing with a girl."

That was the message. But how it related to him, Jesse had no idea. He was relieved when Hamid dropped him off and didn't give it another thought.

19

Michael took out the bobby pins that held her hair in a tight bun at work, and sighed. The pins hurt her scalp, but they were part of her cover. She took a quick hot shower and changed into jeans and a sweatshirt. She was not thinking of Claude, or what she was going to tell her mother. She was not even thinking of making points with Max. She was thinking of Frank Hamid and the death of her predecessor. Law enforcement people do not believe in coincidence.

Hamid was one of the first bank clients she met, and he was the one who was with Allan Faber when he died. Michael didn't have words to explain the way things came together sometimes, no fancy philosophy for it. She didn't think there were ghosts or UFOs or anything like that flying around the atmosphere. But she knew that some people had gut feelings that were so powerful they created a path to the evidence. Other people had heightened perceptions, unusual ways of processing information. She knew a man who could see the way ten thousand pieces of a puzzle fit together when they were just a jumble on the table.

Clean and comfortable after a long day, she started thinking about food. How many miles was it down the hill to a store? She could call a taxi. She could order in. She no longer cared about the house or her possessions on a truck somewhere. Stuff was stuff. What had changed were the crucial pieces of information that led her to reassess her reason for being in Portland. She was now seeing the move as a catalyst for finishing whatever Allan Farber had started.

It was weird karma. Allan's job had been offered to her months ago. But she wouldn't have come on her own. It was Claude's proposal that had gotten her here. Claude was her connector to Allan. As soon as she got here, the connection to Claude was broken. He'd chosen a house and signed her name on a lease. They weren't on the same page. It always came clear in the end. She could cry about her lack of judgment, but she wasn't the weepy type. A girl could change her mind without beating herself to death about it, couldn't she?

Michael stepped into the kitchen and looked out the window to see Mount Hood, snow-capped with tinted clouds from the setting sun arranged around it. So pretty that from afar the image looked completely fake, pasted onto the sky. Her phone vibrated in her pocket. It was Claude. She wasn't in the mood to tell him the engagement was off.

Fifteen minutes later, Claude's brother drove up in his old truck. He got out with a pizza box, a six pack, and a bag.

"Wow," he said when she opened the door.

She shrugged. Yeah, she got that reaction sometimes when people saw her with her hair down. Gloria Steinem, feminist guru, once said, "Hair is everything." And turns out she was right.

"Good timing. I'm starved," she said.

He followed her into the house that was empty except for the bed he'd given her, and she shut the door.

"Mom sent over apple bread. She says welcome," Pete told her. "It's in the bag."

"That's really nice. I say thank you."

Pete smiled. He wasn't classically handsome like his brother, but the smile took him over the top. "Still no furniture?"

"Tomorrow. What brought you here with the fabulous food?"

It was his turn to shrug. "I'm a cop. Checking on people is what I do. After all, you may be my sis some day."

He reacted to the not-likely look on her face. "Did I say something wrong?"

"You and Pam seemed kind of ambivalent about me. I didn't know if it was sibling or Agency rivalry. Your mom baked me cake, but didn't pick up the phone. I'm just wondering what's up with the family."

Pete put the provisions down on the island. "This is deep. How about a beer?"

"Sounds good."

He popped the cap on two beers and handed one to her. Then he pulled out plates, knives and forks. Napkins. The gift from Mom. He'd thought of everything. He drank some beer and put down the can.

"To answer your question, Claude marches to his own drummer. Have you noticed that?" He handed her a slice of pizza.

"Thanks. Last few weeks, I've been seeing a new side of him."

"I'm sure you know he's had a lot of girlfriends. You must be something if you're the one he wants to marry." Pete gave her another of his electric smiles that lit up his whole face.

"Anybody special? I should know the history if I'm going to marry him."

"Probably should," Pete agreed. "Let's see. He brought that nurse, Judy, out here last year. Nice girl, got on with everyone pretty well. Is that who you mean?"

"Judy?" Michael didn't know anything about Judy.

"Yeah, she came twice," Pete said, watching her face carefully. "You knew this, right?"

"Of course. What happened to Judy?" Michael didn't have to hide her face in a beer can. She was an expert at concealment.

"You didn't know about Judy, did you?"

"Of course I did. Claude tells me everything. What about the others?" Maybe not such an expert; Michael needed more than a beer. Unfortunately, the vodka was on the truck. That fucker had been out here twice with fucking Judy? Come on. Did he think she'd never find out?

"Oh, I don't keep track of his love life. You'd have to ask Pam about that. How long have you two been together?" Pete asked.

He gave her a curious look, as if theirs was a brand new story to him. And maybe it was. Maybe Michael had been Claude's secret comfort food, his security blanket, the one he thought would take the best care of him. In that case, he'd underestimated her as a target. She could kill him easy as pie and get away with it.

"Oh, we've been together four years. He gave me your mom's

ring." She held up her hand to show him.

Pete's expression told her it wasn't their mother's ring. Slowly, deliberately, she took another beer. Major thing to remember in conflict situations was not to show vulnerability. Inner strength was pretty much the key to survival. Still, she almost wished she could kill him.

"What made you become a cop?" she asked.

"Somebody got hurt when I was little. The cops were good," he said. "I'm sorry I upset you."

"That's all right. Do you have a specialty?"

"Yeah, DVD," he said and added, "Drugs and vice."

"I know what it is. Do you go undercover?"

"Used to. Long hair, chains around my neck, Harley and everything. Not anymore. In fact, that's my old Harley out there." He pointed out the back door to the bike parked under the breezeway.

"I thought it was Claude's."

Pete laughed. "Nope. Mine. He wanted it as a gift for coming home."

"A gift for coming home?"

"He has his own rationale for getting the things he wants."

Michael nodded. Indeed he did.

"The hospital has a whole wing for biker accidents. We call them road kill. I'm over it. But Claude's a grown man. He can have it if he wants. Are you all right?"

Michael finished her beer and took another slice of pizza. She'd been engaged for a couple of weeks. Her fault; she should have said no the minute she saw the ring. It might have been a shallow reason to turn a man down but would have been the right call. Okay, she wasn't that great at relationships. It wasn't exactly a national secret. Pete stayed for an hour, long enough to feed her and give her the ammunition for her Dear John letter. And he didn't take the last two cans of beer or the pizza leftovers when he left. She appreciated that, too.

20

At 8:30 the next morning, Mary Lou arrived with coffee and more chocolate croissants.

"How did it go last night with Marty?" she asked. She looked even shorter today. Mary Lou was a very short person, wearing a yellow suit that did the opposite of flatter her figure. She carried a huge black patent leather purse and was already looking around the kitchen at the pizza box and empty beer cans with clear disapproval.

Michael sipped the coffee she'd brought. Very good. "Thanks, but you didn't have to come. I know how to move."

"Well, I made an executive decision. I wanted to make sure your car got here—are you all right? You look a little--"

Ragged, Michael thought.

"Everything's fine. I always have a beer when I move." She tossed the box and empty beer cans into the garbage. There were four of them.

"Had a visitor last night?" Mary Lou said, clearly wondering if it was Marty.

"I have a cop friend. He brought me a pizza." But why did she have to explain?

"Nice to have a fiancé who's a cop. But I thought he was a surgeon."

Michael frowned. "I don't think I told you that."

"Oops, sorry."

"Mary Lou, we're going to have to talk about this. My private life can't be grist for the gossip mill. If you're going to work for me, you can't talk about me," Michael said slowly, to prevent herself from killing the woman with one blow.

"I've told you I'm the soul of discretion."

"So you've said, but I don't want you to pass along stories or encourage gossip about me. I can't function that way."

Mary Lou looked chastened. "I'm sorry. I really am."

"We have very serious work to do. Let's focus on that."

"Okay. Enough said, I understand. I won't gossip," Mary Lou held two fingers to her heart.

Michael stared. She'd been a Girl Scout. "All right, I'm sorry. I didn't mean to offend you," Michael muttered. She wasn't used to having an assistant.

"It's okay. I'm on your side. I won't tell anyone about the beer," Mary Lou said.

"Mary Lou!"

"I was kidding. I'm on your side."

She looked so funny with the wild red hair and yellow suit and suddenly really serious expression, that Michael had to laugh. "Well, thanks. I need someone on my side. I really do. You've never worked for a woman, have you?"

"Sure I have," Mary Lou said, but she looked away as she said it.

"I don't think so, but that's all right. I could probably use a little mothering. Never got any from my own. Thanks for the coffee. Tomorrow, I won't need it."

Mary Lou smiled as if she'd won some points. And maybe she had. Michael rolled her eyes.

"All right. You asked about Marty. Does everything I say to him get passed on to HR and Ashland?" Michael asked.

"Marty's a good guy. He was very helpful to us after Allan's accident. I trust him."

"You didn't answer the question, but okay." Michael nodded. "You can go to the office now. I'll take care of this end." She absolutely didn't want the red-haired gnome looking at her stuff. She wasn't exactly unpacking anything but the kitchen.

Mary Lou pulled a stack of crisp twenties from her black plastic bag and left them on the kitchen island before Michael could protest. "For the cleaning girls and the movers, just in case you forgot to get cash," she said.

"Thanks." Michael had forgotten.

"Call me if you need anything," Mary Lou said.

Michael said she would. Then she called Pete on his cell. She just couldn't resist. He answered right away.

"Hey, Mikey, how's it going?"

Caller ID. She was going to have to fix that. "Just had a thought. Is Judy moving here, too?"

"Whoa! Hold the phone. Where did you get that idea?"

"Pete, you told me about Claude's other women. And you mentioned Judy, in particular. Everyone in the family liked her. She was here before me, yada, yada. Your mom didn't stop by. I may be slow, but I'm not an idiot. Is Judy moving here, too? Possibly another fiancé?" Michael had made another assumption, so sue her.

Pete didn't say a word.

She whistled.

"I'm sorry. Are you mad at me? I didn't want to go that far," he said softly.

She could tell he was good in a crisis. Calm, probably told people only what they could absorb. The sympathetic tone was nice, but shit. "You're his brother. Why come by last night with pizza and drop this bomb on me?" she said.

"No, no, no. I did not tell you anything. You figured it out on your own," Pete said slowly.

Strictly speaking, that was not true. She did not figure it out on her own. He told her a lot and hinted at more. "That thing with the bed the first night, what was that about?" she asked.

"You seemed like a nice girl. Shouldn't have to sleep on the floor. Pam wasn't sympathetic, but I crumble like a cookie. And I like an even playing field," he said after a moment.

"Lot of things in this life you just can't fix, but everybody has a right to know the basics."

He was telling this to a professional, but what did she know about real life? "So, I'm guessing Judy is already here." Michael jumped at another assumption.

"Mmmhmmm."

"Okay." Last night she'd suspected Pete was leaking like a sieve because the two brothers were in competition. Doctor beats out cop in every area; so the cop was jealous. But now she didn't think jealousy was Pete's motive. Or that he was interested in her for himself, either. He'd been teasing her with the smile. She'd missed every cue.

"You okay?" Pete asked.

"Absolutely. Would you come and get the motorcycle and the stuff you loaned me? I'm all good now. And Claude won't be moving in," she added. "He's history."

"Okay, but are you really all right?"

"No one likes being taken for a fool, Petey. I saw the red flags, but I overlooked them."

"People do it all the time."

"Yeah, hope springs eternal and all that. Could have been ten years and two kids later, though. I owe you one."

"Don't worry about it. I'm pretty jammed in here right now, but I'll get the bike out by the end of the weekend, that okay?"

"Any time before he gets here would be fine."

Michael checked that task off her list. The moving van arrived with her furniture. The transport truck arrived with her gray Acura. She checked to see if the car had sustained any damage before signing for it. Then she took the day off to get organized.

21

"Do you have a second? Charlie says you wanted to see him."
Mary Lou stood at Michael's office door just before noon the
next day, wearing hot pink, another color that clashed with
her hair.

"Mary Lou, do you make a note of everyone who comes in
here and what they say?" Michael asked.

"Yes, for your protection," she replied.

"Do you listen in on the phone?"

"Allan wanted me to. It's safer."

"Every call?"

"No, not the private ones."

"Do you have notes of what Allan was working on in his last
months here?" She tapped her pen on her own notepad.

"Of course, I keep files on everything." Mary Lou indicated the notebook with the ballet shoes. "I create my files from
these."

"I'd like to take a look at Allan's files. How do you have
them organized?"

"It's not possible. They've been archived," Mary Lou said.

"Archived, already?"

"Why do you want them?" she asked.

"Because I want to see his work product, his operations,
management style, the history of the department. What decisions
were made and why. I need it for my orientation. You'll just have
to get it all back," Michael told her, without showing the annoy-
ance she felt at being questioned.

For the first time the gnome looked helpless. "I can't get it
back. It's out of my jurisdiction."

"What? This is the compliance department, for God's sake.
How can the history not be in our jurisdiction? And what about
all the new transparency requirements?"

"Language," Mary Lou mouthed.

What? Was the place bugged, too? Christ! Now she had to swear under her breath. "Whose jurisdiction is it in?" she demanded.

"That would be legal."

"All right, Mary Lou. Please tell Charlie I'm free."

Mary Lou started to leave.

"And Mary Lou, I want all the notebooks."

"Okay."

Charlie came in a few minutes later. Purple shirt and tie, and the kind of glasses Michael wore. He was an uptight guy. He brought a folder with him, and looked wary, as if she might be a ticking time bomb.

"Everything all right, Charlie?" she asked.

"I've made up a proposal for the audit, but I started doing some preliminary work on what you asked me about."

"That was fast. Have a seat."

"I couldn't remember offhand what Allan had been working on. After he died, we didn't pursue it. But I asked Mary Lou yesterday. And of course, she had it in her notebook."

Michael made a little face. Mary Lou had given him the information yesterday and not told her. The person in question came in and sat down; she didn't want to miss anything.

"No notes, Mary Lou. This is an informal meeting." Michael did not try to chase her away. What was the point? She'd just come back.

"Here's the deal," Charlie said. "I found a pattern of defaults on commercial real estate deals adding up to about $600,000,000."

Michael was surprised at the amount. "Isn't that a lot of money for Portland?"

"It's a lot of money for anywhere, but we've been growing here for the last decade. Real estate was through the roof," Charlie said.

"Okay. Tell me about the defaults."

"Some are understandable, the result of unforeseen issues, including the fall-out that all businesses face in down times. The branches did a good job of tightening up controls and underwriting loan standards to avoid future issues."

Charlie took a moment to star eight properties with his red highlighter. "These are the ones I want you to look at. Here are the four properties that Allan identified right before he died."

He pointed to the others. "But I went further in my search. Here are four more that are not in default yet but have the same characteristics. When I searched for other deals with the same characteristics, they popped right up."

Michael took a look at Charlie's work. Frank Hamid's name came up on both sides of every single deal. A clear signal that something was wrong. Maybe this was what Caulahan was concerned about; maybe he didn't know anything about it. Either way, this was what he hired her to deal with. And this was what she liked to do.

"Go on."

"To anybody who wasn't investigating, the deals would look clean on the surface. Sixteen company names are listed, so it doesn't appear these eight deals are connected to the same three people. But when I checked for principal owners, Hamid's name, as well as Anthony Dominici and a man called Hugh Addem, came up on every single one. They're shadow companies. They don't really exist as more than entities."

"You Add Em. Is that for real?" Mary Lou said.

"Yeah, he's a single practitioner in a commercial real estate appraisal firm. Frank's partner in all these deals is real estate developer Anthony Dominici. Try saying that after a few drinks," Charlie said.

"I don't want to say it sober. Has Anthony ever developed anything?" Michael asked.

Charlie shook his head. "He owns some clubs."

"Clubs and restaurants? Cash clubs?" Michael said, quickly assuming sex trade. Drugs.

Mary Lou saw her expression. "What is it? What's going on?" she asked.

Michael frowned at her. Didn't she get the implications after working there for twenty-seven years?

Charlie explained. "Frank and Tony were buying up real estate at a rapid rate, anything they could get their hands on. Right here in the area, they bought some 2,000 acres at rock bottom prices. They picked up another 2,000 out in the hinterlands, logging properties. They quickly got rezoning for higher density developments here in town. Then they sold the properties at inflated prices based on the new usage potential."

"And You Add Em was the appraiser for the inflated prices?" Mary Lou said.

"Exactly," Charlie said, glancing at Michael with respect.

"I don't get it, isn't this what flipping is all about? Isn't this what everybody does?" Mary Lou asked.

"Mary Lou, they sold the properties to themselves! With the money they borrowed, they bought other properties and sold those to themselves at higher prices, too," Michael said impatiently. "Don't you see?"

"Oh." She still looked as if she didn't get it.

"It's a pyramid. You start small and buy something with half of your own money, then sell it to yourself at a higher price, borrowing more money. Now you have the property and the money you started with. Next time you buy a bigger property, and so on. You get more and more money in your hands, flipping to yourself on OPM."

"Other people's money," Mary Lou said softly. "Our money." Her eyes widened. Now she got it.

"Here, look at this property," Charlie said. "Hamid bought it with shadow company A on Monday morning for $27,000,000. Hugh Adam appraised it Monday afternoon. Tuesday the property was sold to shadow company B for $75,000,000. Shadow B borrowed $18,000,000 from Pac GreenBank, an amount that went under the radar for concerned scrutiny by the bank. Hamid borrowed only $18,000,000 on a $75,000,000 property. Looked like a good deal for us," Charlie said.

"But I found that Shadow B also borrowed the same $18,000,000 from two other banks. In reality, there was no cash transaction between company A and Company B, but Hamid got a very real $54,000,000 in cash from the banks. He has it in his hands. Now he can buy more properties and repeat the process. All he has to do is keep up the payments to stay afloat."

Michael was thinking money laundering. Allan Farber might have been in on it, but he might have just discovered it. She'd already tried searching for documents in his computer, so she knew it had been cleansed. And his files had been archived. It was customary to purge computers when new people came in, but in this case there had been a cleanup.

If Michael were an expert at data recovery, she might be able to find emails and other files that had been erased from Allan's hard drive before she arrived. At FinCEN they had many experts who could do it. Unfortunately, she was not one of them. She flashed to Allan's personal laptop or home computer. He must have had one, everyone did. Maybe it was at his home with his widow, full of incriminating correspondence. She made a note to herself to get it. In any case, Hamid had a motive for killing Allan. And if the bank didn't file SARs, which she guessed it hadn't, then someone at the bank had a motive for covering up criminal activities. She could phone home and make a Federal investigation official, but she was digging in nicely. Why ruin the fun? She got up and turned on the TV. She loved how financial institutions had TVs in every room. CNN played over her voice.

"Charlie, I'd like you to take this a step further. Can you do that for me?" she asked.

He nodded.

"I want you to go into every data bank you have access to and find out all you can about Hamid's business interests. Everywhere one of the names on your list comes up. Let's see what else there is."

"I can do that."

"And I want it strictly confidential between us. We're not ready to report."

"He has a hedge fund. It's called New World," Charlie said.

"Then we're going to need bigger data banks," Michael murmured "Are you okay with this?" She was dragging Charlie into dangerous waters. There'd be some danger involved.

"He was my friend," Charlie said, tearing up just a little.

"All right then." She nodded and turned off the TV.

Mary Lou glanced from one to the other. "Will I get my notebooks back?"

"Does anybody know you still have them?"

Mary Lou shook her head.

"Then don't tell," Michael advised. No, she would never get them back.

At the end of the day Michael's cell phone rang, and Claude's number came up. She decided now was a good time to talk.

"Hi," she said after four rings.

"You sound funny. What's the matter?" Claude replied.

"Well, actually this time something is the matter. Now that I've had a little time to think about our relationship, I don't think we're right for each other."

"What? Are you nuts?" Claude exploded.

"We don't have a true partnership. It's not going to work," she told him.

"What are you talking about? We're a partnership. I rented that house for you."

"You signed my name on a lease without my knowing about it and then waited for me to arrive with the check. Even if we were married, that would not be okay."

"Are you breaking up with me for that? What happened? Did your fucking mother say something?"

Now he was attacking her mother. That was the last straw; only she could attack her mother.

"I'm not going to marry you, Claude. The whole thing was a crazy mistake."

"I can't believe this," he raged.

"A lot of things just don't add up for me. You shouldn't have rented that house."

"What are you saying? I can't afford that house on my own. I'm starting a new job on Monday. I got rid of my furniture for you. I have no place to live. What do you expect me to do?"

Get over it. The gnome opened the door that Michael had

instructed her never to open without permission. Michael spun around and shook her head. Mary Lou closed the door.

"You have family here. Live with them, find your own place. You're a grown up. You'll figure it out."

Mary Lou knocked on the door again.

"I do not believe this. You moved all the way out there to break up with me? You're fucking crazy!"

"I have to go now."

Mary Lou walked in as she hung up. "Marty's on the phone," she announced, holding the high stack of notebooks Michael had asked for.

"Tell him I'll call him back." Michael wondered if there was any way she could train the woman just to take a message. Shit, she'd broken off her engagement. Her next task was to come clean about it to everyone she knew. The last thing in the world she wanted to do.

22

"Don't go to sleep," George yelled at Ali. He was driving with the music loud, but Ali wasn't bobbing his head to the beat. The bastard was gone again.

"Shit. Ali!" George raised his voice. It took a moment for Ali to register. He turned to George, but his eyes showed he wasn't there.

"What?"

"I said don't go to sleep."

Another hour and a half to go on the road, and George could see that Ali was high, in his own head, and didn't care about anything. "What did you take?" George demanded.

"Nothing, man. What's the matter with you?"

"What's the matter with me? What's the matter with you? I don't need this. You told me you wouldn't use anymore."

"I don't do anything but take care of your shit. That's my life, taking care of your shit," Ali grumbled.

"What are we doing today? This is not my shit," George protested.

They were taking supplies up to the lodge; that's what they were doing. But Ali didn't bother to answer. It was totally clear he was high and lying again. George knew it wasn't weed and it wasn't ecstasy or alcohol because Ali didn't drink and he didn't take pills. But he thought meth was okay because the Nazis and Japanese had used it. Kamikaze pilots had used it. Made them better fighters.

"Stupid," George muttered about the rationale. How Ali believed some of the things he believed was beyond understanding. Ali thought it was okay to smoke the meth, but not drink a beer. Okay to snuff two unarmed people. It really burned him up.

George wanted to talk. "Ali, do you think there's any way to get to the President?"

"Nope."

"I'm not kidding, man. I'm getting sick of this indecision. We have to do something."

Driving up there every two weeks to bring supplies to people who couldn't make up their minds who to bomb was driving him crazy. They didn't do anything but run around the woods, shooting at shadows, while he took all the risk, transporting and selling. Didn't anybody get that? He was the one in the car, being watched by the other dealers and the cops. He was the one who had to come up with all the ideas. No one else was pulling down his share. They weren't evolving. They didn't have a plan.

"I can't do this anymore," George muttered.

Maybe at first it had been fun. Maybe. He'd felt charitable like his uncle, doing something for old friends. He reviewed the whole case. The lodge was already fitted out with the beds. But usually people didn't stay there in the winter. He and Ali supplied the place with essentials so their brothers could live there in the off season. They weren't cultists or skinheads; they just didn't want to be part of this corrupt society anymore. They wanted to make improvements in their own way. They had no contact with their parents and wouldn't go to town for anything. And now, like Ali, they were getting worse.

"Ali, you did take something. Do you think I'm an idiot?" George returned to the subject of drugs.

They'd been together for hours. He didn't know when Ali had taken a hit. Maybe when he took a piss? It was like this all the time now. Ali was never really sober. He hadn't been sober when he sprayed the intruders. Now George had two corpses up there at the farm carefully wrapped in plastic but not buried anywhere near deep enough. The shallow grave on his uncle's property worried him. Eventually, they'd have to move them. Moving two corpses was a problem he didn't want to have to deal with. But that's what happened with tweakers. After a while all they could do was get high or think about getting high. They could kill all right, but they couldn't dig a proper grave.

The idea was to kill people you didn't have to bury. That's what everybody else did. Leave them for someone else to deal with. How hard was that?

Certain things Ali could do all right, like meticulously make the grocery list for the brothers at the lodge. It took a couple of days for him to get it done, and more time in the grocery store collecting items. Sometimes he'd stop and try to rearrange cans in a display. But he couldn't carry on a conversation, or think straight. If he was startled, he could lose it and kill somebody. That recent event sealed his fate in George's eyes.

"Ali!"

Ali made some noises that were not speech.

"Shit!"

The meth high disgusted George. He'd taken it by mistake once when he thought it was something else. After snorting the white powder, it hurt so much he'd thought his head would blow off. Then he didn't sleep or eat anything for four days, and coming off of it hurt just as much. Getting that manic was not his idea of a good time. Everybody had their preference, and he liked the downer.

"Ali, it's summer. You have to clean all that garbage out of the farm. Rent a truck and take care of it. This week, okay?"

Ali didn't say anything.

"Why don't you take a couple of the guys? They'll help you."

It was a ridiculous request, of course. Ali couldn't take any responsibility. He'd get high, go off, and forget about it. Or he'd set out to go up to the lodge and get lost. He had no sense of direction. It was a two-and-a half hour drive, and the last half hour was torture, ten miles up a steep logging road that made the driveway to the farm look like a super highway. It was treacherous in fog and worse in snow when the forest closed in and the road disappeared altogether. There were no lights, and they had removed the few markers from the trees a long time ago. There was no way Ali could find it alone.

The previous owners had used the place for hunting parties. They'd liked how far away it was and had kept it Spartan. George couldn't imagine why people like his uncle bought rugged backwoods land. His uncle knew nothing about the logging business, had no idea when the trees could be harvested, or who could do what with the land. There were all kinds of federal laws about logging and development.

But George had good use for it. What made the property so valuable to George were the rain forest conditions that were ideal for growing trees. Growing trees took decades, however. Marijuana grew without any cultivation, and took only a few months. George produced very high quality stuff, and each plant had a street value of three thousand dollars. If they doctored it to make it stronger, it was worth more. He had hundreds of plants, so even if he shut down the meth operation at the farm, he still had a million dollars and the weed plants in several locations, including the lodge and even a public park. His uncle might have his hedge fund money machine. But George had a money machine his uncle didn't know about.

Ali wasn't speaking, so George spent the rest of the trip brooding about how you couldn't reason with an addict. The final ten miles seemed to take longer than usual. Rain had deeply rutted the track that hadn't been leveled in several years. It was steep and bumpy going up. George always worried about getting a flat tire, and worse things than that. It was wet and dark in the forest, and it got really creepy when they arrived. Their brothers, who hadn't bathed or shaved or cut their hair in months, always rushed the car firing their guns in the air as if they'd just won some major battle. The gunfire reminded George of his father's death and all that had happened to him since. It reminded him of everything he wanted to forget. Last time he was here they talked about blowing up the main terminal at SeaTac, the Seattle/Tacoma airport, which wasn't that far away. Two weeks before that, they'd talked about blowing up Boeing, which has a large presence in Seattle and was so important to the U.S. that practically no intelligence of any kind could be done without it. Neither were very practical targets. Now George was thinking about blowing the I5 bridge in Portland. It would be easy to do, a high-profile target, and bringing it down would stop the drug runners who came up from California, through Portland on their way to Canada. It was a very good target.

"Jesus." George heard the shots before he saw the brothers. He braced himself and elbowed Ali awake.

23

Michael met with Marty the next day. And this time she did have some questions. He sent her to a floor in the building that required a key card for access, and there was no information on the phone outside the door. She was about to return to her office when a woman in a business suit came out of the elevator.

"Who are you looking for?" she asked Michael.

"Marty Williams."

"Yeah, he's in here." She held up her card to some hidden eye beam, and the door clicked open. "Third door on the right," she said.

"Thanks."

Michael walked down a corridor that was different from any she'd seen on other floors. No decoration or carpets or names on the doors. Sometimes floors like this were used for data storage, and that would explain the security and the lack of personnel. But it was a funny place for a life coach to be. The third door was open, and she walked into a room with inexpensive furniture, a desk, several chairs, a small conference table. Marty was sitting at the desk where there was a phone but no computer. He got up when he saw her.

"Ah, there you are. Have any trouble getting in?" He came out from behind the desk and offered her a seat at the conference table.

"Was it a test?"

He laughed and shook his head. "I knew someone would let you in."

"Why the security?"

"You have to know how everything works, don't you?" he said, probing just a little.

"It's my training."

"Well, that can be good or bad, depending on the circumstances."

He sounded rabbinical, looking at both sides of the coin. Could be good, could be bad. All he needed was the beard to pull on. She watched him sit down and make himself comfortable before she took the chair opposite him.

"I was hired for the training," she reminded him.

"Indeed. I knew you were trouble the minute I saw you." He gave her a look that was not entirely friendly.

"Really? What kind of trouble?" She smiled, could have told him everyone said it and everyone was right. But she didn't, and he relaxed.

"That was a joke. To answer your question, Pacific Green-Bank is the building's second owner. The security on this floor was already here."

"How come there are no names on the doors?" she persisted.

"This is an empty office. I use it from time to time, but it's not officially mine. I'm just a consultant. That's all I know." He lifted his shoulders.

She glanced at the papers on the table. "Test time?" she said lightly.

"Well, yes. But first, tell me. How is everything going?"

"I'd like your input on a few matters," she said after a pause.

"Good, good. That's what I'm here for. Shoot."

"I told Mr. Upjohn I relocated for personal reasons," she said, watching his face.

"Yes. I believe your fiancé, the doctor." He crossed his legs and smoothed the crease out of his trousers, khaki again, then pinched the crease in again. He was looking down, not at her.

She flashed to their conversation at the restaurant. She'd said nothing about Claude.

"One thing I'm concerned about is the gossip," she murmured.

Marty's eyebrows shot up. "Gossip?"

"Marty, I didn't tell you I'm engaged. Who told you?"

His mouth dropped open. He didn't say anything for so long she had to repeat herself.

"Somebody must have told you," she prompted.

"Honestly, I'm thinking about it." He shook his head. "I can't remember."

"Everybody here talks. And everybody here listens. I have a feeling my office is bugged. Mary Lou told me not to swear." She said this innocently.

Marty shook his head. "I'm sure you're mistaken. Do you think that people are against you? Already?" he joked.

She laughed, too. "No, no. I'm not paranoid. But things get around. I've told Mary Lou not to talk about me, but she has a mind of her own."

"Well, you have to expect that. She's been here a long time. Are you not satisfied with her?"

"She's excellent at her job, but I don't like feeling watched and reported on."

"Surely you have nothing to hide," he said.

"That's not the point."

"I wouldn't worry about this. You're coming into a new situation. Give it some time. I know she means well."

"I completely agree. But along the lines of sharing information and withholding it, I do have another concern."

"Oh."

"Allan's files have been archived."

"Why is that a concern?"

"I'm doing a self audit of random transactions. Checking his files would be part of my research into the department. I want to see the history, the evolution of the progress of the process, if you see what I mean."

"Sort of. Is that common practice?"

"The self audit? Of course, anyone would do it." And the president of the bank asked me to, she didn't add.

"What does that mean exactly?"

"I take a look at a wide sampling of transactions." She didn't elaborate.

"I see. What are you looking for?"

"Nothing," she said.

"I understand. You want to assure yourself that the proper

protocol is being followed."

"Exactly. There are new rules on transparency. I need to see what was going on here before I came."

"That's very interesting. But where's the problem?"

"I don't have access to Allan's files. Mary Lou can't get them without an okay from the legal department. I've never heard of files being archived immediately. It's unusual. What is your take on it?" She leaned forward, elbows on the table.

Marty shrugged. "This is beyond my ken. I have no idea."

"Do you think I should just ask for them?"

"Now you have me. I really don't know. I have to think about this. As I said, you just arrived. You don't want to make it appear that you're looking for problems."

"Right," Michael said slowly. "But those rules on transparency…"

"You want to be a team player. Think of what's best for the company."

Michael nodded. "That's my motive, Marty. I'm here to protect the bank. I know how to do that, but I have to have all the facts in front of me."

"So we're in agreement. Did you know your eyes change color?" he said suddenly.

"They do?" Michael said.

"Yes, they were hazel before. Now they're green."

"You're putting me on."

He gave her a knowing look. "I don't think I need to take your personality test. I have your number." He laughed again.

"Oh, come on. I want to know," she said.

"All right, then." He picked up the pages, popped the point on his pen and took her through a battery of questions, sometimes nodding at her answers as if they confirmed his own view of her. When they finished, he checked his watch. "Okay, we're going to make you very successful here. Let's talk again next week," he said.

She got up to go. "Things are not going well with my engagement," she told him in parting. It was as far as she could go on the subject. Claude had been a good cover story and happened to be the truth, but she was going to need a single status to move to the next step.

Marty looked up, and something flashed in his eyes. Concern, interest, curiosity? "Oh," he murmured. "Thank you for sharing that. I will be discreet," he promised.

"I'm counting on it," she said, as he led her to the door.

After the meeting, Michael went to the mall to get a new BlackBerry and a new cell phone. She needed two in case one got lost. Then she canceled her old number. At the store, the salesman leaned on the counter because there wasn't a stool or chair anywhere in there and programmed the new electronics with her phone lists. With the BlackBerry, she had Internet access at all times and a bunch of other stuff, but not the data she'd had on the BlackBerry she'd been asked to leave behind when she left FinCEN.

She decided against the phone with the iPod in it, but got the video feature. The phone also had a navigation system that told where she was and how to get wherever she needed to go. She figured that would be useful since she didn't know how to get anywhere. Unfortunately, the system didn't include local construction detours, of which there were many.

That evening she made it home with her new toys and quickly composed an email with all her new numbers and addresses. She posted a few glowing details about her new job, but made no mention of Claude. The less said about him the better. She planned to send mass emails as long as she was there--a regular little newsletter about the northwest. Usually she disliked being on the receiving end of trivial mass communications. Even at work, she had to wade through them all day. She didn't understand why so many people had to broadcast everything going on in their lives, as if the most intimate details were of tremendous interest to even their most casual acquaintances.

"I cut my hair today. Thinking of getting Botox in my forehead because people say I look mad all the time. But actually, I am mad all the time. Do you think it will help?" Sent to sixty close friends.

Fifty-five people would answer--reply to all--as if total strangers wanted to hear their opinion. Hundreds of jokes, political newsletters, greeting cards with emoticons and songs, prayers to make the day better, sentimental poetry about friendship, popped up every day. And now she was jumping right in. For once she didn't want to disappear completely. Some novelist, she didn't remember who, said you can't go home again. But that was before the Internet.

She stayed up very late on Friday, walking around the house with her furniture in it, checking on her car that had no garage, working, planning, trying not to think about what she had done for a reason she could no longer remember.

24

Marty met his two bosses at the bank for a drink in the bar at the Heathman Hotel to talk about Michael. He didn't know what was going on. From all the news in the papers, and all the loose talk over the last months, he knew the bank had incurred some heavy losses, toxic debt. People were in trouble. He knew that mistakes had been made. He didn't know the details, and he didn't want to. Plenty of big banks had gone down in the last year, and he just wanted Pac GreenBank to stay on solid ground. His job was there, his money was there. He wanted it to be all right, and no one to be hurt. Who wouldn't?

They frowned as he gave his report. The two old friends and long-time colleagues at the bank exchanged glances.

"We talked about this happening," one said.

"I didn't like her from the first. But you thought she was the perfect target."

At this term Marty shifted uncomfortably in his chair. He'd heard the suggestion they pin a series of bank errors on the new compliance officer at a later date if necessary, and that's the reason they wanted someone good at covering up, who wouldn't talk. The way the law worked, if someone uncovered criminal activity that occurred in his department before his time, he would still be held responsible for it. But they didn't hire a he. They hired Michael Tamlin. Others were tougher than Marty about discrediting girls.

Making a former compliance agent take the fall would be a nice slap at the Treasury and a way to save their own asses at the same time. It would cloud the issue in the media and make everybody look bad. But Marty knew the last thing these two men wanted was for Michael to blow the whistle. He shook his head. Money usually stopped people from biting the hand that fed them. And he knew they'd tried several ways to give Michael extra cash beyond her salary. She wouldn't take a signing bonus of $50,000, however. And she wouldn't take a performance bonus at the end of the year. She'd scratched both line items off her con-tract, and she'd chewed Curtis out for the policy breach. Pac was still up to its old habits. Hoarding bailout money from borrowers who needed it, but spending unauthorized funds when needed.

The younger man pinched his nostrils together as if offend-ed by some bad odor. The older one did that thing with his jaw that made his teeth click. Marty always had to focus on his glass when he did that. Corruption was everywhere, but what could he do about it?

"How the heck did we get into this? I'm disgusted." The more senior man ground his teeth against each other, his lower jaw moving from side to side. His junior had to look away, too.

"Let's not get overexcited. The bottom line is this. Tamlin must remain a loyal employee. We have to accomplish that goal," Marty said.

Even the bite of the two men's favorite single malt whisky was not taking the edge off of the discussion. Marty had had a lot of experience with these two in crisis and needed to neutralize their reaction to the situation.

"Let's just relax for a moment," he said.

"All you ever do is talk about feelings," the grinder said, and held up his hand to order another drink.

"I'm just saying that Tamlin is a strong personality with a lot of integrity. Given your goal, it might have been a mistake bring-ing her in," Marty ventured. "I warned you about that."

The two bankers exchanged glances. Two more scotches appeared. Marty didn't want another.

"I asked if she is loyal," the nose pincher said.

"Loyalty is not an issue for her yet," Marty replied slowly.

"I don't know what you're talking about. She was told loyalty was a requirement of the job," he snapped. "I made that very clear myself. How could we trust a woman with a man's name? Why can't she just call herself Michaela? Or Michelle?"

"What does that have to do with it?"

Marty ignored the squabbling. "I'm sure you told her all about your feelings on the subject of loyalty, but Michael is a person of high integrity; she's somebody who has to have answers. The answers that she needs to hear will be the springboard for her loyalty," he said.

"Jesus, don't give me your fucking mumbo jumbo, Marty."

"She's asked me about Allan's death. It's not an unreasonable question." Marty finally said it. "And I didn't know that Allan was looking into Frank's deals. Did you know that?"

"That has nothing to do with this. What are you suggesting?"

"Nothing. We all know that Frank is an honorable man." Marty looked from one to the other with an unasked question on his lips. For a second no one moved, and he finished the thought. "You're satisfied on that subject. Michael has to be satisfied, too. It's not out of line."

"Then satisfy her, for God's sake. Very unfortunate, this whole thing. I miss poor Allan. He never would have let this happen," the older man said.

"And she was distressed by the archiving of Allan's files. That seemed odd to her," Marty added.

"Oh, for God's sake. I don't give a shit about her distress. Deal with it."

"She's a government person. She likes to dot the i's and cross the t's. It's the kind of person she is," Marty went on. "She won't go down for this easily."

The older man nodded. "We just have to put a plan in place to slow her down, that's all. She can't move forward if we don't want her to move forward," he said thoughtfully.

"Yeah, let's not go overboard about this. There are many ways to bring her down," the other replied.

"I remember you saying that she would be more intimidated than the others because she was unfamiliar with corporate workings, eh, Marty?"

Marty looked away again.

"Well, I still think this is a manageable situation. She's a government lackey, all wrapped up in manuals and response cards. We can handle this."

"I think you misjudged her," Marty said softly.

"You want to try your psycho babble on her? Okay, go for it, Marty. This is what we pay you the big bucks for. Point her in the wrong direction. See if it works."

Marty shifted uneasily in his chair again. "I like her," he said.

"Good. If you like her, then it shouldn't be too hard. I don't want to have to fire her after she's come all this way. The board won't like it."

Marty finished his drink and left them to pay the bill. He spent a lot of time with these guys, but sometimes he had the disturbing feeling that things were a lot worse than he suspected.

25

Saturday was chilly and humid. It was the kind of moody day that was common on Cape Cod and instilled in New Englanders the stony, stoic pride for which they were known. No one ever expected the tropics there. Same here, it seemed. Michael had slept well in her own bed, drank her coffee on the patio by the pool and read The Oregonian, looking for fraud.

There was a feature about a gang attack on the MAX train, and the PPD's promise to hire new police officers to insure safety for commuters. Two articles about fatalities included a cyclist who had been hit by a DUI driver and a wife on a meth high who'd run over her husband with the family RV. Two old people got mugged at McDonald's by gang bangers. Nothing about Frank Hamid. Michael moved on to the Living section, where there were maps of the wine country and the coast. She wanted to drive out to see the Pacific Ocean. But she had something else on her agenda.

Unfortunately the weather wasn't cooperating. Mary Lou had said that unpredictability was the only thing Oregonians could count on. Fog in the morning either burned off, or it didn't. Mist turned to rain suddenly, at any time of day, and stopped as soon as it started. Or didn't. Today, Michael knew waiting until 10:00 a.m. to see if the sun came out would be a futile exercise. Ten was too early for a verdict. At 9:00 a.m. she dressed in jeans and a hoodie and left home with her file of sites that Allan had questioned. She punched the first location, just north of John's Landing, on the car's navigations system and set out in dense fog.

She had created a detailed study of the history of each of the areas where she intended to conduct personal visits. Specifically, she wanted to know what prices had been several years before Hamid had bought, at the time he bought, and what they were now. All she had to do was check public records for comparable properties that had sold during those periods and selling prices for similar properties on the market now. She could have asked Charlie to do it, but she enjoyed the task.

What she'd found did not surprise her. The present values for the eight properties Hamid and his partner Dominici had bought were less than half the original prices. That meant the second deals were a total loss, and there was no way the bank could ever recover its money. Michael didn't tell anybody what she'd found. She wanted to see it for herself.

First, she explored the south waterfront, where the tram went up to the medical center, and new high rises with many unsold condos clung to the river adjacent to an old ship yard that still seemed to be active. A huge, cleared site just north of it was waiting for a plan for its use. Then Michael drove south to a shabbier area of older homes and lower-rent condos that had seen better days. A few years ago this spot might have looked ripe for development, but now it just looked old. There was no indication renewal was imminent. For Rent and For Sale signs up and down the streets gave the area a desperate feeling.

Addem's appraisal for a property that was neither large nor on the water was beyond ridiculous. Only a high rise would give it a view, and there was no new development nearby to give that prospect any credence at all. Obviously, no one had checked this out before approving the loan. Michael got back in her car and programmed an address near the Portland Raceway. She drove north of downtown, into a flat industrial area. The property there had never been much. Formerly it had been used as a storage area for containers, but they were long gone. There was nothing on it now but a small, dejected-looking, one-story building. The property had a chain fence around it.

Michael didn't get out of the car. She could see a hopeful idea behind the waterfront property. In a booming economy, it wasn't such a big stretch to imagine spiffy new housing there. But you would have to wait a long time for this site to have the high-end, industrial-park potential of Addem's overly sunny appraisal. With a feeling of increasing dread, she moved on to the property in the Pearl District.

The Pearl was a mixed neighborhood of high- and low-end streets and condos and houses. Here, Hamid had bought an abandoned warehouse that was the size of a city block on a street that had been rezoned for higher density and mixed-used development. It was more of the same. He'd bought low-end properties in areas that had been hot only for a New York minute. By the third property, she'd had enough.

She drove past Taboule and flashed to the plate of cheeses, crispy flatbreads, dried fruits and nuts she'd seen there. She briefly considered stopping for a late lunch. It was crowded and tempting now. She could use the company. But the sun had finally come out, and she was finally ready for a heart-to-heart with Marjorie.

26

"It's about time I heard from you," Marjorie said irritably when Michael got her on the line.

"It's only been a few days. I emailed, didn't I?" Michael said, a touch defensively.

"Oh please. Your group email yesterday made me feel so special," Marjorie grumbled. "You dropped off the end of the earth. I certainly hope it was worth it." She sounded bitter, almost like a jilted lover.

It was now misting again, and way too cool to try the hot tub. From the kitchen Michael could see steam rising from it, which meant the heater worked, but so what if the last thing you wanted to do was take your clothes off? Michael had taken the top off and turned on the heat to test it. Now she watched the weather deteriorate and knew she wasn't getting in.

"All right, sorry. I'm glad you called." Marjorie's tone softened after the long pause.

"It's only been a week. But I miss you, too." Michael said the last bit softly because she didn't want to seem like a wimp.

"Uh oh, what's going on?"

"I broke up with Claude."

"No shit!" Marjorie erupted. "What happened? He didn't live up to the promise?"

Michael told her about the house. "He signed my name on the lease, and then left it to me to pay the owner."

"Oh geez, that's not good."

"And he had other girlfriends."

"What? What a scum ball. Are you all right?"

"Yeah. I had to watch a Lifetime movie to access my tears."

Marjorie laughed. Neither of them was very good at crying over personal losses without a cheesy movie to get them going. "When are you coming home?" she asked excitedly.

"Not right away. Something came up."

"You've only been there a few days, what could possibly have come up?" Frustration rang in Marjorie's voice.

"Well, it didn't come up this week. It came up before I got here," Michael said.

"All right, what?" Marjorie sighed.

"My predecessor at the bank was shot dead on a bank outing." Michael started with that.

"Oh, God!" Marjorie screamed. "That's all you need. God! What is it with you?"

"They were hunting cougar," Michael added.

"They kill cats out there?"

"Only when it's not deer season."

"That's awful." It shut her up. Marjorie had cats, too. She and Max bonded over them.

Michael was silent for a moment, too. "Yeah, cat killing is bad. But killing people is worse," she said.

"What? You think someone murdered him?" Marjorie was beginning to spin out. "Come on, no."

"I have no way of knowing that for a fact, but it's a situation." Then Michael told her about Frank Hamid, who had been Allan's spotting partner when it happened, and how Allan had been suspicious about some questionable transactions Hamid had made. Real estate flipping deals with a bunch of shadow companies that he and his partner owned, and one appraiser who was over enthusiastic. As well as the fact that other banks were involved, although Pac GreenBank apparently didn't know about that. Michael told her everything she knew and then drew breath.

"They flipped to themselves at much higher prices," Marjorie concluded.

"Yeah, with the help of other banks. And then the market out here totally tanked and my bank is badly exposed."

"How badly?"

"Couple hundred million."

"How many is a couple, Mike?"

"About four fifty that I know of here," Michael said finally.

"Any SAR reports made on these transactions?"

"I read the paperwork. No."

"What about the businesses of this Hamid and his partner?"

"Restaurants and night clubs, looks like."

"Cash businesses? Prostitution, drugs?"

"I just got here, Marj. They were taking large amounts out of banks, not putting it in. But he has a hedge fund. Could be putting the cash there. I'm betting there's something there."

"Still…Was Farber in on it, or on to it, or just fishing?"

"As I said, I don't know yet."

"I see," she said quietly.

"The problem is I don't have access anymore," Michael told her.

"You want to see if they're on any watch lists?"

"Yes, Marj. I need to know if anybody is looking at these guys, if you know anything about them. I want to know if you're looking at Pac GreenBank, too. Do they have any kind of negative points?"

"Ain't that a conflict of interest for you?"

"If I went to another government agency, I'd have to be loyal to the new agency. But I went to the private sector, Marj. So I still have to follow the laws of the land. Right?"

"Especially since you wrote them," Marjorie laughed. "Okay, sounds like this is right up your alley. I'll get on it right away. How are you doing?"

"Oh, I feel humiliated." Michael put it out there, blunt as a hammer.

"Oh, come on. Could have happened to anybody."

"Which part? The bank brought me here on a private jet. Romanced me. And Claude didn't even buy me a ring. He said the ring was his mother's, but it was a fake."

"Aw, honey. You can buy your own ring."

"Right." Michael was silent for a moment. "I did some checking on the bank, but not enough. I wanted to be a vice president and buy designer shoes. What was I thinking?"

"I don't know. You never keep them on," Marjorie said.

"I feel like such a jerk. I didn't ask Claude the right questions. He played me."

"Enough with the pity party. Let's just get you home on good footing." Marjorie was always the practical one.

"Okay."

"Max said you chose a hot spot. Maybe you can be useful. I'll find out what's going on."

"Nice of him to tell me," Michael said before she hung up. The bastard, he knew all along.

A little while later, just as it was getting dark, Frank Hamid called and invited her to a party at one of his restaurants.

"I'm eager to have you meet some people, and I think you'll enjoy it."

Michael cooed her thanks for a few moments while she thought about it. She'd told Marty her engagement was in trouble, so Marty could be leaking information that might inspire a ladies' man to call. But she'd just gotten off the phone with Marjorie, spilling like a fountain on an open line. Everything she knew about precaution right down the drain. What was she thinking? Just because she'd gone all corporate didn't mean this was a game.

She looked around the living room to see if anything had changed since she'd left for her site visits earlier in the day. The place had been messy. She couldn't be sure.

"I can't do it tonight, but I really appreciate the offer," she told Hamid.

"My fault. I should have given you more notice," he replied. "I wanted to personally welcome you to Portland, have you meet some of the bank's important customers."

"Thank you again. Have a good evening." Michael hung up and reviewed. Hamid had called her on an unlisted number, which made her think someone might have been in the house to get it. It wouldn't have been that difficult. The locks were primitive. Outside the weather was kicking up again. It started to pour.

27

All night the wind blew like a bitch. Rain slashed against the windows, and the movement in Michael's house did not feel like a gentle rocking cradle. Outside, not a single light shone. The house had been situated on a bluff with the intention of making it appear alone in the middle of a crowded suburb. So it was dark forest in all directions. Michael couldn't stop second-guessing her unguarded conversation with Marjorie. What if Hamid had heard her tell Marjorie about her suspicions and was now watching her windows, listening to her breathe. She wasn't scared, she just didn't like being stupid.

At 8:00 a.m. she went outside and dialed Pete's number on her cell phone. The fog was beginning to clear. Looked like it might be a nice day. The phone rang many times before he picked up.

"Fleisher," he said. Curt.

"Did I wake you?" Michael wouldn't feel guilty about that.

"No, no. Mikey, how are you?" he asked. He sounded alert now.

"Sorry to call you on a Sunday," she began.

"I've been working, just about to call it a day. What's up?"

Michael licked her lips. She did not want to go public with this. She looked around. All quiet on the eastern front and the western front, too. Maybe she was just being paranoid.

"Mikey?" he said. Now there was a note of concern in his voice.

"I think my place is bugged," she replied softly.

There was a long pause. "Who would do that?"

"I don't know."

"All right. I'll be over in an hour. Okay?"

"Thanks. Really, thanks."

Michael went inside and started frantically cleaning the house, checking again for evidence of a listening device. She hadn't found anything the night before, but bugs could be hidden anywhere and there was no way to find some of them without special equipment. She didn't see one in the phone, but that didn't mean anything. Bugs could be outside the house, too. Could be in the TV, behind the coffee machine, anywhere. In any case, the place was looking pretty dust-free an hour later when a black, generic sort of SUV crunched into the drive and stopped by the gate. Pete was at the wheel. A dark-haired man wearing sunglasses was in the passenger seat.

The two got out of the car, adjusted the holsters at their waists, and glanced quickly around like cops do in the movies. Pete's companion was short and powerfully built. The natty sport jacket he wore did not hide the torso of a serious body builder. The man moved like a wrestler or a fighter, and his expression was all business.

Pete came around the car with the same kind of walk. Don't mess with me. They turned their heads, looking both ways as they moved forward. Pete was the taller of the two and had the lean look of a swimmer, or a skier. Together they made a little army, the kind of men you wouldn't want to annoy. Michael felt a little thrill of apprehension as she came out to meet them. She knew a lot of guys like this, had even slept with a few. The cover had been taken off her pool during the week, and now the water sparkled in the sunshine. Testosterone spiked the air. She inhaled it.

"Hi, Mikey." Pete smiled, but did not shake her hand. "This is Felix Torres, our chief of security. Michael Tamlin."

Felix shook her hand. "Pleased to meet you," he said.

Michael's eyes popped at the title, and Felix laughed. "That doesn't mean I have the rank of a chief," he said. "I'm a detective."

"Well, detectives, thank you both for coming. Is everything okay?"

"You called us."

"Yeah." She looked from one to the other. Was she that important?

Pete glanced at Felix.

"I'll just go over the place. You two can talk," Felix said, and went into the house as if it were his own.

Michael started to follow him, but Pete touched her arm. "Sit down." He pointed to the table and patio chairs. "Why would anyone want to bug you?"

"I have no idea."

He shook his head. "There's more to this. Spill."

"All right." She sat down in the sun and hoped she wouldn't feel sorry later. "Do you know anything about Allan Farber?" she asked after a moment.

"Farber, Farber. The name rings a bell. Was he the guy involved in that shooting incident about six months back?"

Michael nodded and swallowed hard. "Shooting incident. That's an interesting way to put it."

"Hunting accident. It was bad. Yeah, I remember."

"Did you investigate?"

"Not me personally. Why?" Pete gave her a curious look.

"Farber was the Chief Compliance Officer at Pac GreenBank. I am his replacement," she said.

"No kidding." He looked very surprised.

"He was looking into some questionable transactions at the time. It turns out his spotting partner was the man he was investigating, and also the guy who found him. The police report said that he fell out of a deer stand and his gun discharged as he went down. I'm wondering about that. What kind of investigation was done?"

"You talk like a cop, kid," Pete said. "You watch a lot of CSI?"

She shook her head. Firsthand experience.

He smiled. "Go on."

"Look, I feel bad about bringing all this up. I started an audit as soon as I got here. You do that when you come into a new job. The same things that Farber was looking at came up in my check. Funny stuff. It's going to cost the bank a lot of money. This is confidential, okay? I don't want to get anybody in trouble."

He nodded.

"The people at the bank are not going to be happy about this. But if I don't call it now, my career could end over it down the line. The buck stops with me one way or another. I took a step. Yesterday I called a colleague to see if the names I'm looking at are on any watch lists. I want to be on the up and up here."

"And?"

"I don't know yet. But not fifteen minutes later, the person I called D.C. about was on the phone asking me out."

Pete's eyebrows went up. "Name?"

Michael hesitated.

"I'll find out anyway. I can pull the file."

"Frank Hamid. He's a big client of the bank, member of the club. Owns a bunch of restaurants."

"Oh, yeah. Taboule is my favorite. You been there?" Pete gave her one of his little smiles.

"I didn't know Taboule was one of Hamid's restaurants. "Yeah, I was there once, but just for tea," she said.

"You seem to attract a lot of trouble for a person who hasn't been here a full week. Are you sure you're not agency attached?"

"Of course I'm not. I just don't want to be involved in something that might require action I'm not authorized to take. You understand?"

Pete nodded. "And I'm not in homicide. I can't open closed cases."

"Understood. But that guy had my phone number and it's not listed." She paused. "For what it's worth."

He didn't look impressed. "Has he made any threats?"

"No, Petey, he asked me out."

"No law against that," Pete said.

Felix came out of the house, went around the side, looking for where the phone lines came in. A few moments later he was back. One quick shake of his head told Michael she'd made a huge mistake.

"It's clean," he said.

"Okay. Have a nice day. I'll check in with you later," Pete nodded and turned to Felix. "Let's roll."

"Nice meeting you," Felix said.

"Thanks for coming by." Once again Michael felt like a total idiot, but it didn't stop her from her next task.

28

It wasn't hard to locate Christine Farber. Michael got the address from the phone book and called the number to see if she was at home on a Sunday afternoon. A weary-sounding woman picked up after four rings.

"Hello?" she said.

"Is John there?" Michael asked with a British accent.

"There's no John here."

"Too bad. I'll speak with Mary, then."

"No Mary, either."

"Well, who's this?" Michael put on a bit of a prickly tone.

"I'm Christine," the woman said patiently. "You have the wrong number."

"Sorry, my mistake," Michael said and punched the address into her BlackBerry for directions.

Beaverton wasn't that far. She figured half an hour, forty-five minutes max. She got into her Acura, followed directions to a highway, then another highway, past a bunch of shopping centers that weren't doing so well anymore, and found herself in an upscale subdivision with houses that all looked the same—expensive, woody three- and four-bedroom split-levels with shingled roofs. Nice, but not a mansion. About what you'd expect from a bank compliance officer in his prime.

Christine wasn't much of a gardener, though. The bushes were overgrown, and no one had cleaned out the flower beds since the spring thaw. Michael drove into the driveway and parked. After the wild storm Saturday night, Sunday had turned into a gorgeous day. Other people might be taking a day of rest and contemplation, but Michael was feeling like a fool after her fiasco with two of Portland PD's finest. And she wouldn't know what to do with a day off anyway.

Michael got out of the car, stretched and shed her jacket. Then she marched up the Farbers' front walk, rang the doorbell, and waited. Christine had a light step coming to the door. She stopped to look through the sidelight before opening it. A huge ginger cat came to the window and stared out as if looking for someone. The woman was thin. Her baggy jeans suggested a weight loss. Her reading glasses hung around her neck, dispirited. She had short brown hair, just beginning to gray and was carrying a book with her thumb tucked in, marking the page. She was reading *The Year of Magical Thinking* and hadn't been expecting company. One look at Michael and she opened the door.

"Yes?"

"Hi, I'm sorry to bother you." Michael paused. She was so used to making up stories that telling the truth in a case like this didn't come naturally. But something about Christine Farber, the untended grounds, the cat, and the book about a wife mourning the sudden death of her husband made her think Allan's widow might welcome some honesty.

"You're the woman who called on the phone. What do you want?" Christine said. She was sharp.

"Sorry about that. I'm Michael Tamlin. I work at Pac Green-Bank. I'd like to talk with you about Allan."

"Do we know each other?" Christine had steely gray eyes, and a direct gaze that said she knew they had never met.

"No, I'm new."

The cat ran outside and brushed by Michael's legs. Michael was startled. She was allergic to cats.

"It's all right. She won't go anywhere. Come in."

Michael didn't want to go where a cat lived. She had this same problem with Marjorie, but she stepped inside anyway. The living room was pleasant, traditional, clearly used. Family photos covered many of the surfaces, and a lamp was on by the chair where Christine had been sitting. She waited for the cat to come inside before shutting the door.

At thirty seconds in the room, Michael's eyes began to itch. Her first sneeze came in at just under a minute. She was recovering when Christine stepped onto the cat-hairy carpet and looked her over.

"You're Allan's replacement, aren't you?"

Either she was very sharp indeed, or someone had told her.

Michael nodded. "I'm sorry for your loss."

"What do you want to know?"

Michael sneezed again. "Allan was very loved and respected at the bank. No one can take his place," she began slowly. "I wouldn't even try."

Christine nodded and gestured toward a sofa. "Thank you for that. Would you like something to drink?"

Michael shook her head. "I can't stay."

"The cat? I can put her in the other room?"

It wouldn't help, though. "No, thank you. I'm fine," Michael lied, then quickly moved on to the truth.

"The circumstances were very tragic. I know Allan was look-ing into something when he died, something potentially damag-ing to the bank. Were you aware of this?"

"I'll tell you what I told the police. Allan had been preoc-cupied for some time. Everybody at all banks has been worried and concerned. It just came with the territory. You read the pa-per about all the corruption, the bad investments, the greed, the need for bailouts, and of course, you think about it. We've been thinking about it for a long time. But I wasn't aware that there was anything specific, anything to really worry about at Pac. It's a very sturdy institution. Been around a long time."

"Allan wasn't afraid that day?"

"No, far from it. He'd been looking forward to it. He loved those hunting trips."

Michael glanced at the cat. "They were hunting cat."

Christine smiled sadly. "We had some disagreements about the hunting. Every couple has its issues. That was one of ours. Are you sure you wouldn't like some tea? Coffee?"

"No, thanks. Did the police have any interest in his com-puter?"

"They did want to look at it," Christine said. "But by the time they came for it, it wasn't here anymore."

"Really?"

"Yeah, we had a break in," she said, vague for the first time.

"So, the computer was stolen?"

"No, I don't think anything was taken. The alarm went off. The place was a mess, but whoever it was didn't stay here long enough to get anything."

"You have a gated community."

"Yes, but no video. If you have the code you can get in. Hundreds of people have the code."

"It seems pretty safe here. Do you always put on the alarm?"

Christine shook her head. "Never. I don't know why I did it that day. Allan had been killed. It was just like I had to do something to protect myself. I think I wanted to take precautions I'd never needed before, as if I could put on the alarm and it would be all right again. They call it magical thinking." She indicated the book on her lap.

Michael nodded. "I totally understand. But what does this have to do with the computer? Did the police ask for it before or after the break-in?"

"They were different police departments."

"I see."

"They thought his death was an accident, but they kept asking the same questions." Christine mused about that for a moment. "They asked me a lot about his state of mind. Was he depressed, were we having marital problems? Was he in trouble at work?"

"Anything in it?"

"He would not have taken his own life."

"Life insurance?"

"They asked about that, too."

"That must have been hard," Michael murmured. "Did he leave a lot?"

"Enough that I don't have to worry. We were happy. He wouldn't have done that to me. I think they wanted to see his computer to see if he was on porn sites or dating sites to see about the marriage. He wasn't a gambler or anything. When I said he'd given it away they dropped it."

She looked at her feet. "The break-in came after that, and

the local police were concerned about security in the subdivision. You know how it is." She looked up again. "What have you discovered?"

"Nothing yet. Who has the computer?"

"Charlie has it."

"Charlie Dorn?" Her Charlie?

"Yes, Allan ordered a new one. He gave his old laptop to Charlie. The new one came the day after he died. Ironic, huh?"

More than ironic. Michael sneezed again. "He must have backed up his files to download onto the new computer. Did you go through his things?"

Christine looked at her. "You want to know if there was a back-up key, portable hard drive, CDs, that kind of thing."

Michael nodded. That kind of thing.

"I didn't find anything like that. But I wouldn't. You know you're not allowed to put bank information on personal computers. There are blocks. You can't download any bank information."

"But he might have been working on something independently, his own work product."

"Do you think Allan did something wrong?" Christine's gray eyes widened with surprise.

"Did he tell you about any bank accounts, any safe deposit boxes, any extra cash coming in?"

"No! He wouldn't take bribes. I know he wouldn't."

"I believe you. I'm just following up." Tears ran down Michael's face. Her nose was running, too.

"Well, what are you saying? He was good? He was bad? Or just that it wasn't an accident?" Christine was deadly calm, like a person in the eye of a hurricane. She wasn't worried about the good or bad part. She wanted to know about the hunting, the thing they'd disagreed about.

"You want to know if it was his fault—going hunting? If he was careless, falling out of a stand and getting shot with his own gun? Your worst fear, the thing you argued about. Christine, I don't know yet. But I promise you I will find out."

Christine's eyes pooled. "I knew something wasn't right. He was a very careful man. He wouldn't do this to me. I know."

Now they both were crying, but for different reasons.

The cat jumped on Michael's lap, depositing hairs and deadly saliva. It was trying to make friends. Michael patted its head before taking off.

29

Michael thought about Charlie Dorn all the way back to Carl Place, and then she gave him a call on his cell phone. Could he meet her for a coffee and suggest a place? He chose a Starbucks downtown and was already sitting inside by the window when she arrived.

Fifteen middle-aged men, who looked like they might be a fellowship group after an AA meeting, were grouped around a few tables outside, smoking. Michael had the thought Charlie might have been with them when she called. She smiled, and he nodded back.

"Thank you so much for meeting me on such short notice," she said as she moved a chair closer.

"Not a problem, what's up?" He was halfway through a very large, highly caloric-looking cold coffee confection. Wearing shorts and sandals and much cooler glasses than the ones he used at work, he looked like a different person.

She smiled and leaned in. "Just lonely in a new city."

He almost fell off his chair.

"You were expecting maybe something else?" she said.

Charlie took a breath, was actually at a loss for words. She let him agonize for a moment before she came to his rescue.

"We could go a couple of ways with this. I could pretend there's nothing wrong and we could dance around for a few days, or you could tell me what's going on now and get it over with. Either way I'm going to find out." She sounded like a cop, but figured he didn't know that.

"I don't know what you mean." He looked at the guys outside, tapping their ashes into empty cups.

"Yes, you do. It's takes weeks to do the kind of audit you did for me overnight. I asked for something and you gave it to me the next day, and more. So I'm guessing you and Allan had already done that work. Or else you retrieved it from Allan's computer after he died."

Charlie pressed his lips together.

"You were in on these deals, or you covered them up. Or you just discovered them. Which is it?"

Charlie breathed for while. "We found them in an audit. Allan figured it out. He was very smart."

"Who knows?"

"I have no idea. Procedures weren't followed. That's all I know."

"How did it come out?"

"The bank has been vulnerable because of the number and size of defaults. The commercial real estate mortgages stuck out because of their size. Allan was in the early stages of looking at them."

"When I asked you the first day, you said you didn't pursue what he'd been working on. Did someone tell you to drop it?"

"Allan was my boss. After he died, I couldn't take the lead. They blame things on you at the bank. They can make sure people never get another job. I don't know. It can get bad." Charlie sipped his drink to hide his distress.

"It got very bad for Allan, didn't it? Did you see that as some kind of warning to you, or others?"

"I didn't know what to think. The police said it was an accident. Accidents happen all the time. Didn't Dick Cheney shoot his host on a hunting trip?"

Michael smiled and wished she had a coffee. "In the back, as I recall. Why did Allan give you his computer?"

"He wanted something different. An Apple." Charlie looked away. It was a lie.

Michael changed the subject. "Did you get that list for me?"

Charlie nodded. "Been working on it. There's the hedge fund and a jet center. Those are two big ones. The restaurants, of course." He raised his shoulders.

"A jet center?" That was interesting.

"It doesn't have his name on it anywhere, but he's behind it. Bird's Eye Aviation has a couple of jets and a hanger at a small airport near Hillsboro. That's where Nike and Intel are. They don't have a website or anything."

"Is the bank involved in that?"

"No."

"What about the hedge fund? Is money funneled through the bank?"

"We've had regular deposits from a bank in Scotland, Highland's. They're supposed to certify that funds entering the U.S. are in compliance with American regs on source and country of origin." Charlie shook his head. "It always looked clean to us. But there was that case of millions funneled through Lloyds from Iran, or Somalian pirates?"

"Not the exact facts, but something like that." Michael smiled. "The bank there did not reveal where the money came. I remember."

"I went to high school with one of the partners of New World. He would know. The thing is we need a thorough audit on the hedge fund. Things can be hidden in various ways." He gave her a funny look.

"Christine called you, didn't she?" Michael said.

"Yes."

"Have any of you on my team spoken with any government agency about Hamid's activities?" That was the crucial piece of information.

"Not that I know of. But I wouldn't know. I wouldn't know anything." Charlie looked scared.

"You know enough not to talk about it to anyone, yes? We want to keep you safe." It was a dicey situation. Michael didn't know where he stood, who he was really. But she didn't want him to meet the same fate as Allan.

Charlie pressed his lips together again. "Whose side are you on?"

"Same question I have about you, Charlie. But I'm on your side." Michael wouldn't believe it if she's been in his shoes, but he seemed reassured by the answer.

"Can I get you a coffee?" he asked.

"Double espresso. And a piece of cake," she said. "Make that two pieces of cake. And set up a meeting with your friend at the hedge fund, okay? Maybe we could have drinks tomorrow."

The fellows outside dumped their cups in the garbage and moved on. Charlie waved at one of them and went to get coffee. It was a start.

30

Private Caller came up when Michael's new cell phone rang as she pulled into her driveway after consuming way too much sugar and caffeine.

"Yo," she said.

"Bingo. You lucked out." It was Marjorie.

"No kidding. Hot water?" Michael sat down in one of the chairs by her pool and watched the afternoon sun slant through the French doors. Even though the house had been swept that morning, she didn't trust that it was still clean. She didn't trust anything or anybody anymore. Portland was a snake pit.

"You said it, baby. Very hot." Marjorie's voice had the kind of urgency she used only for major situations, and she was advising caution now because Michael's cell phone was not a secure line.

Hot water between the two of them meant a hit. The answer was yes, Hamid was on a watch list. But hot meant more than that. Now it was like bidding in bridge. Which list, who was watching him, and how big an investigation was going on? Michael couldn't ask straight out: how many aces have you got? Her body tingled. Maybe it was all that coffee, but maybe not.

"I went shopping for shoes," she said.

"Really. What kind are you looking for?" Marjorie asked.

"Oh, something a little more special than my usual pumps," she replied.

"I know how you love the bells and whistles, but you should stay away from them this time. You know how they can hurt your feet. You don't want to get bunions."

"Yeah, but how can I resist? I'm a shoe junkie. What can you do? Have you seen anything in any of the major department stores I might like? We have a Nordstrom's out here."

Marjorie's voice got really funny. "Yeah," she said slowly. "I saw just the shape you like in the catalogue. I don't know the brand, though, didn't get the name."

"Really." Michael was silent for a long time.

"Way too expensive even for your new budget. Sweetie, this is a bad connection. Would you call me back?"

Michael cursed and headed for her car. She had to drive back down the hill to find a secure phone. She bought a couple of throw-aways in a convenience store, and an hour later she was talking on one of them. This time she was sitting on a bench up at Council Crest, watching the sun set in the west and listening to Marjorie back in D.C. on the line they'd always used when Michael was in the field.

"Apparently, we've been watching this guy for a while. Lot of cash moving around. Came up in the system, the way it did with Governor Spitzer when he was doing that thing with the hooker. Spitzer changed the law so that lower amounts triggered the system, and that's how they caught him."

"I remember."

"Some of Hamid's restaurants are cash only, and his partner, Dominici, has mob ties," Marjorie added.

Michael thought of the hedge fund, perfect for money laundering.

"We were thinking maybe prostitution at first. Not street activity. There's a lot of high-end call girl stuff in Portland. Some people call it Sin City. A very sophisticated Internet business is going on out there."

"Could have fooled me. This is a pretty crispy, crunchy town," Michael said.

"Only on the surface. Lot of drugs there, too."

"Hamid's into drugs?"

"Listen, nobody has been able to pin anything on this particular individual. Not even a speeding ticket. He appears squeaky clean, a model citizen, into Catholic charities and everything."

"Back up a minute. What agency is looking? You were talking prostitution. Would that be local vice?" She was thinking Pete, from Portland PD. She'd mentioned Hamid's name to him, but he didn't share any intel on the subject.

"I can't tell you if local LE is involved. The structuring came up on IRS software. What got Hamid double-tagged was his sketchy trips abroad."

"Where to?"

"The guy's been to Pakistan a number of times. We don't know what he's doing over there, or who he's meeting up with. Could be a lot of things. He doesn't seem to have connections to any mosques here, any known arms or drug dealers. All we have are dots."

"Pakistan is not exactly a vacation destination. Where was he spotted?" Michael's heart started to pound.

"We've got photos of him in hotels, restaurants. No shots with him and anybody else. He seems to arrive somewhere and quickly disappear from sight. But that's not unusual for this type of individual." Hamid had his own transportation system. He could go anywhere, didn't even need a passport to get in an out of the U.S. Michael didn't mention the jet center. A hawk circled in the sky. She watched it hunt. "Are you sure it's the same guy?" she asked after a moment.

"Computers don't lie."

"Okay, well. Nobody said a word about this when I left." It had been good-bye and good luck. But maybe FinCEN didn't know. DHS, CIA, FBI, Treasury, and IRS didn't cooperate on every case they worked; most cases they worked.

"You know what? You're some kind of frickin' magnet, Tamlin. What is it with you? You can't even go to the movies without turning something up?"

"I didn't come looking for this," Michael protested. All she'd wanted to do was get married and be normal. And look how that turned out. She was eating her own edible undies.

The hawk made lazy circles in the sky. A melody from a Hammerstein musical came into Michael's head. Oklahoma. Her heart thumped away. There were a lot of things to look into. The logs for Hamid's planes, the source of his hedge fund money funneled in from Scotland. Unfortunately, she was just a bank employee.

"What can the locals find out about me by the usual routes?" she asked after a moment.

"Not much. Just the official stuff. You're an intel analyst, compliance specialist. Same thing the bank would know. Why?"

"The case in Louisiana?" Michael prodded.

"I don't think so, why?"

"I've met a local vice guy who looks at me funny."

"Everybody looks at you funny, Mike."

"I'm just saying the locals may think someone sent me here special delivery, okay? Normally, I'd be a plant in a case like this. They may think I'm a wild card."

"You are a wild card."

"So why don't you clear things up and let me in?"

"You wanted out, remember?"

"How long are you going to hold that against me?"

"Forever. You wanted information. I've given you more than your clearance allows. Bye."

"Don't hang up. I am admitting error, okay? Is this being recorded for Max?"

"The whole department, baby."

"Oh, come on. Let a person change her mind without public humiliation. He may be funneling in funds from the Middle East through Highland's Bank in Scotland. I'm in a perfect position to connect the dots for you. There's a big piece missing in your investigation of Hamid, and I can supply it without alerting him."

The hawk disappeared from view. The sky was pink and orange. The clouds looked unreal. Michael held her breath. She wasn't going to tell them about the jet center.

"Max says okay. But you gotta play nice and prove yourself."

"You talked to him?"

"He's right here. Say hello, Max, Mike."

Michael rolled her eyes. "Hello, Max."

"Yeah. Here's the story. We're taking you on as a CI. Stick with the bank investigation and stay away from Hamid. It's an ongoing, not ours. Report what you get to Marjorie. That's it."

"What if there's an overlap?"

"Anything local like vice, homicide--report to the local PD, as any citizen would any crime. You're not on a team. You're strictly CI. That means very limited status. You have to be careful and watch your own back."

"I understand."

"If you get in trouble, bail. Understand? And I'm sorry about the break-up."

Yeah, he was all heart. She understood everything. Max and Marjorie had just turned her. She was a confidential informant now, which made her a whistle blower. What gave her the feeling this had been Max's plan the minute she'd quit her job and said she was going to Portland? Once again, thanks for telling her. Watch her back indeed.

31

Michael Tamlin was a different person by the time she got home. When she opened the door to the Carl house, her eyes swept the living room, looking for subtle changes again. Everything seemed as before, magazines on the coffee table, breakfast coffee cup in the sink. Bed made up, coverlet unwrinkled. Cosmetics in the bathroom were all over the place. Everything looked the same, but everything was different now. She moved quickly through the house, checking her hidey places.

The Glock from the Louisiana incident had been confiscated and was no longer in her possession, but she still had the 9mm automatic with whistle and flashlight that folded up to the size of a paperback. It was a novelty item, advertised for those who might run into trouble while walking their dogs late at night. Click, click to put it together, flash the light, and you're ready. She kept it rolled up with her heating pad underneath the five pound free weights she used from time to time when she remembered. The gun was still there. She'd used it twice, and luckily hadn't needed to hurt anyone. She had a sub-compact Glock, too. Ten round magazine, 5.5lb trigger pull, night sight, extra magazines, holster, decal grip because those plastic grips could get slippery in sweaty hands. Fear and wet conditions do funny things. Six by four inches, it fit in the slow cooker. Both were registered and had traveled in a moving van to Portland in a china box marked fragile. Michael made a mental note to join a gun club far, far away to practice.

She took a deep breath. Claude had not known about this side of her at all, and she'd thought he was secretive. How could she not have known the relationship was weird? As for the guns, she'd learned a few things in the last four years. Once you got used to having a firearm in your possession, you just didn't like being without one. She didn't love them, would never hunt or kill an animal. But mastery of anything was nice, and she liked knowing they were there. When Felix had come into the house that morning, she'd been uncomfortable letting him roam around. He could have found them. It was time to put them in a better place, preferably concealed on her body.

Okay. Complete change of plan. Michael circled back to the kitchen and pulled her bottle of Skyy out of the freezer. She threw some ice in a glass and poured vodka. Not too much, not too little, just enough to help her rethink. It was time to slow way down at the bank and speed up at home. She took a sip and felt the heat. This was more like it.

She took the Glock out of the slow cooker and put it on the counter. Nice small size, same firepower as the bigger, heavier ones with the 8lb trigger pull. She turned away from it and checked the refrigerator. She was finally ready to cook. A bag of spinach, a package of chicken breasts, some slices of fairly recent ham and cheese were about all she had. She decided on chicken Cordon Bleu with ham and cheese.

As she assembled ingredients, some things came clear. Since Pac GreenBank hadn't filed any Suspicious Activity Reports on Hamid's real estate deals, FinCEN and DHS didn't seem to know about them. The shell company names must have hidden his involvement well enough. That was the reason investigators working his case were concentrating on the businesses they knew about. They may not have connected the death of Allan Farber and Pac GreenBank with their investigation of Hamid. Or if they did connect the suspicious death with him, they may not have wanted to nail him for it and jeopardize a bigger investigation. In any case, money from the restaurants interested them, and certainly from the hedge fund, as well. But the primary agency investigating would only follow where they saw Hamid's steps go. If they had subpoenaed his bank records, or authorized a wiretap at his home or one of his businesses, somebody at the bank would know. If the bank was part of a wider investigation, as compliance officer she would know. There wouldn't be any way around that piece of intelligence. And she hadn't been told anything about it. What role Allan had played in this, however, was unclear. If Pete was working the vice side of this, he hadn't shared it. But then he wouldn't. She was just a civilian to him.

Hamid had come up on Homeland Security's radar because faces are routinely screened in airports and hotels in hot spots. If he had jets, they would have to land in major airports. His photo must have prompted an auto match because of the countless photos of him in Portland newspapers. It raised the question: What was a Portland restaurant owner doing in Pakistan? Added to the issue of the cash moving around, it became a big question mark. What was he up to?

It all made sense now. Michael finished her vodka, lit a candle, and sat down to eat. Her plan was made. She was a different person now. She knew exactly what she was there for and what she was doing.

32

After dinner, Michael drew up a strategic plan for herself. Embedded in the bank, she would look like a loyal employee and make friends. Safely ensconced and doing her regular job, she would create a financial picture of Hamid and his projects; examine his properties and see what he did with them. She would try to find links between his real estate holdings and his other businesses. In short, she would follow the cash and see where, and to whom, it led.

This was a method that always worked. It was the way the Feds got Al Capone decades ago, and just recently Sami Al-Arian in Florida, Elliot Spitzer in New York. The worlds of Ponzi kings Bernie Madoff and Art Nadel also completely fell apart when special agents from the IRS or the Treasury started following the money trail, did the forensic drudge work of sifting through accounts, looking for the cash and checks coming in and going out. Huge withdrawals had been made just days or weeks before the announcement that the funds had collapsed, before investors knew their money was gone. The Treasury had unlimited powers to investigate. It could out find anything, and it was much easier now.

In the old days, before the Patriot Act, the banks had to report transfers only of $10,000 or more. To hide illegal activities, people have always done something called structuring. They made their deposits and transfers in lower amounts. It was Elliot Spitzer, the former governor of New York, who changed the law so that all transfers made to the same accounts would be scrutinized. His own transfers of cash to a shell company that turned out to be a prostitution ring was what caught him. IRS investigators thought it was illegal contributions, or a tax dodge; they never suspected he was paying a high-priced hooker.

Software smarter than humans was now able to detect patterns, even the smallest ones. Someone going to the same ATM for four hundred dollars every Friday to pay the housekeeper would be a pattern that would be noted. Hamid's pattern in borrowing tagged him for Charlie when his name was nowhere to be seen. His other dealings would be tagged, too. But Michael's instructions were to stick strictly to Hamid's bank dealings, the loans, the money moving in and out, his relationships with bank officers. Clearly, someone, or several people at the bank were engaged in allowing these commercial deals to stay hidden in the shadows. Whether, they were doing it to protect the bank, or had a deeper involvement in Hamid's criminal activities, it was still criminal activity. There would be prosecutions down the line.

Charlie had some gold stars for producing the incriminating information Michael had requested and finding the jet center. Maybe he'd already known about it. Michael wanted to believe Charlie was on the side of right, but only time would tell. In the meantime, she would not do anything to put him in jeopardy. He could carry on with the self audit, which included a full range of Pac GreenBank financial transactions, to see if other Patriot Act procedures and regulations had been overlooked or avoided. He would not draw attention to himself by looking for anything special, or do any more searches for her that were not strictly bank related.

As for the rest of her team, Michael thought Mary Lou was in the dark except that, like Christine Farber, she was suspicious. Allan's death didn't feel like a simple accident to either of them. It was too soon to speculate about the legal department. Legal was where Allan's archives had been taken. It didn't look good for Ashland. Banks these days were like dead men walking. Any one could go down like a bowling pin at any moment. Ashland might very well be motivated to hide a fraud situation that would discredit the bank. If it came out, he'd never be able to take over from Caulahan as president, and might even go to prison. Ashland was definitely a person of interest.

Around 10 p.m., Michael -- or Tamlin, as she was known in the field -- picked up the phone to call Pete.

"Yeah, Fleisher," he said when he picked up.

"Hey, Pete, it's Michael Tamlin."

"I know who it is, Mikey."

She'd blocked caller ID. "Really? Well, then thanks for picking up. I'm sorry about earlier today. The false alarm."

"It's all right. It's what we're here for."

"Did you find out anything about the Allan Farber investigation?"

"Yeah, the case is closed. Although the evidence was inconclusive as to how the gun discharged, there was no indication of foul play." There was no strain in Pete's voice as he said it.

So why didn't she believe him?

"I see. Well, I'd like to thank you for everything you've done for me. You can take your stuff back. The bed's back in the box. I've washed your sheets. How about I thank you and reciprocate on the dinners you bought me last week?"

Pate was quiet a moment too long. She could hear him thinking. She wanted info, but maybe he thought she was coming onto him. Better clarify.

"I broke up with Claude, but I'm not coming on to you," she said. The second was a white lie. She liked him.

"Does he know about it?"

"Breaking up? Yeah, he knows. He said the usual things. I have to be crazy, right? He doesn't know I'm calling you right now, though. We're no longer in touch."

"You don't sound too broken up about it," Pete said.

"I'm covering my heartache well," she told him.

"Ha, ha."

Finally, she got a laugh. "You people out here don't have much sense of humor, do you?" she said.

"Yeah, you can be funny sometimes. Not now, though."

"Oh, you think moving 3,000 miles for a two-timer isn't a good joke to tell around the water cooler."

He clicked his tongue. "You know, something about this doesn't play for me. You seem smarter than that."

"What if I'm not? People make honest mistakes all the time. You said so yourself." She knew where this was going.

"Yeah, maybe, but not you...Are you still hooked in, Mikey?"

Ah, there it was. He did think she was on the job. That meant Pam thought she was on the job. From the get-go they'd suspected she wasn't here to marry their brother. Should she feed their doubt or tell the truth? She hated telling the truth.

"Would it make any difference?" she asked.

"As I said, I like an even playing field."

"Okay. Well, I'm interested in why my predecessor lost his life. Not that I'm paranoid or anything. Plus, I'm an intel specialist."

"I never get those titles straight in my head. Analyst, specialist? What does it all mean?"

"I snoop. I work with local law enforcement sometimes. It can mean whatever."

"I see."

"But I'm here on the bank's nickel. I don't have status. Why else would I call for help yesterday?"

"All right. Good. You call for help any time. I have your back. So, you're officially in the private sector?"

"Yeah. What do you say, are you on for dinner?"

"Sounds good," he said at last.

They made a date, and she pumped the air. She hated herself for telling the truth yet again, but was glad she got him.

33

"Who turned on your lights?" Mary Lou did a double take when Michael arrived at work the next morning.

"What?" Michael smiled.

"Your hair, your suit. Smile on your face. You look like a different person. What happened?"

Michael had talked long distance and drunk a lot. This morning, with a slight headache, she'd dragged herself out of bed at 5:00 a.m. Then she went online to order an oscilloscope to monitor the electrical waves in her house so she didn't have to rely on local fuzz to see if she was being bugged. Maybe that put the blush on her cheeks. She'd ordered motion detectors for all her perimeters, lights that would flash in the night and provide more security for her beloved souped-up, gun-metal grey Acura TSX. As for the weekend, she hadn't gotten laid or been attacked, so she'd have to call it a wash.

"Not a thing happened," she said. She was wearing the red power suit, the one with the short skirt, and the kind of high strappy heels that hurt just to look at. Her hair was down, and she was trying the new mascara with the vibrator that made lashes outrageously long. She was also feeling a lot better since her personal goal had reverted from enabling a spoiled man and wishing for personal happiness to her original one of protecting the country.

She strode into the office in the short skirt thinking what a relief it was not to have to worry about getting too much attention or pissing anyone off. She deposited her briefcase on her desk with an authoritative thunk. Michael's back.

Mary Lou followed her in, her face screwed up with concern. "What's going on?"

"I'd love some coffee, Mary Lou, if that wouldn't be too much trouble." Michael posed again by her desk.

"Of course it wouldn't. Did something happen?" The gnome looked really alarmed.

"I told you, absolutely nothing happened."

"Are we okay?"

"We are super okay, but we're not going to follow up with that project any longer, okay?"

"Why are we stopping?" Mary Lou frowned.

Michael noted the leopard print shirtwaist with matching glasses and black patent leather belt and shoes she was wearing. "Nice outfit. Would you get Charlie in here right away?"

"What happened? Did someone threaten you?" Mary Lou looked worried.

"I love your dress. Where did you get it?" Michael kept up the girl stuff, and Mary Lou brightened for a moment at the praise.

"You like it, really?"

"Very much. See, we've had a climate change. Look at that great dress. Summer solstice. I like your belt, too."

Mary Lou's expression showed she didn't know what Michael was talking about. Summer solstice had nothing to do with her dress. Did that mean they were going to let the whole thing about Allan go? She didn't look as though she wanted to change course on that. It was very clear Mary Lou would not make a good spy. "What about my notebooks? Can I have them back, then?"

"Coffee?" Michael said again, sinking into her desk chair and shedding a shoe.

Mary Lou lifted a shoulder. "You're the boss. You want Danish with that?"

"Absolutely, two," Michael told her.

Now Mary Lou looked really confused. There was a lot of butter in Danish pastry. Michael had already lectured her many times about the fat and cholesterol in Danish and Cinnabons. Her second personal favorite had eight hundred and thirteen calories, 32 grams of fat and 117 grams of carbs each.

"Okay," the Loughlin gnome said in a tiny voice.

Charlie strode in a few minutes later. "You look good with your hair that way," was the first thing he said.

"Charlie, has anyone asked you how things are going in this

department?" Michael asked, still smiling.

He hesitated. "In what way do you mean?"

"Oh, how I am as a boss. How we're filling our days. That kind of thing." She pushed a pen around on her desk.

Mary Lou was back before he had time to answer. She hurried in with two coffees in Pac GreenBank mugs with the evergreen trees on them. "I have to go downstairs for the Danish. If they don't have Danish, would croissants be all right?"

"Croissants would be great," Michael told her, and Charlie nodded at the prospect of free food.

Mary Lou left looking peevish.

"Well?" Michael asked.

"Nothing specific. Just things like how does the team like you? How are you managing? Any unusual habits, that kind of thing."

The new/old Michael nodded. "I do have unusual habits."

They talked about quirks, but not their real ones, until Mary Lou returned with the Danish. For a while the three sipped the coffee and ate the Danish. Then Mary Lou took the paraphernalia away, and Michael got back to business.

"Charlie, would you email me all your data? I don't want just the hard copy you gave me. I want your work product in a safe place. And you might clean up."

She didn't have to say anything more; he nodded.

The rest of the day she showed off her sparkling personality. She joked around with people in the halls, had lunch in the cafeteria. In response to this effort at sociability, she received an invitation for lunch and to play golf with Ashland and two of his lawyer lackeys on Friday, as well as offers from a variety of other people for drinks and dinners and movies over the weekend. The workplace was always fertile ground for infiltration. She just never did it when she was really working.

When she wasn't out and about revealing her affable, loyal, fun side, she was in her office with the door closed, deep in the system looking for anything she could find on Frank Hamid. His personal account, business accounts, any accounts she could find

under the shell company names. She checked Dominici and Addem for accounts under their names, too, and public records for
other Hamids. There were many, going back in Portland almost a
hundred years. It was an old family in the area.

Creating a complete financial profile was a far bigger job than
Michael could do from the bank's computer alone. She needed tax
returns and several other data banks to make a complete review
of his financial dealings, but she found enough to get started. She
found that Hamid had online banking at Pac GreenBank and a
credit card. She didn't have to get a subpoena to look at those.

She was looking for transfers of small amounts of cash on a
regular basis and didn't see anything unusual. He bought large
amounts of supplies from many different accounts. They'd have
to track where all those supplies went, and of course his pur-
chases from the Internet. He most certainly had accounts at other banks, even offshore accounts, or banks in the Middle East,
that might be receiving and distributing funds in big numbers
that went into his hedge fund, and that Hamid and his partner
Dominici used to seed their first sharp real estate deals. Just the
one failure to report SARs at Pac GreenBank could hide a whole
secret operation. Michael had no idea what the Feds knew. It was
cold out in the cold.

34

When Charlie Dorn called out of the blue, Jesse Halen was finishing up another blue Monday of staring out of the window, wondering when the sun would come out and he could finally take the girls to the beach.

"Hey, Charlie, what's up?"

Jesse was relieved to hear from an old friend and not Frank Hamid or an investor asking for a withdrawal he wasn't authorized to accommodate. People were getting crazy eager to extricate their money from New World. It was scary. Prominent people were hurting from their business losses and houses that wouldn't sell, school and college bills that kept coming, mortgages and credit card debt. They needed more than just interest payments; they wanted their money back. And there wasn't a thing Jesse could do about it. Hamid took the money out whenever it came in and only pretended to invest it. New funds came in from clients in the Middle East and some of it went to pay interest due. There was a word for what he was doing. The fund numbers looked good, but they were cooked. Jesse said he didn't know the real assets of New World, but he did know there wasn't much in it.

"Thought I'd call and see how you're doing," Charlie said.

"Oh, things are pretty secure here at New World. We're pretty diversified. How are you doing? I know how close you were with Allan." He let his voice drop on Allan. Sympathy.

"I still miss him. He was more than a boss," Charlie said.

"I know." Jesse fiddled with a pen.

"So, I thought maybe we'd get together, catch up."

"Yeah. Yeah, that'd be great. What do you have in mind?" Jesse asked.

"Why don't we meet for a drink tonight? There's someone I want you to meet," Charlie said.

Jesse was surprised. "Don't tell me you've finally met someone." Jesse had never seen Charlie with a girlfriend. Could it be, after all these years, that nerd of nerds had found a girl?

"Kind of," Charlie said. "Yeah, I have." He laughed.

"God, that's great." Jesse was enthusiastic. He had always figured Charlie was gay. But maybe the someone was a guy. He didn't want to ask if it was a guy or girl. Not that it mattered as long as an old friend was happy.

"How about Taboule in an hour?" Charlie suggested.

Jesse almost gagged at the suggestion. "Oh, it's so noisy there. Couldn't we go somewhere else?" Last thing he needed was for Hamid or Sami to see him with an auditor from a bank.

"The Brewery?"

"Oh, geez, are you sure?" Jesse knew Charlie wasn't drinking anymore.

"That's not a problem. She's new in town. I think she'll like it."

"Well, I like it," Jesse said, perking up.

"I know you do, buddy. I know you love your brew."

"Well, we had some good times in the old days. Lot of good times," he said, wistful.

"We did indeed. Six thirty?"

It was a she. Ha. Jesse closed the blinds and checked out the back office. He liked to turn everything off when he left. They had a printer and fax machine, mailing room supplies, a sink to wash out the coffee pot. They had a bathroom, and a back door, but no permanent support staff. The place was a just a small storefront. Jesse's desk faced the window, and there was just enough extra room for a small sofa and two chairs. There was no conference room because no meetings or parties were ever held there. Still, because New World's fake money-making record was good, as many people clamored to get in as to get out. That was what made the thing work.

Hamid expected Jesse to be in at 7:00 a.m., half an hour later than the stock market opened in New York. Some days felt so long that Jesse locked the door, closed the blinds, and took a nap in the afternoon, or brought a girl there for a quickie. Few people dropped in. He wasn't expecting anybody to hassle him until later in the week, but he went out the back door just in case. He left his car out front and hopped on the trolley heading into the west hills two stops down.

Jesse got to the Brewery promptly at 6:30. Charlie was there in his banker's suit, his bow tie and gay yellow shirt with white cuffs, and his round accountant's glasses. The girl turned out to be a stunner. Jesse did a double take.

"Well, hello," he said sliding into the booth.

"This is Connie," Charlie said, and put an arm around her. "This is Jesse Halen."

"Pleased to meet you," the girl said. She gave him a big smile, and told him she was interested in the way hedge funds worked. Maybe he could explain it to her.

Jesse ordered the sampler. Six flavors of ale, all made on site. He glanced at Charlie, drinking iced tea, and thought, poor guy. That's no way to get a girl. And then he went into show time. He couldn't help it. He loved pretty girls who looked at him like that and listened so intently to everything he said. Call it a little weakness. He explained to Charlie's girl how the brew was made. And then something in him clicked, call it competition. He just had to show off to the new girl over baby back ribs, the ale, the hearty bread. He even forgot to call Cissy. He started spilling about Hamid's Middle Eastern charity work, and how the hedge fund helped protect so many wealthy families caught in war-torn countries. What a great guy Hamid was. It just came out, like he'd been given some kind of truth serum.

"Why would foreigners want their money here?" the girl asked. "Isn't the U.S. a terrible place to invest right now?"

"They invest to get here," Jesse said. It was like the devil made him say it. If someone had asked him an hour later why he had said that, he wouldn't even know how it happened or what he said. They'd been talking, drinking. Charlie was an old friend. They'd played baseball together in high school, had drunk together many times. The girl was totally adorable and adoring. It just seemed all right. He told them that Hamid was charging wealthy people big money to help with immigration. Nothing wrong with that. He just wasn't supposed to say it.

At 9 p.m. it was just getting dark as Jesse found his way back to First Avenue to retrieve his car. He wasn't exactly drunk, but he wasn't sober, either. He felt good, indestructible even. As he passed the office, he saw a crack of light under the back door. He went to the door and listened. Nothing. For a second he thought he must have left the light on. It nagged at him. Leave it, or go turn it off? He hesitated, walked away, and then came back. He didn't like leaving lights on. He opened the back door to the office. It was a big mistake.

Inside, Sami was waiting for him, and Jesse froze.

"Hey, what's going on?" he said warily.

"I brought you some weed. Just got some new, really good stuff. Want to try it?" Sami offered the baggie and pipe.

Jesse attempted a smile. "That's nice of you." He laughed. "But Frank doesn't like us using."

"Since when has that ever stopped you?" Sami was sitting in the chair by the door. His legs were apart, and he looked relaxed. He'd chosen the back door to wait.

How did he know that Jesse would come back? Or that he would come in the back door? The whole thing made Jesse uneasy. He glanced around his tiny fiefdom with his hand still on the door knob. Something wasn't right. Sami gave him some shit from time to time, but he didn't bring it here. Jesse wasn't a client or a big user. He liked to smoke sometimes, who didn't? But Jesse only used in a party environment, when it was around and easy. He didn't go out looking for it, and didn't smoke the heavy stuff.

Problem was his thoughts didn't come together quickly. He was moving in slow motion, but he knew. He just knew Sami was there to hurt him. He weighed his options.

"Come on, try it," Sami said. "George's best."

Jesse shook his head. "Thanks, Sami. Maybe some other time. Cissy's waiting. I have to get home."

A thought came to him. There was no way to know what was

in that weed. Could be anything at all, could kill him with one drag. Jesse had another thought. It was the oddest thing, he could almost see the shit hitting the fan, splattering him, the walls, everything. Shit everywhere. But he didn't know what to do to stop it. He didn't know how to get away.

"How about a drink, then? I'll give you this for later." Sami held out the baggie.

Jesse looked at it and rolled his eyes. Okay, he could flush it. "Sure, one drink would be fine." He was lulled by the thought of a drink. His drinks were safe.

He went to the cabinet where he kept the booze. It was still locked. "Scotch or tequila?" he asked, bringing out the bottles. Everything looked okay to him. And he reminded himself that he was always safe in here. He poured the shots. Tequila was his favorite. He figured it would go down well after the beer. He and Sami clinked glasses. Down the hatch. The liquid burned Jesse's throat and esophagus going down, but not much more than usual. For a few seconds he felt okay.

Jesse didn't know what happened after that. His thoughts shut down. He didn't feel himself being moved to his desk. He didn't know he was facing the closed blinds for the last time. Of all the things he thought might happen to him, he never in a million years thought that his life would end this way. Sami didn't hit him or ask him a single question. They just had a drink together.

As soon as Jesse was too logy to put up a fight, Sami moved quickly. He put on plastic gloves, moved the two waste baskets around to each side of the desk. He wiped a sharp boning knife clean, pressed Jesse's fingers around the handle and slit one of his wrists. Then he did the same thing to the other. The prints would be smudged, but that's how it had to be in life. A little of Jesse's blood made it to the wastebaskets, but most of it drained out on the floor. Sami scattered Jesse's desk with a variety of pills, the bottles of booze, and the baggie of dope. Jesse was still bleeding out when Sami exited through the front door and locked it behind him.

35

The call came in before Michael was out of the house. She was drinking coffee, preparing for the day, not expecting bad news.

"Where were you last night?" It was Pete, sounding like the cop you wouldn't want to cross.

"I went to the Brewery with a co-worker. What's the matter?"

"Jesse Halen was found dead in his office this morning. Bloody mess, been dead since around ten last night. Just after he left you."

Michael put the cup down and closed her eyes. Oh no. "What happened?" she asked softly.

"Looks like he swallowed a pharmacy and slashed his wrists."

Oh, no. Not death by cop again. Michael opened her eyes and stared out at the ravine. All those huge trees were creepy. For a second the house seemed to sway. Maybe it was her swaying. What was the world coming to when you couldn't ask a few questions without someone offing himself? It was sad.

"I'm really sorry," she said.

"Sorry? You're sorry?"

"Could you be more specific?"

"What are you, some kind of bad penny? Coming to town, breaking hearts and getting people killed?" He sounded really mad about it.

Michael could argue about that, but what was the point. It did turn out that way from time to time. Not that he would even begin to understand. "I mean specific about what happened," she murmured.

"I told you. You and your buddy were the last people to see Halen alive. Okay? You and Charlie Dorn."

Wait a minute. How did he know that? "Am I being surveilled?" she asked.

"No," he said curtly.

"Then how do you know that?"

Pete didn't say anything.

"Was Halen being surveilled?"

More silence. Right, she was a civilian, but he didn't believe it. He said it was a suicide, but she didn't believe it. Games upon games.

"I need to know, Pete. Was he being surveilled? Is that how you know we were with him?"

He still didn't say anything.

"Okay, you're watching me. We went out for a drink. That's it. Charlie and Halen were high school buddies. They reminisced. We had beer and ribs. Pretty good ribs, too. He seemed happy when he left. You can't pin a suicide on our meeting with him. His partner probably killed my predecessor. Don't you see a pattern here?"

"Suddenly touchy, aren't we?"

Michael made a noise. Kind of like a snort. Pete didn't want to listen. Men were so often like that. She wanted to say fuck you. Unfortunately, one little detail was true; people did tend to die around her. And then there was that other little thing about how she'd promised to stick with bank business and instead had strayed to ICE, DHS, and SEC issues. She heaved a great sigh. There were just so many agencies to piss off, you couldn't even have a beer these days without compromising someone's investigation. But if no one wanted to play with her, how was she supposed to navigate around them?

Max wasn't going to like this. For a few moments Michael was seized with guilt for letting him down. Luckily, the feeling didn't last long. She decided she'd better push Pete back.

"Look, do you want me to come in? Put me in a room, you can interrogate me. Bring in the bullies. Let's talk about your two cases. If Halen's body hasn't been taken away, I'd like to see it. Is the lab doing a full range of tox tests? Maybe he was drugged."

All right, so maybe she gave Halen just a little something to help the conversation along. But they'd have to shave her head and pull out her fingernails to get her to tell. Pete replied to her request.

"You'd like to see the body? I don't think that can be arranged," he said.

"And I have some other questions for you. Did anybody else connected with Frank Hamid's operation die recently? Let's check out all your suicides and natural causes. See how many suddenly dead people knew or worked with him."

Pete didn't say anything. Maybe he was thinking about it.

"Look, I don't mean to malign your department. But I talked to Farber's wife over the weekend. She told me your detectives tried to make a case for Farber's killing himself, too. Do you blame every suspicious death in this town on suicide?"

"You're beginning to really piss me off, you know that?" Pete said.

"It comes with the territory," Michael muttered. "Gotta use your brain, or lose it, buddy."

He laughed suddenly. "All right, get off your horse. Lot of drugs on the scene, so it could have been foul play. I'll check it out."

Michael breathed a sigh of relief.

"Thank you. I'm sorry about Halen. Seemed a nice enough crook. And I appreciate the call. Anytime you want to talk, you obviously know where to find me," she said.

They both hung up at the same time. And because he hadn't asked why they'd met, Michael was sure that Charlie was the one they'd bring in for questioning. He'd be much more likely to spill what they'd been talking about than she would. She went outside and called him on one of her throw-away phones. He picked up right away.

"Hi, it's Michael. Did the police question you after Farber died?" she asked.

"Yeah, they wanted to know if he was depressed, why?"

"What did you tell them?" Michael walked out into the driveway and sat in her car.

"He had a breakdown after 9/11. His brother was in the

building. He had a couple of rocky years there, DUIs. I told the detectives he'd been sober for four years and was doing really well. Now you know. That's all Allan cared about, being sober. That and Christine. He would not have shot himself on a hunting trip."

"He got you into the program, didn't he, Charlie?"

"Yes, he was my sponsor. I'm not ashamed of it. Why are you asking me this?"

"Do you have another sponsor now?" Michael's heart thudded. She felt bad for him. Jesse's death wasn't going to be easy news for him.

"Why are you asking me this?" Charlie asked.

"You could take some sick days, go on a vacation. I'd authorize it," Michael said.

"You're freaking me out. What's going on?"

"Jesse died last night. His wrists were slashed. It doesn't mean he did it, though."

Charlie didn't say anything.

"I'm sorry to have to tell you, are you all right?" Michael asked. She'd really like him to get out of sight for a while.

"I feel bad for his wife, but he was a scumbag. She's better off without him," he said finally.

Okay, good healthy response. "Remember what I said last night about the charities?" Michael asked.

"No, what?"

She wanted to laugh. No wonder no one could connect the dots in this town. Nobody shared anything, and she still wasn't sure whose side Charlie was on. But she wanted him to be safe.

"Fine, you can take the rest of the week off," she said. "Go to some place safe. A spa, whatever. I'll cover it."

"Hell, no. I'm not scared. See you in an hour," he said.

Michael dialed Marjorie and told her what happened. She had no choice.

"Okay, that's it. You're in over your head, Chicky," Marjorie exploded.

"I'm sticking to bank business," Michael lied.

"Bail, baby."

"Oh, come on. Where's the fun in that?"

"Do not tease me. This isn't funny. What was the purpose of your meeting with the deceased Jesse Halen?"

She made a disgusted noise. "Jesus. Max will want to know that. And so do I."

"It was a reunion. That's all. One of my staff went to high school with him." Michael didn't want to jump to step two and say she suspected Hamid's jet center was used to import illegal, possibly dangerous people, from the Middle East after she had failed to take step one and tell them about the jets in the first place.

She'd made a promise to herself to check out Hamid's remote properties and see what they were used for. Site visits were part of bank business. She rationalized that it was her job. As soon as she knew that piece, she'd back off.

"Max won't be happy," Marjorie said.

"He can always say I'm not one of his anymore."

"And may never be again. I don't want to lose my best friend. What is the matter with you?" Marjorie demanded.

"Just want the world to be a safer place," Michael told her. It was more or less the truth. She was not here to get married, so she had to do something to justify her existence.

36

Jesse Halen's death made big news in the local media. People at the bank talked about it endlessly. As Michael predicted, Charlie went downtown to talk with the same detectives who had interviewed him about Allan. If he was traumatized about that, he didn't show it. He didn't have a lot to report about the interview, and she didn't probe too much.

The motion detectors and more lights around the Acura were installed at the house. Her oscilloscope arrived, and she swept the rooms and perimeters regularly. It wasn't as small or high tech as the one that Felix Torres had used, but it did the job adequately. Nothing came up. Michael also kept a watchful eye on the cars and people moving around her. Up in the Council Crest neighborhood, it was really quiet. Except for the occasional dog walker and jogger, there were few people out and no unusual traffic activity. As far as she could tell, no one was interested in her. A couple of times when she was working late at night the lights flashed on outside. She hit the switch to black out the room she used as an office, grabbed her gun off the desk, and peered out. Both times it was a pair of raccoons.

It reminded her that every little thing was not about her. The second raccoon invasion made her think no one was watching her, after all. There were other ways Pete could have found out she'd been out with the dead guy. She returned to her original idea that someone had been watching Halen and had taken a photo of them at the restaurant. If there were drugs on the scene where he died, Pete might have been called in to try and trace them. Then if someone had shown him a photo of her, he'd want to know what she was doing there. Who knew, maybe it was a personal interest. That prompted a smile. Later, she was disappointed when he cancelled their dinner date. He said he was working. It didn't matter that he didn't report any details on the case; she would follow up.

The day of Halen's funeral, she noted Frank Hamid's prominent photograph with his widow, Cissy, and the couple's two little girls. She read all Hamid's comments about the stability of New World Fund and denials that it was, or ever had been, under investigation by the SEC, etc. And she read all the obligatory collateral articles Halen's death had generated about bad debt, bad investments, the fate of other hedge funds, stock market woes, and danger of untreated depression. Several times during the week Michael tried to get down to the jet center, but couldn't avoid a host of meetings at the bank.

On Fridays in summer Pac GreenBank execs left at noon for golf, and since Michael had admitted to owning clubs, they expected her to join them. She didn't see any point in going, but couldn't get out of that, either. In the morning she chose her outfit carefully: cargo pants with pockets deep and wide enough to conceal a firearm. She'd promised Max she would stay out of trouble, but she just couldn't risk chasing a ball down in some isolated spot on a golf course unarmed. Two of Hamid's potential whistle blowers were out of the way, and she didn't want to be the third. The outfit was khaki and green. Yellow or pink or turquoise or any other strong color would make a target of her, and Allan Farber hadn't fared well in orange.

Lunch was in the dining room. Michael skipped it to practice at the driving range. She hadn't been on a golf course all winter and thought she'd amuse her co-workers with a comedy act. Swing and miss, swing and connect badly, swing and pockmark the fairways with divots. Five shots to get to the green. She had a whole routine. Still, she had to remember to stick her butt out just right and how to shift her weight from the back foot to the front foot at the exactly right moment to mess up in every single shot. She'd learned all this, of course, from studying Tiger Woods' book, and practicing in the mirror. She knew how to make it look both good and bad. Claude was an excellent golfer. He was the one who'd wanted her to learn.

As Michael was finishing up a methodical warm-up that consisted of hitting at least a dozen balls with each of her eight clubs, starting with the shortest and ending with the driver, Frank Hamid appeared at the range in a golf cart driven by his nephew. She pretended to ignore them as they drew only monster drivers and two irons from their bags and left the rest of their clubs in the cart. Their walk to the driving range was not far. They had to cross a bridge over a tiny stream with a bed of smooth polished river rocks. On the bridge they spotted her, waved, and headed in her direction. Apparently his partner's death did not prevent him from taking his usual pleasures.

"Miss Tamlin, what a surprise. I didn't know you were a golfer. You remember my nephew, George," he said.

"I do indeed. Hi, George," Michael said.

George looked her up and down. She thought it was because her outfit was a bit unusual. Finally, he nodded with a strange expression. "Hi."

"I'm sorry about your loss," she murmured.

Hamid gave her a searching look as if he didn't know what she was talking about. Then he made the connection to his dead hedge fund manager. "Oh, Jesse. Yes, very sad. What's your handicap?"

Michael smiled. "Well, the truth is, I'm not much good at the sport, but you know how it is at the bank. Everything's a team effort. You have to go with the flow."

Hamid tilted his head to one side. "I'm guessing you're a sandbagger, better than you say you are," he said mischievously.

"Alas, no. I'm as bad as I say I am." She wrinkled her nose and glanced up at the sky.

It was fogging up again. If the sun didn't break through in a big way soon, there'd be no way to see the flags on the greens at 160 yards, much less 365. "Do they call the game for rain?" she asked.

"No. Unless there's lightning in the area, and that's very rare, we play through. If you don't have a waterproof in your bag, you might want to run into the pro shop and pick one up."

"I think I'm going to need it. Thanks."

Michael packed up her clubs, slung the bag over her shoulder, and walked the bridge. In the pro shop, she chose a lightweight waterproof jacket with a hood and club emblem on it. Then she went outside and chipped a bunch of times on a hill, tried her wedge in the practice sand trap, raked it clean, and putted around the practice green where everyone still in the dining room could watch her line up the ball. Missed, missed, missed! Perfect. Michael put the cover back on her putter, and the balls in her left hip pocket. They balanced nicely with the Glock in her right one. All right, the hordes were coming off the driving range and the main building. Time to rock and roll.

When she met up with her party outside the pro shop where the carts were lined up, the plan had changed. Ashland Upjohn and lawyer lackey number one, Milo Jackman, were second in line. George was in third place, teamed with Pac GreenBank lackey lawyer number two, Christian Waddle, who looked exactly the way his name sounded. George appeared even more distressed by his designated partner than Chris did. From the fixed gazed of George's eyes, Michael guessed that he was high.

Okay, and here was the kicker. In first place, Michael was paired with Frank Hamid. She felt a little thrill of anticipation as a club worker strapped her bag next to his in the back of the cart. On the passenger side someone had supplied her two cup holders with containers of ice water that she didn't plan to touch.

"Got you some water," he said.

"How nice. This is so fun," she enthused, thinking of Allan Farber crashing out of a tree stand with half his head blown away. She just could not get that image out of her head.

"I've wanted to spend time with you since the day we met." Hamid was striding around like a man on safari. "We get to start at the first hole. I have influence here. Hop in."

They were doing a shotgun start; carts were breaking ranks and heading to different holes so that everyone playing the tournament could begin at the same time. If the irony of the name occurred to Hamid, he didn't show it. She hopped in like a good little camper. Hamid stamped on the pedal and the electric cart lurched forward. She reached out to steady herself as he made a sharp turn that almost tossed her out. It was going to be a fun ride. They arrived at the first tee and the men got out.

Boom. Someone fired a shotgun to signal the start. Hamid was already planting his tee at the first hole. She watched him from the cart, her Glock resting comfortably against her right hip. She didn't need to worry about bodily harm here. Despite the deteriorating weather, the course was teeming with people.

In their foursome, Hamid shot first, then Ashland, and Milo. Michael was last. The lowest handicap played the hardest tee. Michael played the reds, the shortest, easiest route to the green. She didn't slice or shank or whiff. The ball connected with a satisfying ping, took a nice high trajectory straight down the middle of the fairway about a hundred and eighty yards. The three men exchanged glances.

"I knew she was a sandbagger," Hamid said with a chuckle.

The first five holes were very congenial. Michael had to play it straight and stand around pretending to listen with avid interest as the men discussed every shot with great seriousness.

"That'll work," when the ball went where they wanted it to.

"Oh, shanked it again, Milo. You need to work on your set up." Shank was hitting the ball with the toe or the heel of the club.

"Shoot right of the pin, there," Hamid told her when they got about 60 yards from the green on the fourth hole. They'd gotten intimate enough for him to tell her what to do.

She followed his instruction and was rewarded with his approval. "I like a woman who follows advice," he said, nodding.

"Green's slow, breaks right here to the left." Hamid walked a green, pointing out the topography with his wedge. She imagined him using it on her skull.

From twelve feet away she gave her ball a sharp tap. It went straight for the cup, rolled around the edge and then dropped in. Yes.

"Look at that, died right in the hole," Hamid said.

Okay, she could do this. The fairways and greens were wet and slow. The roughs were like dense forests. She could read as well as the best of them.

On the next hole Hamid gave her more advice.

"Now, hit a good drive up the hill, between the two bunkers. It'll roll down about thirty feet and you'll only have a short iron onto the green," Hamid directed.

"Yes, sir." She imagined her short iron cracking his skull.

When they collected their balls on the sixth hole, they were sufficiently chummy for him to speak. "I have heard that you are concerned about my business." He looked straight ahead as he drove.

Michael didn't say anything.

"My business dealings are sound, every single one. And I have many, at many banks. My partners and I can cover any and all mortgages that we have. I want you to know that. I do not think Pac GreenBank would like to lose us as customers," he added. "I hope you understand the repercussions."

A fat raindrop hit Michael in the eye. "Why are you telling me this? I have no influence one way or another."

"Exactly. You're new here. You don't understand how things work. I want to make sure you don't get in any trouble."

"Thank you for thinking of me, Mr. Hamid. And I don't want you to get in any trouble, either."

"Good." He rubbed his hands together and looked at her with his old twinkle. "And I don't want to have to say this again."

A second drop hit Michael in the face. Shit, it was starting to rain and her new mascara was not waterproof. She was not going to look so tough with black tracks all over her cheeks. She pulled out a tissue to clean herself up.

"Call me Frank." He climbed into the driver's seat and hit the electricity.

"Yes, sir," she said.

Funny how those carts worked. They jerked along, open on every side. Small wheels on box that was entirely unstable. If the driver didn't remember to set the brake, they could roll down hills. If he cut too sharp on the steep side of the hill, it could tip over. If he backed up on a bridge wrong, it could land in the water or tumble off a cliff. Men drove crazy, especially when they were playing well, or badly. The beverage girl was showing up at every other hole with the beer cart, and everybody was drinking. But what the hell, Michael thought. It was kind of fun. She hoped that she and Hamid now had an understanding that would give her a few weeks breathing room. Even a week would be fine. She didn't plan to stay long.

She made par on the threes and fours and bogeyed on the two fives. The long holes sometimes unnerved her a little, especially when there were water hazards and bunkers and forests and ditches in the way of the green and she couldn't see a thing. The others had played here dozens of times before and knew the layout. She didn't. A couple of the holes were completely blind. Going into the back nine, Ashland was three under, Hamid was two under, and Milo was one under. Michael was three up, a miracle. Only nine holes to go. Soon it was going to be over and she could get on the road. She looked forward to it.

37

The accident occurred on the eleventh hole. It was the longest on the course and blind, with a water hazard, a big hill between the tee and the green, and a curve to the right in the fairway. By then the fog was pretty intense, and the occasional rain shower added to the general merriment of the foursome.

Ashland and Milo's first balls were good off the tee, and their second balls sailed far down the fairway to the left. Hamid shanked his second ball, sending it right. Michael had tried to shoot high, over the hill to the green on the other side, also right. Her ball disappeared into the mist. She heard a crack. Maybe it hit a tree branch, maybe not. There would be no chance finding either one.

"Let's take another one from here," she suggested.

"No, I want to find the balls. Get in." Hamid shoved his club in the bag and got into the cart, humming a tune as if playing in pea soup was the biggest lark in the world.

Getting in the cart right then was not Michael's first choice. She didn't like the idea of going anywhere near either the hill, which was steep, or the forest which provided too much cover for a man whose associates were dying left and right. She had no good excuse to refuse, however, so she got in the cart. As soon as she was in, Hamid jerked the thing forward and drove over a bridge. On the other side he left the path, making a beeline several hundred yards to the mountain that was covered with slippery grass.

Suddenly it was very quiet. All Michael heard was water dripping from the mist. Dripping mist was very close to rain. The course was beautiful and so spooky even the birds were silenced. Absolutely no one was around. It occurred to her that maybe everyone else had gone home. The closer they got the less she liked the look of the hill. It was too steep for the cart to climb, especially in these conditions.

"We're not going to find those balls," she said.

"Well, we'll take a look," Hamid replied.

Hamid seemed to be one of those guys who can't bear to lose his balls. The change occurred quickly. He turned sharply and picked up speed across the side of the hill. Michael had to hold onto the front pole to keep from crashing into him. The tilt was severe, and it was now quite far to the bottom of the hill. Her stomach lurched up into her throat, and she cursed under her breath when he cut back on a steeper angle. Riding sideways on a steep hill was freaky dumb, but Hamid seemed to enjoy it.

Going faster he made a U-turn, and headed even higher. Smart ass. Now she was on the downside of the cart, leaning left to put her weight on the hill side. She weighed only a hundred and fifteen pounds; lot of help that did. That's when Hamid did a really stupid thing. He steered even steeper, causing the cart finally to lose traction in the slippery grass. The wheels on his side of the cart started to lift. Michael knew they were on the verge of rolling, and when they did, the cart would land on her. There was no jumping clean on the down side of it. And she couldn't get out anyway, gravity pinned her.

"Turn right!" she screamed. Wheel right.

That was about as helpful as putting her foot to the floor on the passenger side of a speeding car. Frantic, she turned away from the roll and saw something her brain couldn't compute. She was tipping alone. Hamid had jumped or fallen out. Lightened without his weight, the cart's wheels lifted higher.

Shit! She lunged for the steering wheel and jerked it toward her, slamming the wheels back on the ground. The cart turned and started rolling down the hill, aimed straight at the copse of trees at the bottom. Michael could not get her body over far enough or fast enough to reach the brake. Shit. Hamid had won. She was going to die an old maid, just as her mother had predicted when she was an ornery ten-year old. That one, often repeated comment, had blighted her whole life. And now it was going to come true because she couldn't reach the damn brake.

She watched death by tree racing at her, and actually had

a vision of her mother's fury at the funeral. All this she previewed in the nanosecond before she made a decision to get out of the cart. Instead of letting Hamid and the tree win, she swore again and jumped into a bush at the last moment where a sharp branch tore through her vest very close to her heart. The breath was knocked out of her, and she must have missed some time because the next thing she knew Hamid was blocking her vision and talking, but not to her.

Someone was touching her, moving her around. Suddenly Michael felt pressure on her neck and couldn't breathe. Someone was choking her. She didn't know what was going on, but instinct kicked in. Her vest and a pair of hands pinned her to the ground, but her feet and legs were free. She bent her knees and kicked, connecting hard.

"Oomp."

The hands released just enough for her to bellow. "Nooooooo!" She kept kicking and bucking as she screamed for help.

"Shit. What are you doing?" Hamid barked at her. "Stop that. You're all right!"

"Someone help!" She screamed louder than she'd ever screamed in her life. Bad victim, good little screamer. Mom would be proud.

"Get your hands off me."

"I didn't touch you," Hamid protested, backing away.

Michael heard the crunch of footsteps in the brush as someone ran away. She tried to sit up and realized her vest was impaled by a branch.

"Don't touch me." She stiff-armed Hamid, and he backed off further.

"I was just trying to find a pulse. Don't move. We'll get an ambulance," he said. "We're going to take care of you."

That was just what she didn't want. Michael's hand went into her pocket. Her fingers gripped her gun for comfort. She was not sure what had happened with the cart or who had been with Hamid when she came around, but it couldn't have been anything good because even now Hamid was not calling 911 for help. She wanted to shoot him like a rabid dog, but Max wouldn't like it.

"What happened?"

"Everybody all right?"

Talking at the same time, Milo and Ashland ran down the hill together, raising the alarm. Seconds later, other people charged after them. Not wanting anyone to see her down, Michael detached herself from the bush and got up.

"Oh, my God. What happened?" Ashland looked at the cart smashed into the tree and then at Michael's torn clothes.

"I'm fine," she told him. "No injuries. Look, I can walk and everything." She glanced at Hamid.

"Were you driving?" Ashland asked her accusingly.

Michael shot him devil rays. Her boss thought she had to be the idiot who couldn't drive a golf cart.

"I was driving," Hamid said quickly. "Damn stupid."

"We should take you to the hospital and check you out," Ashland told Michael.

"No, no. I'm fine, really." She repeated this many times in her nice, cheerful, don't-fuss voice. "I'm fine."

At least some of them were happy to hear that. The bank's lackey lawyers didn't want her suing the club. They even let her drive herself home. Her mother wouldn't have approved. But her mother rarely approved of anything. She got home feeling shaky, and didn't want to tell anyone. She'd set herself up for that one. Damn stupid was right.

Later, after Michael had had a long soak in a hot tub, she saw a van arrive and ducked out of view under the window sill. A young man got out with a huge vase of flowers and restaurant bags of what she assumed was take-out food. She heard the doorbell but didn't run to answer it. The van was from Taboule, and the delivery boy rang the bell about fifty times. No alarms went off because he didn't try to get in. Finally he left the offerings at the door and drove away.

38

At 7:30 that night the three lawyers from Pac GreenBank who had been on the golf course at the time of the accident met in their war room at the Heathman bar. The bank was pretty starchy and had a policy against the national trend of dress down Friday, so they'd changed back into the suits they'd worn to work. Caulahan had been notified immediately, and had flown in from Seattle to join them.

Christian Waddle, the youngest recruit with only four years under his belt, was drinking sparkling water. Milo Jackman was two years older, nearly thirty-five, and had been around long enough to feel comfortable nursing a beer. He was married and had a toddler at home. Ashland Upjohn, the most senior executive at the bank, who had been hoping to become president before the year was out, was drinking single malt and wishing for the good old days when you could light up a cigar anywhere you felt like it and didn't have compliance people from Washington making business so difficult you wanted to slit someone's throat.

"I want to know what we saw, exactly." Ashland was asking Milo this question over and over as if to get it fixed in his mind once and for all. Milo had been his driving partner. Christian had been in the third cart with George Hamid. They hadn't seen anything, didn't know anything. Cross them off.

"I saw the same thing you did, Mr. Upjohn. It was raining. I heard the impact. It wasn't as loud as a car crash—no broken glass in a golf cart. But there was good loud thump. You could hear it clearly all the way across the fairway. You tend to run toward a noise like that."

That was the problem for Ashland. He hadn't heard it, but his hearing was not as good as it used to be. Milo was the one who'd sounded the alarm.

"Something's happened," he shouted. He'd been up ahead on

foot, looking for his ball. He ran back to where Ashland was driving around in circles in the deep wet grass doing the same thing from his cart. He hadn't heard a thing, he'd swear to it.

"What happened?" He'd said when Milo came up to his side of the cart.

"Sounded like a crash. Let me drive," Milo said.

Ashland resisted yielding the wheel. "Get in. We'll never find those balls in this weather."

It was raining. They should give up and go home anyway, he thought.

"Over there," Milo directed.

Ashland still didn't see anything, didn't hear anything. He'd thought Milo was imagining things. Still, he drove across the fairway and around the base of the hill through the rough. By the time they'd reached the cart path, though, they could hear Michael screaming for help. No doubt about it. At this point, neither of them hesitated. They both got out of the cart and ran.

What they saw when they got to the wreck was Michael, on her feet, definitely shaken, but uninjured and vigorously claiming she was all right. It looked to Ashland like just a plain ordinary golf accident, and he'd wondered if she had been driving.

"What I saw was Tamlin. She seemed all right. And Frank trying to comfort her," Milo said.

"But what did you hear before we got there?" Ashland said.

Milo licked his lips. He knew what Ashland was asking.

"Your hearing is better than mine," Ashland prompted. "What exactly did you hear?"

"Was she yelling at him not to touch her? Something like, 'Get off of me. Get away'?" Milo seemed to be asking if that was what he'd heard, not reporting it as a certainty.

"You see, that's where I'm not sure," Ashland said, nodding.

Christian scratched his head and exchanged glances with Milo. What the hell was this all about?

Caulahan strode in and interrupted the discussion by dismissing the two junior lawyers. "Thank you. We'll call you later if you're needed. Have a good weekend."

Milo and Christian got up and trotted away like good doggies.

"Well," Caulahan demanded. "What now?"

"We're just trying to sort it out, Clifton," Ashland said.

"What's our liability?"

"Our employee is all right. That's what matters," Ashland said.

"I mean about not calling 911, not taking her to the hospital, not having any kind of investigation, or at least ask a few questions about what happened."

"I asked Frank. He was very embarrassed. No one likes being a crazy fool in a golf cart."

Caulahan gave his old friend a chilling look. "What are the odds of Hamid's being in the wrong place at the wrong time twice? Don't be an ass. Think about what this means. These are our people."

"I know what you're saying. But there are many issues here," Ashland said slowly.

"Farber is dead. Tamlin is compromised. What else is there?"

"I know, believe me," Ashland was thinking about his future. "Tamlin was not working out anyway. I had my doubts about her, as I told you. Clearly she can't come back to work now."

"I did not agree with you then, and I do not agree with you now. It would not look good to let her go after this," Caulahan said. "Forget it."

"My thinking is, we have a valued employee who's been injured. She needs time off," Ashland said.

"Ash, you told me yourself no one called 911. No ambulance came. She drove home under her own steam. How injured can she be?"

"Obviously she doesn't know what's good for her. Marty said she was paranoid, uncertain about everything. She clearly can't do her job after this; it lets us off the hook." Ashland sat back.

Caulahan pursed his lips and raised his hand to order another drink. "I'm disappointed. I did not expect this from you."

"We can't have her in the building again."

"Listen to me. Do not act like this. She could sue us."

"The woman jumped out of a golf cart, she's obviously

mentally disturbed. We can't have someone like that working for us." Ashland ranted on until Caulahan raised his hand to shut him up.

"If you do anything stupid with this woman that could jeopardize the bank in any way, so help me…" Caulahan said.

Ashland backed off. "Okay, okay. Just for our protection, I'll get Marty to evaluate her."

"Good. Good. Fair enough." Caulahan raised his hand for a waiter.

Two hours later, Ashland called Marty, who was on vacation in Hawaii, to tell him he had to come back right away.

"I need your help."

Marty sighed. "What's going on now?"

"Just get on a plane. I'll tell you when you get here," was all Ashland would tell him.

39

George had a bad day. His uncle yelled at him all the way home from the golf course, as if the accident were his fault. He made a delivery at Taboule around 6:00pm. Sami wasn't there, so he had to come back later. At 7:00, Sami was waiting for him on the street. Sami wasn't in a good mood either. He got into the car, scowling.

"It stinks in here."

"No shit. Where have you been?" George asked.

"I had to make a delivery."

"Did my uncle tell you what happened on the golf course?"

"Oh, yeah. Crazy, right? That was the delivery I had to make. I took some flowers to that girl. She wasn't home." Sami found the package of dope under the seat, checked to see how it was packed, then put it in his backpack. No funny packaging this time. He didn't say anything about that, just lit a cigarette and blew smoke out the window.

"Sami, what were you doing at the golf course?" George hit him with the question that had been bothering him for hours.

"Me? I wasn't there. I was here all afternoon." Sami concentrated on the view out the window.

"Don't lie to me. I saw you."

"If you bug me, I'll tell your uncle you're using. Big time. You and Ali. He won't like that." Sami had a look on his face George hadn't seen before, vicious.

George didn't like being threatened. "After all I've done for you! Get out of the car," he screamed.

"Fine with me, asshole." Sami got out and slammed the door.

Sami walked away without another word. His back had a look of defiance. George was slow on the uptake. It took him a while to realize that Sami hadn't given him his money. Then George hit the roof when he got to the apartment and found Ali doing the same stupid thing that he'd been doing for days: arranging colored paperclips, putting them in rows.

George could not persuade Ali to stop the crazy stuff. They got into an argument because George wanted to eat something, and Ali didn't. A few hours passed in fighting, and then they went out. They were in the car on the way to a club when George told Ali what happened on the golf course. He did not expect the response he got.

"You need to pray more," he said.

"What?" The last thing he needed was to get into old arguments on a night when his head was still spinning from Sami's threat to expose them to his uncle. Why would he suddenly do that?

"You don't go to the mosque. You don't listen to the Imam," Ali went on.

"I told you a thousand times, my family is Catholic. I have no interest."

"It's part of your heritage. You shouldn't forget it."

"My uncle was almost killed today," George said wildly. He'd forgotten that only a few days ago he'd wanted his uncle to die. And maybe he still did want his uncle out of the way, but by his choice, not someone else's.

Ali started babbling about God. George was not in the mood to listen to a crazy tweaker. Ali's head was bobbing, and he smelled like shit.

"Listen to me. Sami was on the golf course when the accident happened. And he told me he wasn't. Do you think he would do something to hurt my uncle?"

The whole idea infuriated George. If Sami was plotting to kill the patriarch of his family, the head of his tribe, it wasn't right. It was worse than stealing his money. It could not stand.

Ali babbled about nothing, rolling his head against the back seat.

"That's right, Ali. For once, I'm talking about my personal honor. I can't stand you anymore." He pulled the car to a spine-wrenching stop. "Get out," he ordered.

"No. I'm not getting out," Ali objected.

"Get the fuck out."

This was the second time he'd chucked a brother from his car today. But Ali crossed his arms over his chest. He didn't want to go. He was a mess, his hands were shaking. George was disgusted. He slammed the steering wheel with his fist and got out of the car.

"I said get out," he screamed.

And then George, who'd been afraid of violence all his life, who had never lifted a finger against anyone, ran around the car to bash his best friend's head in. He opened the passenger door, grabbed Ali by the shirt, and dragged him out on a dark and deserted street in east Portland. No one was going to kill his uncle. He wouldn't permit it. He'd kill the whole world to prevent it. He completely lost it.

"Come on, stop it," Ali yelped.

Ali was twitching all over, smelled like cat piss and the worst BO on earth. He made the car stink, even Sami had commented on it. Ali's hands and upper body jerked so much George got seasick looking at him.

"The fuck!" George was beside himself, overwhelmed by a decade of frustration. One of his sworn brothers was not going to kill his uncle! He shook Ali as if he were a bag of beans. His best friend had no flesh left on his body at all. Ali was a carcass, a nothing!

"What was Sami doing there? Huh? My uncle could have died in that accident."

Ali was loose on his legs, almost falling down. "Aw come on, lighten up," he said.

"This is my uncle. My honor! Sami is not supposed to be anywhere. If he tried to kill my uncle, I have to take care of it, okay?"

"You got it wrong. He's your uncle's number one. He killed that guy. Sami did it." Ali let it out like air from a blown tire. Boom.

George pushed him, almost knocked him down. "What guy?"

"The one from the bank he went hunting with."

"Sami killed that man! You're nuts!" George kicked him and Ali went down. Sami was a dealer. Just a dealer. A front man, nothing more. Sami didn't kill people. George kicked Ali some more until Ali curled up in a ball to protect his head.

George didn't know how Ali knew this or why he told him after all these months, or even how long he kept kicking him. George was supposed to be his uncle's number one. That's all he could think about. He was supposed to be number one, and they kept him in the dark about everything. When he finished pounding Ali, he threw the bag of bones in the car, took him to the apartment and tied him to the bed so he had to come down whether he wanted to or not. George had done this before. Sometimes it helped for a while. Other times it didn't. He needed some time to think.

40

Any reasonable person would have taken one look at the offerings outside the front door and gone to a hotel for the night. Michael didn't think of it. Hamid had almost got her killed on the golf course. The low-tech, almost- successful attempt only served to embarrass her. With the French doors between her and the elaborate floral arrangement with many roses and lilies, she studied the offensive gift.

It was covered with a clear film and way nicer than anything she'd ever gotten from Claude. She happened to be a big fan of Casablancas, the huge white lilies with a strong aroma that could perfume a whole room. Tempting as they were, however, they might be dusted with ricin. The cookies might be laced with strychnine. The innocent-looking food container might go bang when she opened it.

In the kitchen, Michael downed a shot of Skyy to better consider her dilemma. She had no lab to test for poison, no K-9 sniffers to bark at the first whiff of plastic explosives. She could have called Pete to ask for some help in that department, but she didn't want to get the bomb squad or Hazmat over there for nothing again.

She felt she had no choice but to put on a surgical mask and rubber gloves and test the packages with the oscilloscope. Checking them out herself was not smart, but what could she do? The packages were negative for electrical activity. Two possibilities down. There was not a bomb connected to a cell phone detonator, or a timer, or a listening device in the packages. But they could still be booby trapped in a lot of other ways. She took her mask and gloves off, feeling stupid in case a neighbor might be watching, but also relieved that incineration was not in her immediate future.

Her next step was to carefully dispose of Hamid's gifts in the garbage and put the container out on the street. If it went bang in the night at least the house would not go over the cliff. This was not good DHS procedure. You didn't leave possible bombs and chemical contaminants on the street for Sanitation to pick up on Tuesday. It was something she was likely to feel guilty about for the rest of her life, but she was a numbers person, not a bomb or chemical person. It was not her fault that she was only a CI and didn't have a team of experts to help her do things right.

Black and blue and sore all over, she was feeling sorry for herself. But she wasn't the kind of person to call her mother to complain about rolling down a hill in a golf cart and getting impaled by a bush, especially since Farber and Halen had suffered much worse fates. Nor would she tell anyone about putting possible weapons of destruction in her garbage. You could probably go down for that. She didn't even want to tell Marjorie any of this.

Since she'd missed lunch, she was now incredibly hungry. She roasted a chicken and downed a few more shots of Skyy. When the bird was ready, she ate quite a bit of it. When she was comfortably full and a little buzzy, she fell asleep with one Glock under her pillow and the other on her night table next to her bottle of water. She then lost the next ten hours to a series of betrayal dreams: Men who sent her naked into battle, men who broke her heart, men who tried to kill her in a variety of horrifying ways, that kind of thing. Luckily, none of her alarms went off.

She woke up feeling like shit, not remembering who or where she was for at least three minutes. After that, she gingerly crawled into the bathroom to give herself a naked once-over. She was still black and blue, had clearly defined bruises on her neck, and sported some interesting lumps; but her legs worked all right and nothing seemed to need immediate medical attention. She felt lucky that it had been such a crummy day and she'd been wearing long pants, long sleeves, and a padded vest. She took a hot shower, put on a sweat suit, made some very black coffee, and went outside with it. It was the kind of brilliantly sunny day in Portland that makes people forget the lousy weather the rest of the year. She studied Mount Hood with the sun rising over it as she drank the coffee and ate some leftover chicken for breakfast.

Before leaving the house, she emailed the information and reports she'd been working on all week to herself and Marjorie. She was concerned about leaving the laptop at home where there was no security. So she took the computer, the two guns, her throw-away phones, BlackBerry, and cell phone, plus all the paperwork she would not want to be found if there was a home invasion while she was out. She secured the laptop and paperwork in a hidden compartment she'd had built into the car that was not likely to be found except by a professional. She did not have the compartment wired to explode, but anyone who didn't know how to disarm her clever alarm would get a briefly-disabling unpleasant surprise.

Special Ops people, and mercenaries hired by the government to take care of things that required special attention, traveled into the field with a forty-five (or gun of their choice) on each hip and two smaller guns strapped to their ankles. They traveled without passports, in private planes, and carried a lot of fun stuff in their backpacks along with a toothbrush and change of underwear-- assault rifles, grenades, tasers, knives--whatever put them in their comfort zone. If they were discovered by a group of bad people when they were expecting only one bad person, they had to be able to take them all down in seconds. They called the designated enemy of the moment "bad people." And they were prepared to neutralize them whenever necessary. Welcome to the very hot war. A lot of things were happening every day that didn't make the newspaper. Michael could testify to that, not that she'd be allowed to.

She guessed that Hamid traveled that way, too.

Because of the little incident that occurred the day before, she carried both of her guns. She put the one that needed a single click to assemble in her back pocket, and the other was in a hol-ster at her waist. She checked her backpack to make sure she had all the paperwork required to carry a concealed weapon, then put a hoodie on to cover the holster. If the day got too hot, she'd be sweating it. She put two water bottles in the car, and entered her destination in her cell phone with the GPS. Her first stop was Dundee Blackberry Farm.

She did consider alerting someone to where she was going,

but decided against it. Marjorie was too far away to be of help and had warned her to keep her investigation cyber, as it were. Marjorie would not approve of solo road trips. The Loughlin gnome was a possible second choice. But Michael could hit the buddy button on her cell and get Mary Lou at any time. She did not add Pete to her list of possible aids. He was her back-up of last resort.

People knew where she lived so she left nothing incriminating in the Carl Street house. Everything was with her in the car. As she drove slowly down to Dundee, she actually thought about the whole subject of staying out of trouble. The gorgeous weather had brought people out. The road was clogged. She had plenty of time to think about the simple life.

In Dundee, she stopped to pick up a sandwich because she didn't want to get faint from hunger somewhere deep in the back country. Grilled eggplant and mozzarella. As soon as it was in the car she started yearning for it. She'd always been like that as a kid, wanting to have the picnic before they'd even left the house. She promised herself she could eat it later, after she'd seen the farm. It did occur to her that if illegals were staying there, they might be dangerous. But she was feeling lucky.

Just south of what passed in Oregon for a town, she turned off the main highway and went by a number of Vineyards. Twenty minutes later she came to an old mine with a No Trespassers sign and kept on going. It was pretty country. From rolling hills to steep mountainous areas, vineyards took turns with farmland and forest. The paved road ended, and she followed a rutted track up and around the hill. It switched back before climbing higher. The road seemed to lead right up to the summit, and she was glad she was the one in the driver's seat. It was a narrow path, but so isolated up here she wasn't likely to meet a semi coming the other way.

When the car neared the top, it became clear how fantastic Hamid's property was. Drop dead views of the valley and vineyards below spoke of promise here. Apparently Hamid planned to build a resort with a working vineyard and condos with time shares. Michael had read articles about local opinion on the subject. Water issues made it a hot topic. Some conservation groups objected to development that would bring more people and high rises to an Eden where now only day trippers came, small farmhouses dotted the landscape, and water use was light.

The car hit a deep pothole and Michael stopped to scan the road ahead for other hazards. A bird in a tree to the left drew her eye to the small camera fixed to a branch over the road. But for a screech and sudden flash of feathers, she might not have seen it.

Adrenaline shot through her system. She backed the car a long way until she could find a turn-out where she could lock and leave it. Then she headed back in on foot. She left the road and moved into the field long before the camera could catch her image. This side of the road was farmland. Some kind of low bush was growing in rows. Only leaves were visible on them now. She had no idea what crop might develop there later.

As Michael approached the buildings, she had the cover of a stand of trees. There was no fence, no guards, and she didn't see another security camera. As she came out on the other side of the trees, she was looking up. She saw an old barn, small two-story house, and dilapidated trailer on blocks. This property hardly had the appearance of a prosperous farm worth twelve million dollars, and it didn't look occupied by Al Qaeda soldiers, or refugees. Blackout curtains covering the trailer and farmhouse windows, however, were promising signs. Michael moved a few steps forward and tripped over a root. She caught herself and looked down. A patch of earth had been disturbed and the corner of a tarp was exposed. Something was buried there, and a small animal, or several small animals, were working at digging it out. A hidey hole on an isolated farm could conceal drugs, money, guns, explosives, anything. She made a mental note to check it out another time.

She took a picture of the mound with her BlackBerry and moved forward, planning to circle the farm in a wide perimeter. She came on a field of marijuana plants behind the barn where they couldn't be seen from the road and let out her breath in a silent whistle. How simple it was in the country. On one side of the road were acres of grape vines; on the other, acres of some unknown bush, probably berries. Behind the barn, beyond where the road ended, weed, a whole lot of weed. Even legal growers couldn't have more than eight plants, and Michael strongly doubted that Hamid was a legal grower. She got him! Her heart raced as she photographed the marijuana. They could bring him in on this and take their time with the rest of it.

Looking for more cameras, Michael crept closer to the barn. She saw one in a tree trained on some kind of tank and backed away from it. She had no idea what the tank might be used for. Chemical warfare? She took a photo of the barn and the tank. Then she saw the motorcycle parked by the trailer, and looked quickly around. Nobody in sight. She snapped a picture of the bike's license plate and slipped to the barn. Even though the padlock was not attached and the door was cracked open, the place had a vacant feeling about it. She stepped to the door and peeked in.

Every cell in her brain told her to get the hell out before someone saw her, but she could not believe what was in there. The barn was a weed warehouse. No light was on, but it was nice and warm in there, perfect for drying. Must be heaters somewhere. Tables and packaging materials were set up in some of the stalls. A number of people must work here, she thought. Okay, time to leave. She quickly snapped another photo, and ducked low to sneak away.

41

Within 24 hours, Ali was promising everything and anything to get released from George's health watch. He swore up and down that he wouldn't use anymore. He promised he'd eat and sleep, and not talk about God anymore. He whined about wanting to see his mother. He had a thousand arguments for getting out of there.

"I'm not mad at what you did to me. I'm not. You're my brother. I love you for taking care of me. Trust me, man. I'm good now."

"Yeah."

But Ali didn't look so good. George left him food and water and rode to the farm on his bike. He wanted to be free of everything and feel the wind in his face. He arrived at noon and headed into the barn for supplies. He didn't intend to stay there when Ali wasn't working. He told himself it was just a business trip. But, instead of locking up and returning to Portland as he'd planned, he went into the trailer for a smoke. Ali would forget about the fight because he forgot all his fights, but George wouldn't ever get over it. He wouldn't ever forgive Sami for threatening him, either. The business was suffering, too. People were clamoring for the meth, and Ali wasn't out here making it. Sami had stolen his money, but he'd also killed some people. That was part of the scary news.

The other part was now George had to worry about Jesse Halen and the drugs found in the office. He'd read about the drugs in the newspaper and knew where they came from. He wasn't sure if they could be traced to him in real life the way they could on *CSI*. You never knew what was made up in those shows. He also had known Jesse well, had worked for him one summer, and he knew that Jesse was way too chicken to slash his wrists. He'd once freaked out over a paper cut on his thumb. There was no way he would cut open a vein. So somebody else did that to him. The thought that Sami had hacked away at Jesse's wrists and then used George's drugs to set him up was extremely terrifying.

George couldn't trust anybody anymore. That's how it was now. A war zone. By 12:15, the weed had brought him way down. He'd started to nod off when a flicker on the monitor catapulted him out of his stupor. He jumped up as if he'd been shot. At first he thought he was dreaming. He couldn't believe what was on the monitor. The woman from the bank, the one who'd been in the accident with his uncle, was sniffing around the garbage Ali was supposed to have cleaned up weeks ago.

"Jesus! Jesus!" George started hopping around, furious and frightened. Who sent her? What was she doing? What was he supposed to do? He grabbed his gun. Shit, shit, shit. He was alone there. Fuck, and he couldn't let her get away.

Michael ran, crouching low, glad she'd worn her sneakers. She stopped on the far side of the farmhouse near the field with the mystery bushes. Then she crept closer to the crummy house to listen. There was no sound from within, but that did not surprise her. The building was in bad shape. The paint was long gone, the window frames were rotten, and the place had an unmistakable odor. Not the smell of mold or abandonment, not the smell of fertilizer or gasoline. This place wasn't a bomb factory. Whoever worked here was making something else very nasty.

It was clear the property was a regular Eli Lilly of illegal drug production. She was elated and beyond by the discovery. She experienced another burst of adrenaline that made her feel brilliant and invincible, the way the explorers must have felt when they conquered new worlds, or gladiators when they conquered their enemies and lived to fight another day. She'd found what the locals and the Feds hadn't, and she couldn't wait to see what Hamid did on the rest of his properties.

This was DVD, stuff that Max had told her to report to local authorities. Happy for a reason to make contact, she popped open her phone and dialed Pete. He answered right away.

"Hey, Mikey. What's up?"

"How big is your territory?" she asked.

"My territory?" He sounded puzzled.

"Yeah, you're DVD. Do you keep to the city limits? Or do you travel?"

"Where are you?"

"I'm down in Yamhill County."

"What are you doing there, Mikey?"

She'd moved low around the house, was now closer to what appeared to be a mountain of garbage bags. "I've found something of interest to you."

"I'm very far away from there. So get yourself to safety," he said. Then, "What are we looking at?"

"Well, I can't talk about this on the phone," she told him irritably.

"You listen to me. Wherever you are, get out of there. Now," he ordered.

"How about meeting me for a coffee?" she said. "You had lunch yet?"

She heard him swear.

"Get out and call me when you're in a safe place. Got it?"

"All right, I'll call. But pick up even if you see a number you don't recognize."

"Now," he ordered.

How did he know where she was, or whether or not she was in danger?

"God, you're bossy," she muttered. She snapped the phone closed, and moved out, into the field.

George wanted to get out and follow her, but his doubts about so many things kept him paralyzed at the trailer window. He had his gun in his hand and was peeking around the edge of the black-out curtain like a nosy old lady in a housing project. This impotence, like so many others from the past, infuriated him. Sami was like someone from The Sopranos, and even Ali could run out and kill with no hesitation. What was the matter with him that he couldn't walk out there and put a bullet in that woman's head?

It was an impossibly painful moment, even more shocking to George than the day the tweakers showed up. His heart raced with a wild desire to shoot that girl who'd smiled and led him on the first time they met, and then wouldn't even look at him yesterday. She'd seemed like a friend to both of them, and turned out to be an enemy.

George had felt the hot throb of rejection all afternoon when he'd been forced to trail around the golf course with that bank asshole, Waddle. The woman had joked with his uncle but wouldn't give him the time of day. Not once. George had been glad when she got hurt. He thought she'd deserved to suffer. And his uncle must have thought so, too, because he didn't bother to mention the incident in the car. George didn't give it another thought after they left the club. His uncle had been in such a terrible mood. Now he realized his uncle must have wanted that girl dead. What Ali had told him shocked him. Sami sold drugs for him and killed for his uncle.

He didn't know what to think about his uncle now. All the plaques on his wall for good citizenship were lies? Jesus. Jesus. George could not imagine his uncle having any part in a killing. He just could not, but Jesse's death wasn't an accident. And there was the other guy, Farber. And now there was this woman creeping around the house. Who told her to come here? Who told her what George was doing there? Sami told her. It couldn't be his uncle. His uncle didn't know. George's head reeled with so many painful thoughts. There was no car on any of the monitors. How did she even get here?

George stood at the window as he'd seen snipers stand at windows back home. He had a gun in his hand and knew how to shoot it. But he could not shoot the gun. He'd never been able to shoot a gun. Even when he went hunting for deer, he could not shoot the gun. He hunted with explosives. It took guts to do that, real guts to blow something up. Blowing up he could do. Shooting, he couldn't.

The woman finished poking around and started to walk away. George struggled with thoughts that he was a nothing, a pussy, worse than a girl. He couldn't deal with his enemies like a man. He was a person so low that his own uncle conspired against him. A mere woman, not even a tall one, was turning her back on him and walking away just like the tweakers Ali had killed. And he couldn't stop her with a bullet. His helplessness made him want to rip his face off, destroy the whole world. And then he had his first brilliant thought in a long time. He would do what Sami hadn't been able to do. He would follow that girl home and blow her up. That he could do.

42

Piece of cake. Michael found her car exactly as she'd left it and drove down the hill to the paved section of the road, and from there to the highway. When she got back into Dundee she stopped for gas, used the restroom, then called Pete on one of her throw-away phones. Once again, he picked up right away. This time she had the goods. She was in no mood to be coy.

"Mikey?" he said.

"Yeah, but you can call me Tamlin from now on."

"Nah, you'll always be Mikey to me. Are you in a secure location?" he asked.

She got out of the car and walked a short distance from the pumps while a station attendant filled her tank. People in Oregon weren't allowed to fuel up themselves. "Yes, getting gas in Dundee," she told him, looking around to see if anyone could listen in. Nope, all clear.

"Okay. You're really beginning to worry me, you know that? What made you go down there alone?" Pete demanded.

"I wanted to see what Hamid was doing on his properties."

"Is that common procedure for compliance VPs?"

"Don't be ungrateful. I told you I was doing an audit. Site visits are part of the process."

"Not for VPs. Come clean, Mikey. You're back in the game?"

"Not enough to make anyone nervous. Very limited status." She couldn't believe she was telling the truth.

"Congratulations, I'm listening," he said.

"You told me you weren't involved with the Farber case."

"Correct," he confirmed.

"But your department has been looking at a certain individual for other things."

"Maybe. What do you have?"

"The individual I told you about last week has a marijuana

farm on one of his properties. He's got a lot of it. You can bring him and his partner in for that alone. I know you're looking for more, though. Maybe I can help you." She put the offer out.

There was a long silence on the other end. "You saw this?"

"It's a weed farm, Petey. They dry and package the stuff in the barn. They're making meth down here, too."

"In a barn with the weed?" His voice said nobody could be that stupid.

"No, the meth lab is in the farmhouse. Is that so surprising?"

"We've shut down a lot of labs in recent years. That would be unusual. Not impossible, but unusual. Are you sure?"

She didn't like the patronizing attitude. "Well, they must be starting them up again. I've smelled it before. They have a big tank out there, like a natural gas tank. What would that be for?"

"Liquid fertilizer. Okay, where is this place?"

"I guess I know stuff you don't know. Can you meet me there?"

"No, I want you to go to a safe place. I hear you had a little accident on the golf course yesterday. What happened there, something PD should know about?"

The gas tank was full. Four dollars-plus a gallon. Michael walked back to the car and handed over three twenties to pay for it. No credit card trail for her. She'd paid cash for the sandwich, too, but had forgotten to eat it. The day was getting expensive. She got in the car but didn't start it up.

"You heard about the accident and didn't come to my rescue? Now I'm really hurt," she said, teasing a little more.

"I wanted to, Mikey. But I'm working on something else out of town. And your guy isn't my case." He sounded seriously apologetic.

"That's a pretty lame excuse." She needled him a little more.

"It couldn't have been that bad if you drove home," he said slowly.

"It was that bad."

"Then I'm truly sorry."

"All right. Where are you?" she asked.

"I'll be back Monday. Can you meet me at Central Station early a.m.?"

"How early?" she asked.

"I get in at seven. Look, I've got to go. I'm sorry I didn't call."

"Nothing like surveillance without protection, Petey." She didn't want him to go. She wanted him to stay on the line with her a little longer.

"You're not under surveillance. Certain people's movements are monitored, but not yours. If you don't come to us to report an incident, we can't assume an assault and offer you protection. That's how the system works."

"I know that." But she didn't want to compromise an ongoing investigation with an attempted murder charge. And she was an employee at the bank. It was complicated.

"I'm not supposed to make waves," she said after a moment.

"Very thoughtful, but do you have any back-up from your end?"

"There is no my end. I told you, I'm very limited status."

Michael turned on the engine and looked around to see if anyone was spying on her now. "So, there's no one watching me?"

"Not unless you picked up a friend of your own," he said.

"Okay." She pulled back on the highway.

"How are you feeling, by the way?" He sounded sincere, his trademark.

"Hard to kill," she said, perky as she could.

"Good. I can't force you, but my advice is to stay somewhere else tonight. You want me to arrange something?"

"How about your place?"

"Can't get you there. I'm working."

"In that case, I can take care of myself. See you Monday." She shut the phone and glanced in the rear view mirror. Oh, ho ho. Now, two cars back, there was motorcycle like the one she'd seen up at the farm. Maybe she had picked up a friend. It didn't worry her, but her options were limited. She could kill the guy, which would serve no purpose whatsoever, or lose him. It wasn't a hard choice, she decided to lose him.

George left the farm without taking the time to lock up the barn. He was surprised by how easy it was to find that woman who'd evaded his security. He saw Michael talking on her cell phone beside her car at a gas station in Dundee as if she didn't have a care in the world. He stopped on the opposite side of the street and kept his helmet on while he watched her. She looked like a college kid in jeans and a hoodie, which seemed like a strange outfit because it was a really hot day. She was driving an Acura TSX, though, not a kid's car.

When she finished gassing up, she pulled back onto Route 99, heading north toward Portland; and he followed her with no clear plan. He just wanted to see what she was up to, where she was going. He knew he didn't have to do this, since he could easily find out where she lived, but it was a matter of principle with him. He didn't want to let her get away. He had to do something on his own, had to recover the honor he felt Sami had stripped from him. His second ride of the day felt good. George was in control with the bike roaring between his legs. He loved the motorcycle. Even on a hot day like this, it was cool and free on the road. He felt he could ride like this forever.

About five miles on, the Acura turned onto a country road. He turned onto it, curious about where Michael was going. As far as he knew, this was a road to nowhere. The Acura sped up on a straight line. George hit the gas going up a hill. At the top of a steep rise, a tractor inching along the other way scared the shit out of him. Trying to avoid it, he almost spun out into the ditch on the side of the road. He skidded to a stop, stalled out, and swore. The motor started right up again, and he was back on the road in minutes. But by the time he'd gone another few miles he realized the Acura was long gone.

43

Michael saw the motorcycle swerve and begin its spin. Break your neck, she thought. Ahead the two-lane road was clear, so she put her foot to the floor to see how fast the Acura would go. At ninety-five, it was doing fine, and no more road test was necessary. She slowed down and consulted her GPS for the best route to Hillsboro. On the seat beside her, she had the maps and information on four other of Hamid's remote properties, but they were all north and east of the city, three and four hours' drive from where she was. Much as she wanted to take a bigger file with her to Central Station on Monday, she knew she could go only as far as the jet center in Hillsboro today. She found the right highway and headed west towards the coast, then settled back to review her research.

Now it was clear that Hamid was involved in many more illegal activities than his pyramid scheme milking banks. He was also growing and making drugs that he might well be selling at his own restaurants and strips clubs. His hedge fund had required silencing his partner Jesse Halen, so there had to be a story there. Michael had observed many times that people like Hamid who acquired wealth and power thought they could get away with anything. Look at what he had done yesterday in a place teeming with witnesses and only a little fog as a foil. It's not so easy to jump out of a tipping golf cart. Attempting that was kind of crazy in itself. He could have tripped getting out. He could have crashed and killed them both. The man was bold and foolish, and she was going to get him. It gave her a thrill thinking about it.

Bird's Eye Aviation added yet another dimension. Hamid's sightings in Pakistan could be related to arms sales or drugs, but Jesse had told them that clients from the Middle East were paying big money to get into the U.S. This international component involved human trafficking for one purpose or another. The questions were who were the people he brought in? Where did they come from? Where did they go when they got in the U.S.? And what did they plan to do here? A recent case right in the state of Oregon involved a man who had traveled to Pakistan and brought recruits back to his training camp in the woods. It was wild country, but they hadn't come to hunt cougars.

Michael had spent some late nights researching the Hamid family background. They were Lebanese, from a town that had been Syrian at one time, so she figured there might still be a tribal connection. Their official religion was Catholic, but in times of war, a different religion did not rule out an even stronger national or cultural identification. True religious affinity could be ambiguous. Jews who had converted during the Spanish Inquisition and at other perilous times in more recent history often continued to practice their religion in secret until it was safe to practice openly again. And in some countries that time never came.

There were layers upon layers of loyalties in the Middle East, beliefs and biases people didn't even know they carried from their ancestors. Just because Hamid had no known ties to terrorist activities didn't mean there weren't any. For Michael, that made finding out what he was doing with the other remote properties even more pressing. Could be just drugs out there, but she doubted it. Based on Hamid's attempt on her life at the golf course, it seemed clear he was willing to murder anybody at any time to safeguard his secrets. She figured they had to be big ones.

An hour later, she passed the headquarters of Intel and Nike and found the small private airport. It was easy to observe from the parking lot. One building served as a terminal with the controller's tower up on the second floor. Another building stood on the other side of the parking lot. Looked like a barracks building. Mid afternoon on a summer Saturday there was some small plane activity. As she entered the parking lot, a single engine propeller plane was taking off. A number of others like it and small jets were parked on the tarmac.

Michael pulled a baseball hat over her hair. She was already wearing large sunglasses. She circled the parking lot slowly. Her plan was to park, get out, and walk around, see who was in the terminal, and what was going on at Bird's Eye Aviation. Two hangers had the company name on them. The doors of one of them stood open. She drove closer and was shocked to see one of the pilots who had flown her there from D.C. He was checking out a jet that was the same size and had the same red stripe on the tail as the snappy one that had brought her here.

He glanced in her direction and she felt an instant jolt of discomfort. She was several hundred yards from where he stood in the building, but she had recognized him. And immediately she had second thoughts about hanging around. As she made a U-turn, a blue Sebring convertible came into the parking lot. Pat, the flight attendant, was at the wheel. Either the pretty blonde worked here, or she and the pilot were going somewhere. She had the appearance of someone going to work. A bag with take-out food was on the seat beside her. The food reminded Michael of the sandwich she'd bought in Dundee hours ago and forgotten to eat. She pushed thoughts of food out of her mind. Okay, it was the same jet, same crew, and they knew her. She put her foot on the gas, and drove out the exit. Pat was too busy parking to look her way as she made her escape.

From Hillsboro it wasn't that far to the coast. Michael thought it was safer not to go home and decided to check out the Pacific Ocean, find a place, and spend the night. She took her time driving, and was awed by the rugged coast when she got there. She had twenty-four hours to think about yet another layer.

Pat was the one who had told her that Pac GreenBank had sold the jet to a leasing company. Now she knew that leasing company was owned by Frank Hamid. That meant the bank leased, or borrowed, the plane whenever they needed it. It was another bank relationship to think about. Michael would love to get a look at the terms of that deal. Hamid and the bank were in tight with the jet, the real estate and the funds funneled though it from Scotland. She wondered how much of all this Caulahan knew, and when, how, or even whether she should tell him at all.

44

George returned to the farm, picked up the stash he needed for the week, and locked the place up. Then he rode back into the city to the apartment near the Pearl to check on Ali. Ali had been tied to the bed in the second bedroom for over twenty-four hours and had made a mess of the place. Pee, vomit. The man was an animal. He'd drunk two bottles of Vitamin Water and the Gatorade but not eaten any of his food. George hoped that at least he hadn't shit his pants. That always grossed him out.

"You got to let me go now, man. I'm fine." Ali started wailing the minute the door opened. "I'm good now.

George looked in and swore.

"Fuck. Look at what you did to my place. You know how disgusting you are?" George went into the other room for the cleaning stuff. He hated this.

"You beat the shit out of me. I could have died." Ali was sobbing now. "I could have died here all alone."

George returned with a garbage bag, two rolls of paper towels and bucket of hot water, heavily laced with Mr. Clean. "You are dying anyway, asshole. I'd be doing you a favor."

"I can't make the meth without inhaling some of it. Doesn't mean I'm using." Ali looked bad in a soiled T shirt and jeans.

"Fucking addict. Take off your clothes." George held out the garbage bag.

"Oh, come on. I don't have anything else."

"You made so much noise my neighbor was going to call the police." George was furious. He had to listen to the complaints when he came in.

"He should have. They could put you away for this."

"Yeah, and you, too." George shook the bag. "Come on. I have to go to work."

"Go on then. I'll clean the place up."

"Like fuck you will." George shook the bag again. "Because

you're incompetent I had to go out to the farm alone. Guess who I found nosing around this morning?"

"I don't know. Let me take a bath. I'm good now," Ali put his hands together. He was really begging now.

His ankles were caked with dried blood from fighting with a rope. The fact that if he'd just concentrated a little bit, he could have untied it disgusted George even more. He didn't make the knots tight at all, but they were too tight to untie now. He cut the rope with a knife and deprived Ali of his filthy clothes. Oh, God, Ali had shit his pants. George swore some more and made him throw them in the garbage bag, trying not to look. The bruises and shit smears on Ali's bony body were anathema to him. Ali had finally gone over the top and forced George to beat him. This didn't have to happen. George grabbed the bucket of soapy water and flung it at Ali.

Ali yelped, coughing from the ammonia. "What's the matter with you?"

The protest brought on another fight. They went at it for a while, fighting old battles and new ones. Ali's pathetic condition made George want to kill him, or cry. Muttering and complaining, near the end of his rope again, he got the place cleaned up at much as he could. At least there was no rug in that bedroom. He made Ali take a shower and stood there to make sure he washed his hair and got clean. Finally he gave him one of the sandwiches he'd bought.

"She was at the farm," he said when Ali was relatively calm, sitting at the table, dressed in George's too-big jeans and sweatshirt.

"Who?" Ali had no interest in food whatsoever.

"Tamlin, the woman from the bank. We played golf with her on Friday, and Sami was there, remember?"

Whenever Ali was relatively lucid, George always thought they were friends again and Ali was going to be all right. But of course Ali didn't know what he was talking about. His brain was fried, he forgot everything.

"I told you about this," George said, angrily. "Don't get me mad again."

"So what?" Ali said.

"Try to pay attention. She knows about the farm, and you weren't there to take care of her." George scowled. "You're supposed to take care of things like that."

Ali stared at him. "Oh."

"Oh. Is that all you have to say?" George ranted.

"What do you want to do?" Ali asked.

"We're going to rig her car in the parking lot where she works. When she turns on the ignition, toast."

Ali did that thing with his head that showed he wasn't listening. Bobbed to the side. Once, twice, three times.

"Christ. Do you know what I'm talking about?" George demanded. Ali knew devices better than anyone. He'd blown up his mother's kitchen sink, practicing when he was twelve. George knew dynamite. But this required plastics and a detonator. It wasn't hard to do, but he didn't like to touch that stuff.

"I want to go home, man. I need rest," Ali whined.

"You can go home after you've done it."

Ali shook his head. "You're an asshole, you know that?"

George could agree with him there. He didn't want to tell Ali how Michael had outraced him on a back road, and that was the reason she had to die inside her car and nowhere else. He hated the car, and he hated her. He didn't want to admit he hadn't been able to shoot her from the trailer, either. He was just one of those people who needed someone to help him. That wasn't a crime, was it? Ali should be grateful. Without George to clean up after him and make him eat, Ali would probably be dead already.

"Ali, I'm doing this in your best interest. You have to pull yourself together. I'm not going to have to force feed you, am I?"

Ali made a face at the sandwich. If he didn't eat it George was going to have to do something else. George considered other menus. Ali could eat ice cream sometimes. Power Bars. But he needed real protein. Meat.

"Ali, you listening to me? I don't like being your nurse."

"You beat me up. I'm supposed to forget about that?"

"Other people would beat you worse. Okay?"

They fought for another hour. Ali caved in and agreed to rig the car with a blast just big enough to take care of Michael but not blow the whole building, wherever it was she parked. That way they'd accomplish what Sami hadn't been able to, and George could earn some points with his uncle. That was the plan. It didn't go off that way.

45

Sunday afternoon, after not a restful night in a crummy motel but a pretty morning walking the beach and having splendid seafood in a deli-like diner, Michael drove back to Portland in heavy traffic. She parked the Acura down the street and walked back to the house, entering through the basement door. She had expected a visitor, and there had been one. Her alarm was not connected to a loud noise, or the police. If she had been at home, it would have let her know which point of entry was breached. Since she was out, she didn't know about it until she returned.

She could see the changes in the house right away. A black lacquer box that was always in the middle of the coffee table was now on the floor. The coffee table itself was not in exactly the same place. The legs were off from the marks in the carpet. On her desk in the study, the top drawer had been opened and not closed all the way. The filing cabinet had been rifled. She'd stuffed it with fashion magazines. Her closets had been examined. Nothing exciting in there, either, she could vouch for that. And the telephone in her bedroom had been moved. There might be fingerprints on the phone and the box, so she bagged what was portable and put it away for later reference. The rest she tried to not to touch.

Neither of the doors she was likely to enter was rigged to go boom when opened. She used the oscilloscope to check the rest of the place for bugs and bombs. Again it detected no unusual electrical activity. The intruder had come in through the kitchen door, which had a simple lock that any idiot could open; and he must have left the same way. It would lock automatically when he shut the door.

Michael checked the place from top to bottom, looking for something that might go bang when she touched it. She even went into the empty bedroom upstairs. It was five in the afternoon. No one was there now, and she had no way of telling who had been there or when. She didn't find anything. For all she knew, her intruder had been Claude looking for the iPod he'd given her two years ago. Nope, it was still there where she'd left it.

She returned to her car and parked it in its usual spot where alarms of many kinds would go off if anyone came near it. She removed her computer and Hamid files from the secret space that could be accessed from the back seat. She'd already downloaded the photographs she'd taken at the farm, as well as the photos of Bird's Eye Aviation and memos about Hamid's properties and their relationship to the bank. She had already emailed all the information she had to Marjorie. It wasn't a game, so there was no holding back on anything now. If something happened to her, somebody had to know everything she knew. She then printed, and added all the photos and memos to her file.

Outside by the pool a few minutes later, she called Marjorie.

"Where have you been? I've been calling you since Friday."

"I went to the beach."

"There isn't phone service at the beach?"

"Did you get my email?"

"I got your email. Thank you, very nice. Now get out of there. No more fooling around."

"Don't worry. I just have a few loose ends to tie up. I'll be home by the end of the week."

"What about now don't you understand?"

"I have to get the movers back, give my notice…" Michael didn't tell Marjorie about the golf cart incident or the visitor to her house.

"You don't have to give notice. You can call them later."

Michael didn't say anything. There was plenty more that she could do at the bank, but it wasn't the job she'd come for. And Marjorie was right. It was all very complicated as long as she was employed there.

"Okay. I'll move as fast as I can. Call you tomorrow."

Then Michael had an uneasy but uneventful night. She was up early and checked out the area at 6:00 a.m. No one was lurking around Carl Place. She got in the car and cruised slowly around the quiet neighborhood streets, searching for any strange vehicle parked close enough to watch her house. She didn't see anything out of the ordinary. She took a few minutes to check around the house, under the house, and in the house. No funny packages had been wired to the supports that held up the addition, stuffed into the basement, or hidden in the pool equipment room on the other side of the living room wall. Her oscilloscope read negative again. Good, she had a phobia about dying in a fiery blast.

Then she removed the guns and the laptop from the house and secured them in the car's safe box. She put a copy of her file in her briefcase and placed it on the seat beside her. At 7:00 a.m. sharp, she backed out of her driveway. She saw the dirty Toyota right away. Although there was still a pretty dense mist, almost fog, at this altitude this early in the morning, the two guys inside were wearing baseball hats and sunglasses. With the Ralph Lauren shades on their faces these guys were not likely to be gardeners or construction workers. Michael thought one of them could be George Hamid, but wasn't sure. Neither one was the guy who'd delivered the flowers on Friday. She paused for a moment pretending to check her hair in the mirror while she took some photos of the car and faces. Partials, but it was the best she could do.

She reapplied her lipstick and noted that she still looked like shit. Oh well. She made a sharp right and tested the Acura on a fast ride down the hill, taking the switchbacks at close to seventy where traffic was light. She was able to get a license plate then. It would have been fun to be picked up for speeding, but that didn't happen.

46

Central Station was on Second Avenue, and closer to the Willamette River than the bank. Michael located the building and drove around the block. The driveway into the jail entrance was not what she wanted. She turned the corner and found the PD parking garage. Expecting to be stopped, she drove into it slowly. When no one questioned her, she parked the Acura and got out with her briefcase.

Security was in the lobby. It took a little while for her belongings to be screened by the metal detector and for Pete to escort her upstairs to a conference room where four tough-looking guys, including Detective Torres, had gathered. That made five against one in the male to female department, but in her line of work she was used to the odds. Pete did the honors.

"This is Michael Tamlin, of FinCEN. You know Felix Torres. Chief Henry Rangel, Major Case Squad; Sergeant Brickle, commander of DVD; Chief Craig Olson, head of operations."

"How do you do?" Michael shook hands with each of them in turn. They were very polite, clean cut; several wore uniforms that indicated their rank. And they refrained from looking her up and down the way arrogant cops did from the really big-city agencies. That was a nice touch.

"Thank you for coming. Can we get you something?" Chief Olson was tall, wore his blond hair in a military crew cut, and had steely blue eyes. Really cute. He was also wearing a wedding ring and seemed to be the one in charge.

"I'm fine, thanks," Michael said. She took one of two empty places at the table and glanced at Pete. Although he said almost nothing in the elevator, he'd sent a charge through her elbow as he steered her into the right room. Probably didn't mean to.

Michael studied the faces around the table. "Thank you for seeing me this morning. I know you're busy." She said this without irony. She was sure they were busy.

"What can we do for you?" Chief Olson asked.

The classic cop phrase implying that assistance was needed on her side, instead of the other way around, did not provoke her. She wanted to inform Chief Torres that their building presented an extremely soft target and needed more security, and their Homicide Unit sucked. But maybe they already knew that. She glanced at Chief Rangel and wondered what constituted a major case in this city.

"A black 2003 Toyota Highlander, license plate partially obscured by mud, occupied by two ethnic males, early twenties wearing Ralph Lauren wrap-around sunglasses and Portland Beaver baseball hats, was waiting for me outside my house this morning and followed me here."

The car had picked up her trail again when she slowed to tour around the building looking for an entrance. They knew where she was and how to get in.

"Why would these individuals do that?" Olson asked.

Michael shrugged. "You don't know me from Adam, sir. But I did not come to Portland to become embroiled in ongoing cases. I retired from the Treasury and replaced Allan Farber as a bank compliance officer at Pacific GreenBank." There she was, telling the truth again.

Chief Rangel nodded. "Go on."

"In a routine audit, I discovered some bank irregularities involving some of Frank Hamid's real estate deals that Farber had been looking into at the time of his murder."

She let that hang out there for a moment. No one said anything. "I believe Farber's discovery of the deals was the precipitating event that resulted in his death, made to look like a hunting accident, as you well know."

A pin could have dropped.

"Of course you know that Frank Hamid was the one who discovered his body. There are Federal issues involved in the case, so all I'm authorized to do is raise local law enforcement awareness regarding the crimes about which I have personal knowledge. I was not present at the death of Farber, or last Monday's incident involving Jesse Halen." She stopped again.

"Go ahead," Rangel said.

"On Friday, at a bank outing at the country club, I was in a golf cart accident that occurred when Frank Hamid was driving. It may have been carelessness on his part that caused the cart to smash into a tree, but that wouldn't account for these."

Michael untied the silk scarf she was wearing around her neck and displayed the tell-tale bruises on her neck. She could feel the air sucked out of the room in the silence that followed her little show and tell.

"I may have lost a second or two, but he, or someone else, tried to strangle me. I was lucky. The instinct to breathe is a reflex action. Choking woke me right up."

"Have you seen a doctor?" Chief Olson asked.

Michael shook her head. "I'm all right, thank you for asking."

The Chief exchanged glances with Pete. It was clear they hadn't known about this. "Why didn't you come to us with this on Friday?" he asked. "We would have gotten you checked out and given you protection."

"I am a civilian, just a bank employee now. Obviously, this is a complicated case. I don't know who's running the wider investigation on Hamid." She retied her scarf. "Just wanted to do the right thing," she added. She didn't mention that Pete had blown her off when she suggested going to his place for the weekend. Said he was busy Saturday night.

"For us, attempted murder takes precedence over everything else. You should have alerted us."

Go ahead and scold me, she thought. Everyone else does. That didn't change the fact that in this town, homicide did not seem to take precedence over everything else when it came to Frank Hamid.

"I've heard from my people that you haven't been able to pin anything on Hamid. As part of my bank audit, I went for a site visit to Blackberry Farm on Saturday. That's one of the eight properties that I am looking at. I thought you might like to see what I found at this location." She glanced at Pete quickly.

She fanned out the photos she'd taken. The five men leaned forward and passed around the blurry images of the barn interior, the farmhouse exterior, the piles of trash, the trailer on blocks, the ammonia tank, the marijuana plants, the mound with the edge of tarp uncovered, and the Honda motorcycle. When the Honda came up, with the license plate clearly visible, Olson's face came alive. He turned to Pete. "Would you get Richardson in here?"

"You know the bike?" Michael asked.

"Sure you don't want some coffee?"

"Thanks, I would like some. White, no sugar," she said, then sat back to wait as Olson went out of the room. Nice to be waited on by a man. It didn't happen often.

"Why did you ever leave Treasury? Too exciting for you?" Chief Rangel said while they waited.

Michael replied with a shrug. "It had its days."

Pete returned with a disheveled, chubby man in jeans and a T-shirt. Chief Olson brought the coffee and a tall, distinguished gentleman in a very starched uniform. It was now seven to one male to female in the crowded room. Chief Olson put the coffee on the table and introduced the Chief of Police, Derek Stanley.

"This is Michael Tamlin," he said.

"Pleased to meet you." Michael wondered which part of her story had gotten his attention.

"This is Toby Richardson, who handles our MPs," Pete said.

Michael shook his hand, said she was glad to meet him too, and shot Pete a questioning look.

"I look for missing persons," Toby said.

"Oh." That explained the hair standing on end. She was served the only coffee in the room. She nodded her thank you and drank some. For a bean city, it was pretty bad. Maybe the rest of them went out for theirs.

First things first, Richardson put two photos on the table. "This is Cheli Abrio and Matthew Brand."

Michael studied them long enough to know she'd never seen

them. "I've not seen them. Who are they?"

"He's an engineering graduate student from the university in Eugene. He was supposed to graduate on June 2. Cheli is an undergraduate. They disappeared back in May. They were staying in Portland, took a day trip and never came back. No one knows exactly what day they left or where they went. It was already a cold case when we got the call."

"How can I help you?" Michael asked.

Richardson poked at one of her photos. "That's his bike."

"Oh." Her eyes slid over to the photo of the dirt mound she'd stumbled on. Seven pairs of eyes watched her reaction. She told herself not to jump to conclusions. Then she remembered the cameras and drug operation. "Were they users?" she asked softly.

"He wasn't. She'd had her wild times," Richardson answered. "Did you see anyone at the farm?"

Michael shook her head. "But I think the bike might have followed me when I left. I did notice one like it on the highway."

"Did you see the driver?"

She shook her head. "He was wearing a helmet. I lost him," she added.

"No, you found him. Congratulations. This is our first break in the case," Richardson said.

"Well, I'm glad I've been useful. Does this have any connection to Mr. Hamid?"

Silence followed the question.

"Can you download these for me? I need to keep my phone." She displayed the photos she'd just taken from her driveway.

"And this is?" Richardson asked.

"This is the Toyota that was waiting for me this morning at my home. These are the two individuals in the vehicle. Maybe you can do a face-recognition on them. The driver could be George Hamid. He's Frank's nephew. George was on the scene at the golfing incident on Friday," she said. "Although I doubt he'd try to kill anyone. He's kind of a wuss."

Pete shook his head. "We should have done some tests on you before you took a shower. Didn't you ever hear of DNA testing?"

"Sorry, I just wanted to go home. Oh, and Hamid sent me some gifts from one of his restaurants. They're in the garbage. Pickup is tomorrow, in case you want to test them to see if they're toxic or something."

She was careful not to look at anyone as she said this. "One more thing. Hamid's real estate deals were a kind of pyramid scheme. FinCEN is working on the money trail. It involves his hedge fund, where Halen died last Monday, and his jet center down in Hillsboro. Hamid is an extremely dangerous individual. I have made a detailed map with all the data we have on the properties. I'm not certain they were in play in the investigation. They were hidden pretty well. One is a warehouse near the race-track. One is down by John's Landing. Three properties are in logging country. And of course, the farm, where I was yesterday. I'm guessing these other properties are used for other illicit activities of one kind or another. He uses his jets out of Hillsboro to fly abroad." She paused for a moment before going on.

"Drugs are likely to be only a sideline. Halen told me Hamid is bringing people in from the Middle East. That means the pilot and crew should be picked up to insure he doesn't fly away. The warehouse and logging sites should be checked very carefully. Blackberry Farm has video cameras. For all I know, the buildings there are booby trapped, so go in carefully. And keep an eye on the Toyota. They saw me come in here." Michael sat back. She'd given them everything she had.

Different investigators took turns asking questions in a more private setting, including many questions about her and Charlie's evening with Jesse Halen. She answered as truthfully as she could. She then told the appropriate chiefs who her contacts were in D.C. and how she'd been told to take local criminal activity to the local authorities. She was confident that she'd stayed within the boundaries set for her. People would be debriefing her for a long time, but it was now up to local and federal agencies to collaborate on who got to take Hamid down and when. Unfortunately, as an outsider, she was just a CI and would not to be there to see it.

Finally, a female officer asked her to remove her skirt and

blouse and took some photos of her injuries. Finally, Chief Olson thanked her for coming in.

"I hope to hear from you soon," she told him, but had no real expectations. She knew her job was done.

Pete took her downstairs. "Why didn't you tell me this sooner?"

"I tried, but you've been holding out on me, too, Petey. Will they search the farm today?"

"We're a five-man drug unit, and finishing something up at the moment. My bad that I put you off until today. I'm sorry."

"It's okay. I spent the weekend at the beach. It wasn't too bad."

He gave her a look. "I'm really sorry."

"It's really okay. What about those kids?"

"I don't know. There will have to be some haggling among other agencies. Some of it is Federal. We have some different jurisdictions, more than one state. A lot of ducks to get in a row. Today is unlikely. But I'm concerned about you." He took a step closer, and she could tell he was concerned.

"Don't worry, I know how to take care of myself." She wondered what he meant about more than one state.

"I believe it, but I wouldn't want anything to happen to you. Where are you going now?"

"Work. Five blocks away."

"Okay, you'll be all right there. But I'd like you to stay with me or Pam as long as you're here. I'll put a BOLO on the vehicle that followed you, but if you see anything suspicious, alert me right away. Don't be a hero. I'll call you later about tonight." He touched her arm and she felt the excitement again.

"Okay," she said. Maybe their date was on again.

"It's an order," he added.

She smiled. For her, orders were for restaurants. "You want me to pick up some steaks?"

"We'll see."

"You're not a vegan or anything, are you?" she asked, suspicious.

"No." He shook his head. "See you later."

Michael went down to the garage smiling. It wasn't going to be a picnic at work anymore, but it never was. At least two things were going her way. She wouldn't have to be alone tonight. And the Toyota wasn't waiting for her when she left the station.

47

Ali's head shook like a Parkinson's patient. George wondered if he could get through the next two days--long enough to do his last job. As far as George knew, Ali hadn't been alone for a second, but there were definite signs he was getting weird again.

"Are you telling me no? Or did you take something behind my back again, you idiot?" George wanted to pound him. When did Ali have an opportunity to inject himself? Damn, George hated working like this. Last time, he told himself. This was it with him and Ali.

"I can do it." Ali pressed his index finger against the side of his nose.

Oh, of course. He'd sniffed it. George was pacing around between the three buildings at the farm, planning his big move. All right, they couldn't blow up Michael's car in the parking lot. It was too late for that. She'd gone to the cops, so now they had to blow up the police station instead. It did not require a rocket scientist to figure this out. One simple blast would put the whole of downtown Portland in chaos. A light finally came on in his head. This was the statement he'd been put on earth to make. The quiet rage and indecision he'd felt ever since losing his father and leaving his home half a world away ignited into a purpose that made perfect sense.

"You're renting a van and meeting me. Repeat it," George said.

"I know," Ali replied, but he looked as if he didn't know his own name.

"Say it, Ali."

"I'm renting a van," Ali said.

"Where are you going with the van, Ali?"

"I don't know, brother, where?"

"Not after it's armed, dummy! Where are you going as soon as you get the van?" Talking to him was crazy-making.

"I'm going home," Ali said.

"No! You're going to my place to pick me up. Can you remember that?"

Ali nodded, but George rolled his eyes, doubtful.

"Say it again," he demanded.

Ali's head went from side to side. Shaking his head that he wouldn't repeat it, or that he'd forgotten already? George couldn't fight the battle of clarification anymore. Looking around at the mess the farm had become, he was overwhelmed by the sheer amount of shit that had collected over the winter. Why hadn't he seen it before? Ali had just piled up the bags everywhere and never dealt with it. George had known it was there, of course, but it didn't register with him exactly how much garbage there was until that bank woman showed up yesterday. So now everything needed to be cleared out pronto: the bags, the equipment in the farmhouse, all the weed in the barn.

These were separate challenges to deal with. The weed had to be harvested. Transporting it would not be an issue, but the meth waste (which was contaminated) could not be moved in the Toyota. Then there was the question of Ali's corpses. They had to be moved, too. It was mind boggling how much trouble Ali's addiction had caused him. George tried to figure the logistics. If he used the rented van to blow the police station, he couldn't use it to haul the garbage out.

He considered the situation. Maybe he needed a Ryder truck instead. Get the brothers down here to harvest the weed, dig up the corpses, and clean the property. They'd been making bombs up there. They'd help. He stood there in the yard trying to categorize the steps in order of their importance. Blow up the police station was first. Forget the clean up and bodies for now.

Ali was sitting on the ground arranging pebbles. That repetitive activity convinced George that he'd have to go with Ali to rent the van. Ali couldn't be trusted to get it, remember to bring it back, or drive it up to the lodge to collect the plastics and detonator they needed to blow the building. Truth was, he couldn't be trusted to do anything. As George reviewed his plan of action, a new catastrophe occurred.

Without any warning at all, his uncle Frank drove up the driveway to the farmhouse in his powder-blue custom Bentley sports car that had taken a year between order and delivery. George swore. Once again he had not been watching the monitor when security was breached.

"Get into the trailer," he ordered Ali.

Ali gave no sign of hearing him. His uncle had to stop the car to avoid hitting him.

"What's the matter with you?" His uncle got out of his expensive car, shaking his head at the bag of bones in his way.

Then, by degrees, his uncle registered the pebbles Ali was playing with and the mountains of garbage around the farm house. And then he registered the trailer on blocks that had not been there the last time he'd visited, over a year ago. George didn't know why his uncle had come here, but it was clear this ruin of his property was not what he'd expected to find. For several long seconds his uncle was speechless. And then he erupted.

"What's going on here? I trusted you to take care of this place." He looked around, horrified.

"Uncle. We were just cleaning up."

"Sonny, this is disgusting! What's that awful smell? God! Smells like someone died."

"No, it's--" He didn't have a chance to finish.

His uncle marched over to the house and looked inside. He started screaming when he saw the make-shift lab in the kitchen.

"Are you trying to kill me?" he yelled. "Are you trying to send me to prison for the rest of my life?" His uncle closed the front door of the house and covered his face with his hands.

"Uncle, I can explain," George began.

His uncle released his face and made two fists. "You are! You're trying to kill me! What's wrong with you? I gave you everything." Then he marched across the yard to the trailer and opened that door.

George groaned. The monitors, the porno videos, the magazines, the packaging for the meth: everything was in plain sight.

"Oh, my God!" his uncle screamed. "My God, you're the

devil. You are the devil, sent to destroy everything I've spent my entire life building." He spun around like a dancer, and came at George with his fists raised.

From long history, dating all the way back to babyhood, George had learned to shrink and cower when attacked. Now he was afraid to move even a tiny muscle lest he be beaten to death. Then, as his uncle came at him, George suddenly realized that he had the upper hand for the first time in his life. His uncle was alone. The man was twice his age, was taller than he, and weighed more, but George knew he and Ali could take him if they wanted to. He glanced at the hose from the nurse tank that Ali had been too sick to use for over a week.

"Ali, get up," he said. If his uncle died, George could keep everything. He stood taller. He would not cower in front of his uncle anymore. It was not his fault that the farm looked like this. All the brothers were involved. Many people were involved. His uncle's favorite was involved.

"Uncle, do not upset yourself. We will fix everything. I promise."

"You were supposed to look after this place. How could you do this?"

"I am looking after it." George willed Ali to get up, but Ali was having one of his out of body experiences. No one was home in his head.

"You're making drugs on my property!" his uncle yelled. "We don't do that in this family. We don't sell drugs. I was told you were taking drugs, not making them. What's the matter with you?"

His uncle kept screaming, and that infuriated George even more. That's all his uncle could ever think about him: that something was wrong with him. Nothing was wrong with him. He was doing a job, just like everybody else. Doing an important job, helping people, but he couldn't argue that case with his uncle right now. The thing that bothered him was that he didn't want to be nailed as a user. It hurt his feelings, challenged his honor, and put him on the defensive.

"Who said I was using drugs? I don't use drugs. Did Sami tell you that?"

"Sami is very worried about you. And him." His uncle pointed at the tweaking Ali.

"Don't get me started on him. He has the flu." George couldn't help defending his brother. "But we don't do drugs, okay? And your precious Sami deals at Taboule, did you know that? He's a drug dealer. Everybody's involved, not just me."

"What?" His uncle stamped his foot. "You're a damned liar."

"I'm not stupid, Uncle. I know Sami killed that banker, and he killed Jesse, too. Get on your feet, Ali. Show Uncle you're all right."

"Liar!" his uncle yelled.

"You can tell me the truth. I'm family. Sami can't be trusted. He's not family." George started pleading his case. He couldn't help it. He wanted to be accepted even now.

"Family! You've been like a son to me. I don't care what your mother has to say about it. I'm not getting over what you've done here. I'll tell you one thing, asshole. If that bank bitch finds out about this, we are all cooked. Everything I've worked for. Every bit of good I've done. Down the drain. Do you understand?"

George leaned against his uncle's car. Well, the bank bitch already knew about it, but he wasn't going to tell his uncle that.

"Did you and Sami try to kill her, Uncle? Because I know how to do it. I can take care of it for you." He said this eagerly, wanted to prove himself. If his uncle was a killer, he could be a killer.

"Are you crazy? You dishonored me. You defiled your family with this." He waved his arms at the two buildings. "You're finished." His uncle was beside himself. "You're not touching anybody. Get away from my car."

George hastily backed away from the Bentley. "All right. But I said I would clean this up. I keep my promises."

"Then do it. Today."

His uncle got into the car and fired the engine. He was really steaming, but George had seen him go off like this a hundred times. He always got over it. Right then it was almost comical. His uncle was so mad he could hardly maneuver the car in the small space. He nearly ran Ali over a second time, and scattered all of his stones.

When his uncle finally executed the U-turn and tore off down the road, Ali stood up and acted relatively normal for the first time in weeks.

"Let's go rent the van," he said.

In the past Ali had always liked planning and carrying out the jobs. He had a technical mind. Now he almost sounded like his old self again. George nodded. What the fuck? They were still blowing up the police station. That would earn some respect.

48

When Michael arrived at her office just before eleven, the Lough-lin gnome was pacing the hallway outside the elevator. She was wearing a pantsuit of hunter green with a belt and necklace of seashells, and seashell earrings. Her outfit was further decorated with some fiber art that looked like a fish net. Indescribable.

"Oh, my God. Oh, my God. Where have you been? I've been worried sick." Mary Lou pounced on Michael the moment she limped off the elevator.

"Wow. That's some outfit," Michael remarked.

"You like it? I got it in a cool store in Cannon Beach, kind of funky, huh? Want to go shopping with me some time?"

Michael didn't think so. She was in the end game, on her way home. The gnome did a quick spin to show off before she remembered her distress about the accident. "Oh, my God, it's true."

Michael was wearing her hair down to cover a bunch of scratches on one cheek. The bruises on her neck, which were still deep red and purple, and had not yet started to yellow around the edges, were mostly hidden by her blue and white scarf. Other small scrapes on her hands, wrists and arms were healing nicely. But there was no doubt about it. Anyone looking at her would know she'd seen action.

Mary Lou followed her into her office and shut the door. "I just heard this morning. Why didn't you call me? I would have taken you to the doctor. I would have gone food shopping and cooked for you." She took one of Michael's hands and turned it over. "My God, what's the matter with you? Why didn't you go to the hospital?"

Michael shrugged. "You know lawyers. They didn't want a lawsuit." She sat in her desk chair gingerly, acting just a little. It wasn't as bad as it looked.

"But you could have been…I'm really upset." The gnome fell into a leather wing chair and covered her face with both hands.

"I didn't know about this. This is scary--"

Michael cut her off. "It was an unfortunate accident, Mary Lou. Accidents happen on golf courses all the time."

"I heard Frank pushed you to safety. Is that true?" Mary Lou leaned forward in her chair. She didn't know what to believe.

"Is that what he says? I'm kind of foggy on the details. You should see my clothes. I was impaled by a branch." Michael laughed.

"I'm scared," the gnome said softly. "Honestly, I am. I called Marty. He came back from vacation to see you."

"What!" It was Michael's turn to scream. "I didn't tell you to do that!"

"Well, I thought you needed some support, and he's so good in a crisis." Mary Lou tried to be soothing.

"I don't want him in my crisis. That was not a decision for you to make."

"Calm down. He'll be here in an hour."

"He must not have gone very far." Michael spun around and looked out the window. Smarty Marty was the last person she wanted to talk to.

"I wasn't the first. Ashland called him Friday after it happened. Marty flew home yesterday."

"No. No. No! I won't do it." Michael considered a huge tantrum. And then she realized that Marty's appearance explained the silence from team Upjohn. They wanted him to take care of her, threaten her with paranoia and other mental illnesses. Nice. She wouldn't have thought of that. End game, she told herself. Time to make a graceful exit.

"Too bad, I've already cleared your calendar, and Ashland called. He wants to take you to lunch after your meeting with Marty."

"Oh, Jesus!" Soften me up, give me a salad, and then call me crazy. That pretty much covered the corporate life. Except for the homicide risk. I'm hungrier than that, she thought.

"You need some support. Everybody's very worried," Mary Lou went on.

"How comforting. But tell everybody this. I'm not leaving the building. Lunch will have to be in the board roam. I'll want a taster, and if Marty comes in, he has to meet me here in my office. And I want you with me."

"He won't like that."

"You know, Mary Lou, I don't care what anybody likes. I want you with me all day, even in the ladies' room. Copy?"

Mary Lou frowned. "Copy what?"

"Copy means you understand."

"Oh. Do you really want a taster?"

Michael shook her head. The gnome had the weird look down. She'd be fine for the Agatha Christie period, but she just wasn't working as a contemporary spy. Michael would have to brief her and Charlie on how to behave and what to say when she was gone.

"Now, I'd love something really gooey for breakfast. I need some calories." And a couple of shots of vodka, she didn't say. She was feeling that peevish. She didn't like things at the bank ending this way. It wasn't going to look good on her record.

49

On the way back from the farm, Hamid checked his watch and called Sami. The phone rang and rang before Sami picked up. Seven rings, to be exact.

"Where are you?" Hamid demanded.

"In the shower."

Hamid could hear the lie in Sami's sleepy voice. He wasn't up yet.

"You're still in bed. Meet me at the warehouse in an hour," he told him.

"Is everything all right?" Sami asked.

Hamid didn't have to gauge the tension in Sami's voice. Sami had reason to be very scared. He'd messed up on Friday. He'd tried to break Michael's neck when all he had to do was put a rubber-gloved hand over the unconscious girl's mouth and pinch her nostrils. Death would have been quick, and no one would have figured it out. Why make things harder than they had to be? If you have a second to get something done, you do it in half a second. You don't leave bruises all over her for people to analyze. Hamid didn't blame himself for not helping to finish her off. It was not his job to kill people. It was his job to be the innocent bystander. He'd trusted Sami, and now he was worried about that trust.

Sami had told him he'd watched Michael and knew her habits. He reported how she walked to the top of Council Crest once, went to work and the grocery store, and didn't have visitors. Hamid thought that part was odd. Everybody at the bank said she had a fiancé. If she had a boyfriend, he should be around. Sami was sure she wasn't an agent; Hamid wasn't so sure. Her behavior was agent behavior.

Sami said she'd stayed put at home all weekend after the accident on the golf course, except for the time the day before when he'd searched her house and found nothing. So where had she been when he was searching her house? Sami didn't know. It took a lot of people to do proper surveillance. Hamid always knew when someone was following him. Sami, who had a night job and slept late in the morning, was not up to the job.

He wasn't telling the truth about a lot of things. That was clear now. He shouldn't be asking his boss if everything was all right. He should already know. Sami should have known everything about George, not just the using part. If he didn't know that George was making meth at the farm, he was a loser. If he did know, he was a traitor. In Hamid's world, traitors didn't live long.

"You tell me if everything's all right," Hamid barked.

"Everything's all right," Sami told him.

"I had just had a little talk with George about what you told me," Hamid said.

"Where are you?" Sami asked.

"On my way back from the farm."

"George was there?"

"You know what he told me?"

"He and I don't have the same values. He lies about everything," Sami said.

"You know what I found there?"

"No." The word came out flat and fast. There was no hesitation.

"One hour," Hamid said and hung up. Let him stew.

Hamid drove 99 from Dundee as fast as the traffic would allow, thinking about how he'd purposely kept his operation small. He didn't want a lot of people knowing what he was doing, where he was going, what he did there and who he knew. He had built his business on two beliefs: His number one belief was anything that Americans didn't want to see could be hidden forever. Second, he believed that anyone could be managed. Just two exceptions in forty-four years. Michael Tamlin and his own nephew.

The Bentley wove in and out of RVs, SUVs, and farm trucks, honking at vehicles that didn't get out of the way fast enough. Hamid didn't worry about scratching the $250,000 vehicle. There were more where that one came from. He took his eyes off the road frequently to gauge the sky. The forecast was for rain later in the day. He loved rain, loved that his city was full of it, famous for it. Water mattered as much as oil. That's why he thought about water all the way back to the city. He had to be careful about his blood pressure.

When he got to the warehouse, Sami was waiting in the office, playing with an empty container of coffee. The warehouse was empty at the moment, but sometimes they stored things there. When Hamid came in, Sami got to his feet and waited.

"Tell me about George," Hamid said.

"You know everything I do," Sami said with an open face.

"I didn't know George was making drugs in my farmhouse. I didn't know you were selling it at my restaurants." Hamid gave Sami a look that scared his enemies.

"I'm not. It's a lie." Sami's face was empty.

Hamid opened and closed his fist. "You should have taken that girl out like I told you to."

Sami shook his head. "I thought she was already dead."

"Then why put your hands on her?"

Sami shook his head some more.

Hamid changed the subject. "George trashed the farm. It's a meth lab now. The whole place has to be cleaned up, and then burned to the ground. Nothing fancy, nothing traceable."

Sami rubbed his nose with the back of his right hand.

"You upset about that?"

"No, sir."

"You have to burn the barn, too. There's no alarm up there, but it still has to go fast."

Sami indicated he understood.

"Tell me the truth. Is everybody involved in this, like George said?"

"No, sir. It's a lie."

"Then you won't mind cleansing the lie. I want it done right away. I don't want him to risk my whole operation."

Sami cleared his throat. "Does George know about this?"

"George is finished. I won't see him again."

Hamid turned his back so he didn't see Sami's smile. Then

he turned around again. "And I want you to do what you were supposed to do Friday."

"I thought you wanted to cool it on that--"

"Well, I changed my mind, didn't I? Get her when she's in the car. Take her up to the farm. Make that fire very, very hot. And do it quickly. Don't wait around on this."

Sami nodded wearily. It was only Monday, but already he looked very tired. Hamid didn't believe a word he said.

50

Smarty Marty arrived promptly at eleven. Mary Lou was already sitting at the conference table in Michael's office, but there was no sign of the Cinnabons they'd consumed with gusto only a few minutes ago. The gnome had her spiral out and was taking notes on nothing at all. She and Michael were both flying on sugar highs.

"I just heard." Marty marched up to the desk to make a quick assessment of Michael's visible injuries. "How are you doing?" he asked.

Their meeting must be very important to him because he was wearing a dark suit and conservative tie. Michael was speeding from sugar, but otherwise not well enough to come out from behind the desk to shake the hand he held out.

"I thought Ashland called you on Friday," she replied.

Marty heard a noise and looked around to see that the green gnome was at the table behind him. He shot Mary Lou a pained look, but it might have been a reaction to the outfit.

"It's all right, we have no secrets here," Michael told him. "What a pity you had to come home early. Where were you?"

"Ah, Hawaii." Marty seemed uncertain about it.

"Oh, double pity." Michael's lip jumped just a little. She hoped it didn't look too much like a sneer. "You certainly didn't need to come back on my account. Your wife must be disappointed."

"I'm not married," he said slowly.

"Oh." Michael smiled again. "Well, somebody must be disappointed."

Mary Lou stopped writing little nothings long enough to giggle.

"Thank you, Mary Lou, you can go now," Marty told her.

"Miss Tamlin asked me to stay," the gnome replied.

Marty looked from one to the other. "This is highly unusual," he said after a pause.

"Well, so is crashing into a tree. And so would be the murder of two Pac GreenBank compliance VPs in a six month period. We're in strange times. Have a seat," Michael offered.

"I don't follow." But he took a wing chair by the desk all the same.

This was the part where Michael turned into a super bitch. From time to time, with the right people, she let herself go. Whenever she did, it felt really good. The golf cart incident and the two missing students, and the flight out here that she took on a jet that most certainly brought bad people to the U.S. from war zones, took her right over the top. The four dead people that she knew of were likely to be only the tip of Hamid's death squad iceberg. Her eyes were green. Her face was small and stony.

"I'll try to be clear. What are your instructions?" she asked.

He had the gall to look hurt. "My instructions? You're my client. You had a bad accident. I'm sure you have feelings about that and need some help to process and work on the future."

Michael cut him off at the knees. "I don't pay for your services. The bank is your client," she corrected him. "So, let's process that first. Your client is my boss. Second, the accident that I was lucky to survive happened on a bank outing with a bank client driving. I believe Ashland is on the board of the club, so he has a kind of double jeopardy in all this."

"I wouldn't know." Marty suddenly looked gray.

"Even I know," Michael said.

"Well, maybe he is. Where are you going with this?"

"Marty, although I like you personally very much, I'm not going to play mind games with you. I'm not and never have been paranoid." She took her scarf off and showed him the bruises on her neck. "Someone tried to strangle me. It's a fact."

He gasped. "Oh, my!" It was the first thing he said since they met that wasn't an act.

Mary Lou gasped, too.

"How did that happen?" Marty asked.

"As I told the police this morning, I'm a little foggy on the details. I'm not pointing any fingers. But I do remember that in one of our sessions you suggested that I was paranoid about Allan's death and overreacting to other worrying bank matters. You particularly advised me to go with the flow. If I ever have to testify about it, I will have to tell the truth about all of your recommendations about my job and well-being, and whatever you have to tell me now. Your relationship and payments from the bank will be scrutinized, and your actions with regard to other employees will be investigated. So think carefully what you are about to say to me now. If you perjure yourself later about any of this, you could go to prison. Understood? Someone else I know got forty-five years. Okay?"

Marty shook his head as if she'd betrayed his trust and he was deeply disappointed in her. Michael twisted the scarf around her fingers. It was a good one, pure silk. One of her lovers had given it to her a long time ago. Unfortunately, she'd been drunk at the time and couldn't remember which one. However, Marty had never been a friend. She wouldn't mind if his soft ass went to prison. "Mary Lou. Would you turn on the news?"

Mary Lou got out of her chair and turned on the TV. It ran over Michael's voice. Marty had to lean in to hear her.

"So, dear life coach. I took your advice and relaxed. I went golfing. On that outing I made it very clear to all involved that I did not intend to create difficulties of any kind for the bank. I had every intention of cooling it." Lying put her back in her comfort zone.

She lifted her shoulders in simulation of a sad little shrug. "I'm a loyal employee of the company. I certainly didn't want the bank in trouble, or anyone to get hurt. But you did not keep your side of the bargain."

"What are you suggesting?"

"I'm suggesting you set me up to cover up the bank's wrongdoing."

Marty crumbled like a cookie. Michael could see it happening. The man had no guts, no conviction. He probably had knowledge and now he felt remorse.

"I'm very sorry," he said. "I had no way of knowing anything like this would happen."

He was a lackey, a corporate tool. Pretty far down the ladder of importance. She could see him struggle with some new and really disturbing questions to which he did not ultimately want to know the answers. She put the scarf back on to give him a moment to process.

"What do you want?" he asked finally. It was clear he didn't want to know who hurt her.

"I want protection. My mother would mind if something else happened to me now. The local police and my former employers at FinCEN would be all over any accident that befell me now. I can guarantee that certain people at the bank would suffer even more than they inevitably will. Forty-five years looks good for money laundering, fraud."

Mary Lou looked like she was going to faint.

"There will be a lot of charges. Some people will go to prison for a long time. You probably know who they are. I'm not going to ask who your boss in this is. Obviously there is a conspiracy here at the bank. But others will ask and will find out. It won't make any difference if something happens to me now. But I think Mary Lou would mind, too, wouldn't you Mary Lou?"

The gnome gasped. "My God. Of course I would."

"I understand your anxiety, but--"

"You asked me what I want, Marty. I want you to go back and tell your client that I need to die another day. That's from James Bond, remember it? And I don't want any harm to come to anyone on my team. Is that clear?"

He nodded meekly. "No one here had any intention of hurting you. I can assure you of that."

"That's not my job to determine. All I want is to get out of here with no more accidents to anyone, okay?"

The poor man licked his lips. He had no idea what he was doing, but he was a life coach and went with the flow. "Of course," he said. "Of course! You are safe with us. We will keep you safe. That's a promise." He looked like he'd swallowed a death pill himself as he spoke the words.

"Good. Thank you for stopping by," she said. "This meeting has been recorded. If anything happens to me, our conversation will be sent to the Treasury and the Justice Departments in Washington. I hope we're clear on my issues." What a liar she was, and how very good she felt. Marty looked pretty scared, and Mary Lou did, too.

Michael did not look at him as the gnome showed him out. She had about fifteen minutes of quiet before Mary Lou returned to tell her that the lunch with Ashland had been canceled. Apparently he had a conflict he hadn't known about. Michael figured they would now be working on a dollar amount. It wouldn't affect a single thing. When the time of reckoning came, she wasn't going to help their defense. Someone else was going to have to find out if Caulahan was involved.

51

Pete called as Michael was packing up to leave the office after a very quiet afternoon. No contact from anybody. No reason to stay. She had some calls to make.

"What's going on?" he asked.

"You first," she replied.

"You were very impressive here this morning," he said. "A lot of people are rushing around now. Looks like I'm not going home tonight."

"Ah, I'm disappointed," Michael said. "And here, I thought we had a date."

"Can I take a rain check on that?" He sounded sincere.

"Well, thanks. But I don't plan on sticking around much longer." She stood behind her desk looking out at the view. She'd probably never have one like it again, and maybe not a boyfriend, either. But maybe she wasn't suited for it.

"I'm sorry to hear that. Are you going back to your old job?" He said it matter-of-factly.

"No," she said, "But I'm clearly not a corporate player. I'm only hanging in long enough to work out my exit terms."

"That's too bad. I'll be sorry to see you go. Look, I'd like to secure you in another location for the time being. Keep you safe. Will you go to my sister's? She's working, too. But it's closer than my place. Or PD could assign an officer."

"I don't think that will be necessary now. I've had a heart to heart with my employers. I think they'll make sure I'm secure in my own location. What action are you taking? What about those missing kids?" She studied the river and beyond. Clouds were gathering out east where the mountains met the sky. She felt she had a right to know.

"I can't talk about that on the phone," Pete said. "A lot of people are involved in a coordinated effort. Your information has been very helpful. All I can tell you is that it's big, and soon. Your individual won't be sleeping at home tonight."

"That's good to know. If I can't be there, I guess I'll go home soon."

"Call me when you get there," he said. "I want to keep in close contact."

"You mean it?" Michael said.

"Of course, and I still want you to see my place. Won't be tonight. But maybe tomorrow?"

"Okay. I'd like that."

Michael hung up feeling at loose ends. She wasn't exactly one to walk away when the water came to a boil, but what could she do? She put on her jacket and threw her cell phone in the pocket. She collected her purse and some files that she didn't want to leave around. As soon as she was outside she was going to call Marjorie. Done. Safe, on her way home. Marjorie would be pleased.

When she passed Mary Lou's desk on her way out, Mary Lou jumped up. "Why don't you stay at my place tonight? I know my lover won't mind."

Michael's eyes popped, and not only because she suspected Mary Lou had been eavesdropping again. "You have a boyfriend?"

The gnome bristled like an angry porcupine. "I don't call him my boyfriend. He's my lover."

"Oh, now I understand why you're such a hot dresser." Michael couldn't help feeling even more depressed. Mary Lou had a live-in lover and she couldn't even get a one-night stand.

"Come on, it will be fun," the gnome urged.

"Thanks anyway, but I don't do threesomes."

"I'm worried about you," Mary Lou confided.

Michael shook her head. "Just because of that little incident on Friday? Come on. After our conversation with Marty, I don't think it will happen again."

"Will someone be guarding your house?"

"It would be a smart move."

Mary Lou walked with her to the elevator. "Do you want me to stay with you? I'd like to stay with you," she said eagerly. "I want to hear all about this."

"Thanks. I'll be fine. I have a lot of calls to make." She had to make contact with her mother, too. Another M word. Why did she feel depressed? She should have known Pete would be busy. She'd given them a lot to do, and they wouldn't let her play with them. That's how the game was played. The CI didn't get to ride with the cavalry. She told herself to get over it.

They got to the elevator and Michael pushed the down button.

"I'm coming with you," Mary Lou said. "Executive decision."

"No."

"Just to the car."

The elevator door slid open. The gnome stepped forward and Michael put her hand up to stop her from going any farther. "Don't worry, I'll see you tomorrow." She surprised herself and gave the gnome a quick hug.

Then she got into the elevator with several other people who left on different floors. Michael was all alone on the second level of the garage when she walked out and looked around. It was a large space, and quiet. She didn't like the quiet. Even during peak hours of the day when plenty of people were around, she was uneasy in public garages where there were no attendants and the entry and exit gates opened automatically to anyone.

She glanced around twice before hurrying over to the Acura. Then she walked around the car looking for a wire, or something that didn't look right. She didn't see anything. This was the awkward moment that she hadn't wanted Mary Lou to witness. She was going to have to look under the car to make sure it was clean. Checking for a car bomb wasn't, strictly speaking, something she wanted people to know she could do. And it was clumsy.

She thought about just getting into the car and hoping for the best. She was tempted to do that, but knew that people who didn't take precautions were the ones who got blown up. The enemy didn't have to blow up the building or himself if he wanted to take her out. All he had to do was to wait until the car emerged on the street and then dial a cell phone number that activated a bundle attached somewhere under it. Or he could blow the car in the garage. There were a lot of ways to do it. She unlocked the driver's door and hesitated, debating. Open the door, don't open the door. She had that sinking feeling that despite her bravado all day, she wasn't safe at all. A lot of people would breathe easier if she just wasn't around anymore. She had to check the car. She took a breath and got down on her knees.

She had a fifty/fifty chance of making the right decision. She made the wrong one. As soon as she was as low as she could get, someone in sneakers darted out from behind a pillar. She saw the feet under the car, running around to her side. Nike Airs. She reached up and opened the car door. She was trying to haul herself inside the car when he got to the open door.

She was sprawled across the seat facing the passenger door, not in all the way. She kicked out. Nike man took a few hits with her stilettos before he launched himself on top of her, and pinned her arms. She rolled toward the dashboard and opened her mouth to scream. He hit her on the head with something hard, and her lights went out before a single sound came out of her mouth. Second time in less than a week.

52

George was silent at the wheel driving the Toyota down the hill to 99. The last thing he wanted to do was go all the way up to the lodge, which was northeast of Portland, and then drive back down that terrible road with a van full of explosives. He didn't know how much explosive was needed to do what he wanted to do. He didn't know how the detonators worked. This wasn't his area of expertise.

He liked dynamite and knew how to manage it. Dynamite had to be lighted. It was simple. He had some sticks, but not enough. Ali had told him a thousand times that military grade C-4 (which was made all over Eastern Europe and blew up the Cole and other U.S. targets all over the place) was as stable as soap, easier to mold than Play Doh, and readily available on the black market. And the brothers had a lot of it. George knew you could pack it inside anything, but he didn't understand what kind of device was needed to set it off--how it could be rigged, or propelled in a rocket. He knew the guys were working on all these things, and that they had other explosives, too. Fertilizer and gasoline, both of which were easy to get. Ali told him how they dried it out and packed it in drums. There was some method they had read about that had killed a lot of people in Iraq. Burying the stuff so deep it couldn't be detected. But he wasn't burying anything deep.

As soon as his uncle was gone, George started questioning Ali about all this. "How about we use the ammonia instead of C-4?" he began.

"Doesn't burn," Ali said.

"So what? It goes up, doesn't it?"

Ali nodded. "Yeah."

"So, a bang is all we need."

"It just mixes with oxygen and pops. It won't do enough damage without added fire power. You want to blow a whole building, you need more."

"What if we used a lot?"

"Would just make a bigger pop."

"But we have the ammonia right here. Why not use it?"

"Whatever." Ali didn't care what they did. All he wanted was more dope. That much was clear.

For the first time George started thinking about using Ali's addiction to his own advantage. So, they drove down to the feed store, about five miles south on 99. It didn't take long.

"How much do you want to get high?" George asked when they hit the highway.

"I don't want to talk about it." Ali was sucking on a cigarette in the passenger seat, looking out of the window. Couple hundred yards up on the left was the farm store they were looking for. Big place; it sold all kind of farm supplies, tools, and the kind of tanks they were looking for.

"Well, I do want to talk about it," George said.

"Let it go. We're here." Ali pointed.

George let it go, for the moment. Bernie's Farm Supply had a chain link fence around it because so much stuff was kept outside. George drove in through the open gate. The gas tanks for barbeque grills were kept around the back, near the back door. George didn't think Ali was strong enough to lift the tanks, so he loaded the back of the Toyota himself. With the seats down, six fit comfortably in two rows. George didn't want to set them on top of each other; he needed to see out the back window. He considered sending Ali in to pay, but Ali looked too much like a tweaker. Somebody might ask what he wanted them for, so George went in himself. No one asked why he wanted six empty propane gas tanks.

Back at the farm, Ali put on his mask and gloves and filled the tanks with the liquid ammonia. He'd drunk two bottles of Gatorade and finally had some energy, but maybe he'd taken something. George couldn't be bothered screaming about something he couldn't control any more than he could control the weather. You weren't supposed to put anhydrous ammonia in propane tanks because it corroded the seals very quickly and caused the tanks to blow, but meth makers were gamblers. They did it all the time. George was pretty sure the seals would hold for quite some time. He needed only twenty-four hours.

While Ali filled the tanks, George checked his laptop for a place to rent a van. When the Toyota was loaded with the full tanks, they headed back to town. George was jittery as hell.

"Ali, how is this going to go off?" he asked.

"Impact would be good," he answered.

"Huh?"

"Drive the van into another vehicle. Impact, plus the full gas tanks of police cars in the garage, plus the full tank in the van, you'll get your result. Might not bring the whole building down, but there will be a major explosion and resulting fire. Should take care of it."

George liked how simple it was. All they needed was a driver. "Ali, will you drive the truck?"

"Now?" he asked, innocent.

"No. Tomorrow morning."

Ali flipped his cigarette out the window, shaking his head.

"You want dope, don't you?"

"More than you do, brother." Ali lit another cigarette.

"I'll give you anything you want if you drive the van."

Ali snorted. "Why don't you do it?"

"You want me to do it?"

"Yeah. If you give me enough, I'll go with you," Ali said.

"You'll be with me when I drive the van?" George laughed. That wasn't his plan. "How about this? Is there any way we can get the van to crash itself?"

"You mean, robot truck?" Ali asked.

"Yeah, can you rig it?"

Ali's head rocked from side to side.

"Are you laughing?" George demanded.

"No. I could do it in a field. At the farm. I can't do it blind, down two levels in a garage. We'd need a camera in the van so we could see to make the turns. Too sophisticated. It would take months and equipment."

They had less than twenty-four hours. George was quiet. So it wasn't just a point and shoot. The van had to be driven. Who could they get to do it?

"Any ideas?" he asked, meek now.

"I told you. Detonator, C-4, ammonia, gasoline."

George licked his lips. "Good." He was sure he could get Ali to drive the van when the time came.

He decided to drive straight through. They had to go north, up to 84. He stopped at an exit north of the city and found a rental place. He left the Toyota in the lot, bought some coffee and a dozen Power Bars in the adjoining convenience store. He made Ali eat one. It wasn't enough nutrition for him, but it was something. Then they loaded the van he'd rented using Ali's name and driver's license. It was 5:15 p.m. He wanted to get to the lodge before dark.

53

Mary Lou had been frightened by everything she'd learned since Michael Tamlin came to work at Pac GreenBank, and she was even more terrified after she saw the bruises on Michael's neck. People did this kind of thing in Portland? Really? Two of her bosses had been targeted by highly respected clients of the bank, people she'd thought were good? Her superiors at the bank were involved in a conspiracy of some kind and Marty was in on it? It was horrifying. She couldn't sit there and ignore this.

She watched the elevator go down with Michael Tamlin in it, and rebelled at how stubborn she was. Fifteen minutes later, when Michael didn't answer her phone, Mary Lou made another executive decision. She drove to Michael's house to check on her. The car wasn't there. Mary Lou shook her head, got out of her Prius, and slogged through the rain to try the front door anyway. No answer. That alarmed her even more. Why couldn't Michael just do what she said she was going to? She muttered to herself and went back to her car, where she waited inside for another fifteen minutes.

The rain intensified, slowed, then pounded down again as Mary Lou sat there wondering what to do. She felt she'd messed up a bunch of times since Allan started this ball rolling, and she didn't want to take a passive role again. She still thought about him every day. She'd taken all his notes, listened in on his calls, and then failed him in the end. He just hadn't told her what his concerns meant. She hadn't known.

Pretty much as soon as Michael Tamlin arrived on the job, Mary Lou guessed something was up. No one at the bank had ever worked the way Michael did. Stayed to herself, didn't make friends, kept asking questions no one else had ever asked. And from the get-go, she'd acted like she wasn't sticking around long. She wouldn't explore the city. Even her team didn't understand what she was up to.

Maybe Charlie did. Mary Lou wondered what Charlie knew. The whole department had heard about Michael's golf accident. Charlie didn't have anything special to add, and Mary Lou didn't want to tell him about the meeting with Marty Williams. She could tell Marty was scared. A bigger question was, how could something like this happen at a stuffy place like Pac GreenBank?

Not a patient person, Mary Lou sat in the driveway of the Carl Place house in the rain for fifteen long minutes. She drummed her fingers on her steering wheel and tried to put herself in Michael's head even though she had not been very successful at this exercise in the past. What was Michael's motivation? If she'd suspected Hamid, why go golfing with him? If she was in danger in her home, or anywhere else, why be alone? What was the matter with her? Mary Lou could not begin to guess.

She hit Michael's number on speed dial five times. Nothing. She got tired of sitting there and drove back downtown to Zupan's, where she cruised the parking lot of the high-end grocery store, getting more worried by the minute. She tried Whole Foods. Michael wasn't shopping there, either. Finally she made another executive decision. She'd listened in on Michael's phone conversations enough to know Michael had broken up with her doctor fiancé, but talked frequently with a cop called Fleisher. He was probably the cop she'd been drinking beer with the night she moved.

Mary Lou reasoned it this way. Michael had gone to the police this morning. For all she knew, Michael could be with the cops at this very moment. That would make sense. If Michael was with the cops right now, she wouldn't have to worry about her anymore. She'd be sure Michael was safe. If, on the other hand, Michael wasn't with the cops, they would be in a better position to find her. At 6:30, she was in the lobby of Central Station asking for a cop named Fleisher. He was busy, so she waited for a long time.

54

A male voice came from far away. "Shut up, bitch, or I'll kill you right now."

Michael heard groans and heavy breathing, but didn't know they came from her. Her head was a solid wall of pain. She was crumpled on the back seat of her car, mumbling and groaning, unaware that she was the one making the noise. "Oh, no. Oh, no."

"Shut up!"

A waterfall splashed. Michael felt motion, the buzz of a bee. The ZZZZZZ teased her hip. The pulse stopped, then started again. The fourth time her eyes opened. It didn't help much. Her vision came down a long tunnel through a deep fog. Everything was blurry and weird, as if she were under water, not in heaven or fiery hell.

Moving room, plus spins, plus headache equals--hangover? She groaned, unable to pinpoint any catastrophic bar scene in recent history. Her brain struggled for clarity, which was not entirely a new experience for her. Okay, not dead. Was she on that boat trip Claude had talked about, river rafting? Her head throbbed as she tried to break free of confusion. "What happened?" she moaned.

A hand struck out at her from nowhere. "Shut up!"

She did see the hand. It came at her over a shoulder and didn't quite reach her. Then she registered rain sleeting on the window and saw the back door of the car. Her car. Moving. Okay. This much she knew: her head was not covered and she was not taking a nap on her own back seat. She saw the head of the driver--familiar enough to make her think she'd seen him before. But not familiar enough to be a friend. Got it. She was with an enemy.

Bits and pieces painfully returned. She was in Portland, not Maine, working in a bank. She recalled being at her big desk, looking out the window at clouds. Now she was in her car in the rain, trying unsuccessfully to get her hands out from under her. She heard the ragged breathing and finally understood it was hers. She felt the loops of the plastic restraints on her wrists. She was missing some time, figured she'd been carjacked, but didn't know when. Didn't take a genius to figure that out. Then she thought, stupid as she might have been to get herself caught, at least she was alive. She took some comfort there.

"You have a chip on your shoulder," one of her bosses used to tell her. "But you're the one who gets you in trouble every single time."

"Ya think?" she muttered now.

Judgment is all. If she lived long enough to have a motto for the future, she would be sure to remember it.

"What?"

The driver was asking her what? Jesus. Michael's jacket pocket started vibrating again. She could reach the phone but not lift it to her ear, didn't want to make contact yet anyway. She was coming around, already working another plan.

"All right, you got me. Where are we going?" she asked. Why not strike up a conversation. Maybe she could learn something before she ended the game.

"Guantanamo. Abu Ghraib. Your choice." He laughed.

Oh, very funny.

"If you have your ricin tab with you, you better take it now," he added.

The guy was a real joker, and he wanted to talk. If her head didn't ache so much, she'd laugh. She rolled on the seat to get more comfortable. Less than six inches from where she lay were her two guns, a knife, a wire cutter (from a fence job she'd done a while ago) mace, taser, a few other essential tools, her laptop and files. Everything that mattered to her, every protection she had was in this car. As long as she was in it, there were things she could do.

Michael hated headaches and nausea, but still had a few brain cells left. Whoever had grabbed her wasn't very smart. Her hands were in plastic restraints, but that was about it. He hadn't thrown anything over her to hide her from view, or tied her ankles. How dumb was that? Must have been a spur of the moment thing; he didn't have any equipment with him. Or maybe he'd thought she wouldn't wake up. In any case he didn't have a lot of common sense.

"Did you hear me? I said you should take the poison now. Save yourself a lot of trouble."

Only his forehead was visible in the rearview mirror, but Michael could see the back of his head, his hair, his forehead, the curve of his cheek. He had a high forehead, well cut black hair and didn't need a shave. No hat. His right arm and hand on her steering wheel were relaxed, and he didn't look back at her. This was definitely not a pro. Whatever he might be thinking about, there were many things he was ignoring.

Michael's hands were behind her. With some contortion into a fetal position she could get her arms in front of her and garrote him from the back seat. It would be easy to take him down, but not a brilliant choice while the car was moving.

"I don't have poison," she told him.

"Frank says you're an agent."

"I work in a bank."

"If you're an agent, you have poison."

If she were an agent, forget the poison. She'd have a team.

"Frank is wrong."

"I'm going to find out everything about you, just the way you people do it."

"We people?"

"You're getting the special treatment--the same thing my people get from you. You tell me if it's torture."

"Is this little stunt a political thing?"

"Call it an opportunity to get even."

"If you want to talk politics, we have some areas of agreement."

"You're my prisoner of war," he said. "We have no areas of agreement."

"Oh, come on." She rolled a little more to keep her circulation going. She could smell him now. Sweat and the onions he'd eaten for lunch. "Look, I don't hurt people. I work in a bank."

He didn't say anything for maybe a minute and a half. It seemed a really long time.

"I think we agree on a lot of things. Why be enemies?" Michael had never interrogated anyone while she was in handcuffs. Never been alone in the wind. Never been hijacked or threatened with torture. What could she say, I'm sorry, people do bad things to each other, but that's not what this is about. Maybe that's what it was about for him. Hamid was a big time bad guy. Could politics be at the core of it, after all? Sleeper cells all over the country? Al Qaeda training camps?

Michael's immediate concern, however, was what he wanted to do to her. Waterboarding came to mind first. Being shackled to the floor naked and forced to stand up for days at a time. Shocked and beaten with electrical cords. She knew what torture he was talking about. Allan Farber had been shot in the head with his own gun. That was quick. Other people got beheaded. She had to put torture out of her mind. She was still in Oregon, still in the back seat of her own car. And she wouldn't mind knowing what Hamid was really up to.

It was hard to think with her head throbbing like a jackhammer, but her captor was definitely not an experienced operative. She had that on her side. Whoever and whatever he was, she could feel him dying to talk as much as she was dying to listen. She just didn't want either of them to perish before she found out. She wondered where they were going, how far it was, their ETA, and how many people would be there waiting for them when they arrived. She hoped he was the only one she'd have to fight, and it would be fully dark by then.

55

Pete Fleisher was distracted when he brought the woman to an interview room. He didn't have much time and checked his watch. Two minutes was all he could give her. He took his cell phone out of his pocket and put it on the table. Before he could hear her story, one of his officers came in and whispered in his ear. He looked away from his visitor and tapped the phone as he listened.

"Right. I'll be there in a minute," he said and checked his watch again. Now he had one minute.

He refocused on the woman opposite him: definitely a character with wild red hair, crimson lipstick, big black glasses, a green outfit with seashells and fishnets. And she wasn't a patient waiter. Her expressive face was an angry pantomime of hurry it up.

Pete's cell phone rang. He was the kind of guy who preferred the straight chime to the musical theme song, and his ringer was loud and insistent. He picked up the offending object and checked caller ID before answering. Then he said a few words and closed the phone. When he glanced back at the woman she looked ready to pummel him. He smiled.

"I'm sorry. It's been a busy day. You're…?"

"Mary Lou Loughlin, Michael Tamlin's assistant at the bank."

He nodded. "That's right. You told me that. What's the problem?"

"You're her friend, right?"

He tilted his head, unsure what she meant.

The woman gave him the most obvious kind of once-over for the third or fourth time. The clear sexual implication almost made him laugh out loud.

"You're the one who came over to her house with the beer," she said.

He nodded slowly.

"So, you're the friend." She kept prompting until she felt he got it.

Even though she was wrong in her assumption, he'd been attracted to Michael from the first moment he saw her in the uptight hairdo and uptight business suit. Now that he knew her better, he'd still like nothing more than the opportunity to make love to her. But he didn't let that show in his face. It wasn't likely ever to happen.

"Yes, yes. I'm her friend. What can I do for you?"

"She didn't get home tonight, and it looks like she isn't here with you. So I think something happened to her."

"Does she have other friends she might have visited?" Pete asked.

Mary Lou shook her head. "You're her only friend."

Pete frowned. He hated to hear that. Claude's bringing a woman out here with the (probably) false promise of marriage wasn't the first asshole thing his brother had done, but it was the incident that ended Pete's live-and-let-live attitude towards him. No one in the family had known Michael was coming until the day she arrived. They knew about the other girlfriend, Nurse Judy, the one who'd come six months ago, and with whom Claude was now staying. Which hadn't been his plan at all.

Pete glanced at his watch again, realizing that Michael hadn't called him as she'd said she would. "What time did she leave?" he asked.

"Five forty-five."

Pete shrugged. "Well, Mary Lou. That's not even an hour ago. What makes you think there's a problem?"

"She promised me she'd call when she got home. She told me that people would be watching her back, that she'd be all right. I thought she meant you. And now she doesn't answer her phone."

That was two people Michael had promised, and failed, to contact. He picked up his phone and dialed her number, watching Mary Lou's face as the cell phone rang and rang. He left a message to call him right away and returned to Mary Lou.

"Why don't you tell me what happened at work that's got you so alarmed?" he suggested.

"How did you know?" Mary Lou flashed him a grateful look.

"My job is to read people." He smiled again. "Go ahead. You have my full attention."

Mary Lou told him about the meeting with Marty Williams, the life coach.

"Life coach, what's that?" Peter asked.

"It's a benefit the bank gives to senior executives to help them adjust to the company."

Pete scratched his cheek. "Michael had a life coach?"

"Yeah, and when Allan Farber was killed, he helped us all process."

"Process? Is that what they call it?"

"Uh huh. Marty came back from his vacation to talk to Michael after her accident." Mary Lou stopped.

"To help her process?" Pete prompted.

"Yes, and she wanted me there with her. She showed us the bruises on her neck and told Marty we were sending a tape of the conversation to the FBI."

"Oh." Pete closed his eyes. "Did you make the tape for the FBI?" Pam hadn't mentioned anything about this.

"No, it was a bluff. But she wanted to put the company on notice, you know. Make them responsible for her safety. She said she'd better die another day. From James Bond, you know."

What was she up to now? Pete tapped his phone. For someone who claimed to dislike heights, Michael Tamlin jumped off a lot of cliffs. He didn't like this at all.

"How did Marty take it?" he asked.

"He was scared. Everybody in the office is scared. I'm really scared. I worked for Allan, and I work for Michael. I know stuff. Charlie knows stuff, too."

"Charlie is the one who was with Michael and Jesse Halen the night he died."

Mary Lou nodded. Then she told him how Ashland Upjohn,

the general counsel, had set up a lunch with Michael. "After he heard from Marty that she'd been to the police station, he canceled the lunch."

She was getting tearful. She reached into her huge purse for a tissue to blow her nose. "Michael said she didn't want any of us hurt, either."

"What did she mean by that?"

"I told you, we know stuff. We worked uncovering the details of the Hamid deals. You know about that?"

Pete nodded. They knew about them now.

"After we analyzed those transactions and knew there was a major problem with them, Michael told us to back off. But Charlie did all the work, found out about other mortgages at other banks. We both know everything."

"Why did she tell you to back off?"

"It could be she didn't want us to get fired. But I think she was worried about what happened to Allan. She told us to shelf the project and came to work the next day in a red suit with her hair down. You know how pretty she is. She always wore her hair in that bun, so it caused quite a stir. That's when the golf date was made. It was the day Jesse Halen died. You know, the atmosphere got different."

Peter did know. Michael had gotten some clearance to do a little spying, and dove right in. "So she started making friends."

Mary Lou nodded. "Yes, I guess you could say that."

"Well, thank you, Mary Lou. You've been a big help." Pete put his phone back in his pocket.

He was thinking that Michael was like a force of nature. You couldn't tell her what to do, and you didn't have a clue what she was going to do next. She worked on her own, almost got herself killed, called him from some meth lab in Dundee, came to the police station to trigger a major alarm, then went to work and told everyone in her office that she didn't want any trouble. Figure that one out. And now she was in the wind where a lot of people who didn't like her had opportunity to finish what they'd started.

"Michael wouldn't stay with me tonight. She wouldn't even let me go down in the elevator with her to the garage to get her car. She just disappeared."

"Are there security cameras in the garage?" Pete asked.

Mary Lou shook her head. "Not all over. But definitely at the entrance and exit."

"Well, thanks again for coming so quickly. I appreciate it." He got up from the table to end the interview.

"What are you going to do?" Mary Lou asked as he escorted her to the elevator.

"Don't you worry, we'll find her," he said.

The minute the door closed on Mary Lou, however, Pete lost his calm. "Ah, shit," he muttered. He shouldn't have let her go home alone.

What Michael had given them this morning changed everything. She had mapped remote sites owned by Hamid that were across the state line in Washington. The locations were up Route 84, past where Pete lived on the river. The Columbia River was the state line. On the south side of the Columbia was Oregon. The north side was Washington State. Lot of wilderness up there, state parks, and some wasteland made by the St. Helens eruption a few years back. Not much farther north, the U.S.-Canadian border was largely un- patrolled. Hamid could be taking things in or out of the country up there. He could be up to a lot of things.

Michael's intelligence on these locations in Washington State had triggered a massive response. Restaurant owners with ties to Pakistan didn't buy hunting lodges without electricity or water in the back woods, where there were no ski trails or lakes or rivers, without a good reason. Further delay in bringing Hamid in was out of the question. They had to get him now.

Hamid, who lived alone in a house in Beaverton, was scheduled to be picked up in the early a.m. His known associates would be roused from their beds at dawn. Morning, when people were sleepy and vulnerable, was the best time for bringing them in. Then everything would come down at the same time. All the locations would be searched at the same time. Teams from a host of different agencies were presently flying in and gathering for raids on all Hamid's properties. DHS, FBI, a SWAT team out of Seattle, Special Ops from the military and the Justice Department were among the teams involved, birds in the sky, the whole nine yards. They didn't know what they would find, but they wanted to be prepared. Now they had to remove Hamid from the picture a lot sooner.

Pete knew he should have handled Michael differently. He should have confined her until the operation was over. If she talked to the wrong person now, she could blow the whole operation. Plus he didn't want her to get killed. And he should have told her she'd done a great job. Shit. He dialed Torres to get the security tapes from the garage where she parked her car. See if she was driving when she left. Check if there was a tracking device on her car. And start searching for her cell phone signal. There were a lot of ways to track people who didn't want to be lost. Torres knew them all.

56

As George drove east on 84, the sky darkened and the weather deteriorated steadily. First fog, then drizzle, then rain, and finally pour which persisted all the way to Carson. These were not ideal conditions for travel to the lodge. George was dogged by a sick feeling that intensified the closer he got to that steep, nameless track that would take them twelve miles deeper into the wilderness, where it was dark even in daylight.

Ali crashed around four, abandoning him to a range of agonizing fears that Ali's behavior always stirred up in George. The way Ali's mouth hung open, mile after agonizing mile, and his body sprawled on the seat suggested more a coma than a nap. The bone-rattling snores of a person out cold increased the feeling of desertion and rejection George felt when people let him down. The reaction was like a rock thrown in a lake with ripples that spread to every shore of his life, shocking his fragile psyche over and over until he couldn't stand it any more. People he should be able to trust betrayed him left and right. His uncle screamed at him for stuff that wasn't his fault. Sami got away with all kinds of shit, and Ali was unconscious as usual.

Since being humiliated at the farm, George felt exposed in every way. And now the van was a white blob that stood out on the road. It infuriated him. He'd asked for a less noticeable color, but all they had was white. Must have been a blow-out sale on that model, he thought. And for good reason, he soon found out. The vehicle had no power or maneuverability. It didn't accelerate or slow down without a fight and tilted dangerously on even minor curves.

George had never driven a boat like this. Worse than the old Toyota, it was a truck built for short hauls, not the highway in bad weather. Speed would have been out of the question with the cargo in the back in any case, but George worried about what would happen on the road to the lodge. Even if the tires held traction up thousands of feet, through a dozen cut-backs, and didn't slide off into one of the many deep ravines, there was the added stress of appearing in an unfamiliar vehicle. He wanted to call ahead to tell the brothers he was arriving in a van a week earlier than he was scheduled to arrive, but there were problems with that, too. He didn't have a pre-paid phone with him and couldn't stop to buy one. The pre-paids they had up there were used only once and thrown away. They weren't kept on because of the risk posed by a signal emitted from a place that was supposed to be uninhabited. This rule didn't exactly jibe with all the noise they made with their shooting practice, but he was hardly the one to tell them what to do. They pretty much did what they wanted anyway. He wondered how the brothers would react when he told them he was blowing up the police station. That thought was the only bright spot in his day.

57

Michael woke after the phone rang twice. Loud ones, not her ring. Her eyes had closed when her captor stopped talking, and the backseat motion of the car had made her too queasy to cope. Migraine, hangover? She went over the possibilities the same way she had the first time. What, when, where, how, and came up empty. At some point she had turned over and was now in a fetal position facing the back of the car. She smelled the reassuring leather of the seat, but clarity couldn't be rushed.

Her head pounded to the beat of her heart. What, what, what was happening? Her bound hands hung over the edge where the secret panel under the seat dropped down to the floor. Only half conscious, she had been stroking the access to her hiding place like a lover's cheek. She tested the plastic restraint on her wrists. The two loops clipped together were like so much packaging these days, impossible to open. They were not loose enough to slip out of and didn't give like rope. That was the point. You needed clippers to escape. The thud of her heart demanded answers. What, what, what was she going to do?

"Yeah, I have her."

Then she heard the voice and remembered. Her eyes opened, but she didn't see anything except car seat, gray as a whale. She was traveling in the rain. Her head throbbed with the beat. Where, where, where were they going?

"No, easy as pie," the voice said. "She kicked me a few times. But I wouldn't call it a problem. I told you. It's fine."

She could feel him turn around quickly to check and smelled him again, sweat and onions.

"Don't worry, she's out cold. No, of course not. No one saw me. Don't worry! I'll take care of it."

Pause. "I said I was sorry. I'll get it done this time."

And there it was, whole. Michael flashed to the same voice she'd heard without entirely being aware of it on the golf course.

She couldn't remember what exactly had happened. Just that she'd had an impression of two people leaning over her. One exuded the odors of sweat and onions so strongly they'd acted like smelling salts in her nose. Their panic, their moving her body, their hands on her neck, and their smell. Woke her right out of a death grip.

"I can find that out...well, everything. What she knows, who she told. No sir, I'm not arguing with you." He made the sound of impatience, air pushed through his lips.

"There wouldn't be any signs of that. Please, Mr. Hamid, I know how to ask questions."

A sound of resignation. "Okay, but there wouldn't be anything left—Yeah, I'll do what you want. May take me a while—"

Pause. "All right, tonight. I understand. I said I would."

He hung up. "Fucking asshole," he muttered.

"What's the matter?" Michael said.

"He thinks I'm stupid," the guy muttered.

"Are you stupid?"

"FUCK!"

He turned around to strike at her. She moved a few inches and he struck air. "You're listening."

"What's your name?" Michael asked.

"You're dead. You're going to tell me everything you know and then you're dead."

All right. Cards on the table.

"Fine. I'll tell you anything you want to know. We can trade. You tell me everything I want to know. Then we'll see who dies."

"See, you are an agent."

"I must be a pretty stupid agent if I let you catch me."

He laughed. The guy needed an Altoid real bad.

"Why is Frank a fucking asshole?"

"You want to know his plan for you? Burn you up in the barn the minute I get there. He said it was a mess. How does he think I can clean that place up in an hour? Huh? Take an army a week."

"So, what do you want?"

He kind of slipped into his own reverie, driving in the

rain. "Do what you assholes do to us. The bitch is my dog on a leash as long as I want."

Okay, Michael got the picture. He described it anyway.

"Stand naked all night in a cold shower with a rope around your neck. I slap you all over. You fall, you choke. Most people die before they hang. Hypothermia. If you live 'til morning, you get a bag over your head, stand chained to the floor. You fall, you die. If you live past that, waterboard express."

"Is that what you did to the two college kids?"

"What?"

"You take care of things for Frank. You must have taken care of Farber. Must have taken care of them."

"I take care of things, but not college kids. You got the wrong guy on that."

"Okay. So your specialty is bank people." She'd turned around on the seat again and was looking at the back of his head. Now she made him for the guy who'd come to her house in the restaurant van. Okay, progress.

He didn't say anything. She sighed.

"Come on. You're not going to tell me Frank killed Farber. A pussycat like him?"

"Shut up."

"I'll tell you, if you tell me. We could be friends." It was amazing how normal her voice sounded to her. As long as she was in the car, him driving, she wasn't at risk.

"You're gonna die with your head in the toilet."

"I thought I was going to burn in the barn." She had to remind him.

"Die by water first."

Oh. What she knew about torture was that everyone spilled. Everyone. With water in your lungs, you'd send your mother down. Brother, sister, children, anyone. People in the know said McCain dropped the dime on his buddies. Didn't matter if it was true or not. She wouldn't be any braver than anybody else. She'd never liked cold showers, and nudist camps were not her thing. On a case once, she'd gone into a public sauna in Finland in a bathing suit with a skirt. Well, she had to have a hiding place for her stuff, didn't she? And this guy was going to need help if he wanted to string her up in the shower. Please.

Her heart thudded, but not with fear. Not by any means. She was pissed off, but spoke pleasantly. "My name is Mike. What's yours?"

"I know. Stupid fucking name for a girl," he muttered.

"True. What's yours?"

"Samir."

She laughed softly.

"What's wrong with it?" he demanded.

"Nothing, it's perfect. You're my companion in evening talk."

"How the fuck do you know Arabic?"

She didn't answer. If you were a guy named Sue, you'd think about names every day of your life, too. Michael. What the hell was wrong with being Michele, Michelle, Misha, Masha, Marilyn, Maria, MaryAnn, Marlene, even Mary George? But Michael! The embarrassment of being on the boys' list at school every year had been agonizing as a kid and a teenager. And she'd stuck with it all the way through grad school. She'd never softened it up, or taken a sissy nickname. Her dad had wanted her to carry the name. In the Bible, Michael was the archangel, leader of heaven's armies. Patron saint of soldiers. Her father was gone now, but the name still resonated. She was half guy in her head; that was the way he'd wanted it. God only knew why.

So Michael had a passionate interest in names. Samir meant "companion in evening talk" in Arabic. Samuel in the Old Testament was the prophet and judge who'd anointed Saul and David as kings of Israel. The Qur'an told the same Old Testament stories with different emphasis. Samir's parents could also have used his name to dedicate him to God.

"Samir, do you serve the Lord with all your heart?" she asked, as if it were the most natural question in the world.

Samir swerved to avoid a drifting truck. Michael bumped around on the seat. "Hey," she complained.

"You know," he said, amazed.

"We're on the same side," she whispered. "Didn't you know that?"

"You know?" Samir was not the sharpest blade in the drawer. Most crooks weren't.

"Where are we going?" she asked.

"The farm," he said without hesitation.

Okay. They couldn't go very fast in this weather. She had some time to rest up. She wished she'd eaten more for lunch. But you couldn't have everything. She closed her eyes for another nap. When they arrived in that hellish place, she was going to need a lot more fight in her than she had right now.

58

It did not take long for an officer to collect the video from the garage in the Pac GreenBank building where Michael parked her car (only a few blocks away from Central Station). Pete and Torres sat in a small room and reviewed Michael's arrival in the Acura at 10:58 a.m., and the departure of the same car at 5:17 p.m. with someone else in the driver's seat.

"Shit." Pete rubbed at his chin as if a stain was there that he needed to remove. He'd dropped the ball big time.

Surveillance cameras at the garage exit showed an ethnic male driving Michael's car when it left the garage.

"Okay, it's been jacked. That guy looks familiar." Torres said.

"Yeah, I've seen him around. Handsome devil," Pete muttered. "Look at that haircut. Bouncer? Bartender?"

"Let's get the files, see who he is."

There was only a tiny pause.

"Jesus, Felix. She came to us a week ago," Pete said softly. "We let it drop."

Felix didn't say anything as they watched the tape again. There was no sign of a passenger in the car. He played it back one last time. Officers of every rank kept coming to the door, asking what they needed.

"Give us a minute," Pete said. They needed a lot.

"My bet she's in the car," Felix said. "But we should check the building anyway."

Pete nodded.

Felix got on his phone. He sent two officers to search the garage and the building in case Michael was still there, injured or incapacitated in some way. Pete popped in another tape just to be sure--the one of the elevator on the employee level where there was no surveillance in the garage itself. Michael appeared only twice, in the morning going in with several people; in the afternoon going out alone. She did not return to the elevator again after her car departed. She did not raise an alarm. And she did not leave on foot.

"She's in the car," Pete said.

"Okay. We need traces on the car, the phone and the Black-Berry."

"I'll do it," Pete said.

"I'll get the files."

They joined up a few minutes later in the conference room where the brass had gathered with Michael only that morning. Felix had the Michael files, complete with the photos she'd taken with her cell phone of the Toyota that had been parked outside her house that morning. He also brought in some stills from the video of the man driving her car in the afternoon. They compared the images of the two men in the Highlander with the clearer shot of the driver of Michael's Acura.

"Not a match. We have three separate guys," Felix said. "And a snatch is Federal."

He and Pete locked eyes. They had three different (probably ethnic—Mediterranean, Italian, Arab, Hispanic--could be anything) males. One was in Michael's Acura and two were in the battered Toyota. Pete got on the horn and put BOLOs out on both vehicles. Three bad guys in the wind. Michael was out there with them. He had to get the news out.

The only good thing was they had Hamid on the ropes now. He had been careful up to now. They hadn't been able to nail him for Farber's death. In fact, that whole incident had been murky as hell. Lots of people had believed in the accident theory at the time, but Michael's assessment of Farber's death, and then Jesse Halen's, had changed everything. This wasn't the way anyone wanted it to go down. They'd wanted to catch him in the act, but Michael was not supposed to be the bait.

A license search earlier in the day revealed the Toyota High-lander dogging Michael that morning was registered to Windsong Realty, one of Hamid's shell companies, with an address that had a mailbox but no office. It didn't surprise anybody, but now they needed to find that car fast. Get the chickens out of the road.

Time to open up. Pete called his FBI contact. All right, he called his sister.

"Hey, Pam. What's going on?" he said. It was a little slimy on the uptake, but he felt like shit and didn't want to say sorrysorrysorry right off the bat.

"I heard," she said. Cold.

He could not miss the sarcastic "Good job, PPD" in her older sister silence. So the febs, or feebles, (as he called them) knew everything before the news was even out of the building. They'd let an informant down. More than an informant, somebody whose back he should have started watching a long time ago.

"Yeah," he muttered.

Enough said. There'd always been rivalry between him and Pam, even when they worked together and spoke five times a day. He was local, she was federal. FBI had the toys and the big bucks, thought they were the hottest shit. Local agencies were dependent on local money, which was always shorter than the shortest hairs on the human body. PPD had big territory to cover and not enough people or toys for the job they had to do. They had to fly by the seat of their pants every damn day. And this was an especially bad day for Pete. He'd lost the informant who'd dated his brother, apparently for three or more years. Wanted to marry him, even, misguided as that idea was. Good job, indeed.

"I'll find her," he said more confident than he felt.

"How can I help?" Pam said, colder than any sister had a right to be.

"You're all heart. Any chatter from the prince of darkness?"

"He took a drive this morning to one of the locations Tamlin pinpointed. Out by Dundee."

"Okay." The file was on the table. Pete reached for it and pulled out Michael's maps. "Blackberry Farm?"

"Yeah."

"That's the place Tamlin found Matt Brand's bike. Anyone go in after him?" Pete asked.

"Nope. Our guy had to stay back and rely on the tracking

device we had in his car because of the road. It's isolated up there. Hamid would have seen him on the trail. But there isn't any other way out. Hamid stayed only a few minutes, came right back to town. Hid out in the Pearl Warehouse for a while, then made his usual restaurant rounds. No chatter on the phones at all. But we know he uses pre-paids and then destroys them."

"Did he meet anybody at the warehouse?"

"Yes, bro, he did. Samir Yassin. Works at Tabloule. He has a sheet. You can pull him up. Anything else?"

"Can you get me a bird, Pammy? I'll be your best friend."

"I'm already your best friend, buttwipe. I haven't killed you for this yet. What do you need it for?"

"Would be faster. Somebody's got to have one. Call in a favor for me?"

"I don't know if I can get anything in this weather. And you have to tell me where we're going."

"You're not coming. This is my thing." He didn't want to say he didn't know yet. It was a wishful thinking kind of ask.

"Fuck you." She always knew everything.

"Okay, thanks," he said into the dead phone.

Then he spread out the files, including the super fat one that included all known associates of Frank Hamid. Hamid was a bachelor around town, who dated a lot and was involved in charity functions of every description. His social connections were many and varied. Nevertheless, it didn't take more than a few minutes to find matches for the three men in the two cars. George Hamid and Ali Satan were in the Toyota.

"Nice moniker," Pete said about Satan. "Poor Ali must have taken a lot of shit for that in school. What do we have on him?"

"Let's get Tracy in here on that."

Pete rolled his eyes. Tracy was a curvy, drop dead blonde with a pony tail halfway down her back. Pete had dated her for a very hot while when she'd been on the outs with the longtime boy-friend she finally ended up marrying. She was a uniformed officer who wanted to be a detective, and was as tough as they come. Her defection in favor of past passion had broken Pete's heart at the time. It was a while ago now. He wasn't exactly holding his breath for the inevitable breakup.

Tracy came in with a stack of files, tossed the pony tail and winked at Pete before joining the party. "Hey." As if everything was as sweet as lemonade between them.

"You have background for us?" Pete didn't react.

"What do you need?" She gave him a big smile.

Nothing from you, sweetheart, he didn't say. "Got a few people for you. How about Ali Satan for starters?"

"Got him." She pulled him out of a file and started to read. "Chemical Ali. Blew up the kitchen sink at home just before his twelfth birthday. Blew up a lab sink in eighth grade. Studied chemistry and communications in college, right up the street. Expert in computers and electronics. He was involved in the Islam club. He's got a sheet. Couple of DUIs, drug arrests. He was on a watch list for a while."

She pulled out some photos of a swarm of young men smeared with ketchup, carrying a sign that read Nuke the Killer Jews. "That was a protest rally. 2003, just after the Iraq war started."

"That's a while ago. What's he been up to lately?"

"Not much. He's a tweaker."

"How about Samir Yassin?"

"He's right here." She pointed him out at the rally.

Samir looked younger and not so pretty with a red smear on his face, but it was definitely the same man who was driving Michael's Acura. Bingo for that.

"Who are the rest of these guys?"

"Ah, interesting that you ask. This is George Hamid, Frank Hamid's nephew. Ali Satan, Samir Yassim you know. Daniel Anajoe and Paul Othman went missing six months ago. Kal Boustany, likewise. No sign of any of them for quite a while." She pointed at three more, one at a time.

"They were friends in college, got sucked in by some radical thinkers. It happens in the very best families. Some get over it. Some don't. These guys now own a couple of clubs. Tony Hampar, Michael Ezz, Bill Goldberg. They're playboys, but clean, nothing on them since this."

"Goldberg?" Felix said.

Tracy shrugged. "That's his name."

"Thanks, Tracy. You're a brick," Pete said.

A few minutes shy of 7:00 p.m., he heard they'd picked up signals from the Acura. It was moving south on 99. Okay, now he needed the bird.

59

Seven fifteen p.m. Whereabouts known: Frank Hamid was downtown, a few blocks away from Central Station, just beginning to greet guests at a party in his fish restaurant on Sixth Avenue. Place was called Pacific Fresh. Occasionally, when the trendy restaurant was taken over for private parties, there were wild scenes in there with exotic dancers from one of his partners' clubs. Gentleman's Choice and Cheetah were two of the prominent ones. But tonight looked to be a quiet one.

Hamid was a domestic animal who liked to return to his lair at night. Sometimes he took a woman with him, sometimes he stopped somewhere for an hour or two and then drove himself home in one of his flashy cars. He had different women, different vehicles, but his final destination never varied. The plan had been to let him follow his routine, and pick him up as soon as his head hit the pillow. If a woman was with him, she'd be coming in, too. But that was changed. Now they were going to take him before dinner was over. Cut him off from all communication. Pronto.

Whereabouts unknown: George Hamid and Ali Satan. So far there was no sign of the Toyota that George had been driving earlier in the day. All patrol officers on duty were looking for it--driving around, scanning parking lots, checking George Hamid's known places of work, the clubs where he and Ali were known to hang out. No sign of them yet.

Whereabouts hypothesized: Michael Tamlin and Samir Yassim. Signals showed that the Acura was still heading south on 99. Pete and Felix figured they were going to the farm, where Frank Hamid had been earlier in the day and Michael had been on Saturday. Since this was not a location Hamid had been known to visit in the last nine months at least, it seemed clear something was heating up there. Michael's phones were in the car. A reasonable guess was that she was still with them, unable to use them. Local law enforcement was notified, but the weather had caused several car and truck crashes that claimed priority. No one could break away.

Pete spent some agonizing minutes trying to get the transportation he needed. No sense in driving when there was a better way. The accidents, and a Search and Rescue operation, were claiming all county resources. He did not luck out. He had to reach wider. He was forced to make the call he didn't want to make. He jumped in the elevator to get away from a gathering crowd. Then he had to listen to excuses from his sister all the way down. When he got outside the building, he walked away from the clot of fools who still went out there to smoke, and recommenced the begging.

"Look, I'm not asking here, Pam. The guy has two hours on us. Mikey may be in the trunk. How much air has she got? If I get on the road now, it could be too late. I have maybe twenty minutes. Maybe thirty. I need a bird."

"Well, she could be gone by now, too," Pam said, still cold.

"Hey!" Pete said sharply. "Let's not make that leap. That's wrong."

"All right, all right." Pam was pulling his chain a little, stalling. "How do you know the farm's where they're going?"

Pete moved further away from the building. He didn't want to beg for help where anyone could hear. "Look, Mikey identified the bike of two missing college kids down there. We've got some other missing individuals, associates of George and Ali and Samir. This may be their killing ground. Ya know? He could be taking Mikey to a place he's comfortable."

"I hear you. But like I said before, everything's requisitioned for tomorrow already. I asked. I can't get you one. What's wrong with your people? You dropped the ball. Last sighting of Tamlin was on your turf. You should bear."

"Shit." She was ticking him off big time. And so was the weather. The rain on Pete's face felt like sweat after a marathon, only a lot colder. His tension level was off the charts. Even when it wasn't raining, Portland wasn't exactly packed with helicopters you could hail like cruising taxis. The county had its Search and Rescue birds. There were the med vac ambulances, DHS had some.

"What about the county?" Pam asked.

"They're occupied," he admitted. He'd gotten a bunch of answers to his request, all of them no. What could he say, the chief wanted them to drive?

Pam clicked her tongue. "Well, there you go."

"I think we both bear some responsibility here." Pete finally ducked for shelter.

Pam didn't respond.

"She's an agent, Pam. Come on."

"Not anymore."

"C'mon. Could be one of us. We didn't do well by one of our own. Let's face it. She came to town, we ignored her. We treated her almost as bad as brother Claude. You know we did. If she dies, our fault."

"I'd say more your fault than mine. She came to you; you didn't help. But you do have a point. Why don't you get someone private? How about Med Flights? You know people. Get one of your hotshot pilot friends to take you."

"Just tell me straight out, Pam. You can't get one because of the weather, right?" Pete prodded.

"Something like that," she admitted finally.

"Well, it's looking much better out here now." He looked up, got rain in his face, and shivered. "Do I have to go to the Pentagon with the story that the Feebles let an agent go? Huh?"

"All right. I know someone who loves to fly in the rain." She caved for him, but then she always did.

"Good. Tell him we can land in the parking lot of Archery Summit. Know where that is? They've got good sodium lamps up there, and the farm is located five miles up the hill on the same road. I can get some cars."

"It's a her." Pam told him.

"Who's a her?" Pete was confused.

"The pilot is a her. She's ex-military."

Pete scratched his nose. "Okay. I'll congratulate her on that when I see her. You're sure she'll do it?"

"Yeah, she's kind of different. Real low on the fear factor chart, no boss to tell her what to do. See you on the OHSU roof in ten."

Pam hung up.

"I love you, too, sis."

Pete went in to get Felix. When he told him he'd gotten a copter but the pilot was a girl, and sister Pam was coming along, Felix's expression was a joy to behold. He raised his thick line of black eyebrows, and his face read, Whaddyagonnado? If it was a single pilot, launching from Pill Hill, it was clearly not law enforcement.

Ten minutes on the roof was not a long time. Pete guessed that Pam had responded after his first request and called in a favor from Medvac. Nice of her to tell him she was on it.

60

Michael woke when the car left the main road and began the last stage of its climb to the summit. It was gray outside, not yet dark. She was fully awake in an instant. The driving rain had stopped, but fog hugged the ground like a blanket, dimming the light outside the car to almost nothing. No one would find her here. No one was coming. She had that thought. This was worse than Louisiana, where at least she'd believed backup would keep her safe. There'd been a lot of it. In the end, though, you can't rely on anyone. It's always just you and the other guy. And if you think about him for even a second, you're gone. That was a fact.

In Louisiana, she'd fired as fast as she could, and still there were two bullets in her vest. Any time she wanted, she could conjure that moment of impact when the slugs slammed into her, hard enough to knock her down but not stop her. She'd probably never forget firing when she should have been dead. How many people get shot in the heart twice and live to remember it? That was the good part. It felt like shit to take someone out, especially when you hadn't seen it coming. But still, you got a certain confidence knowing you wouldn't wimp out with a bad guy's cannon in your face. She comforted herself now with that experience under her belt, even though it had seemed disgraceful at the time.

All right, all right. This time she'd been really stupid. She'd been taken by an amateur. One tap on the head, and she was down. Managed the big one, lost on an easy one, it didn't feel good. But she'd get this Samir. No doubt about that. She'd get him.

From the front seat there was the faint glow from the dashboard lights. The headlights were on. She didn't know how long she'd been sleeping in that cramped position on the backseat. Maybe it had been a half an hour, probably not much more. The car was small. She was closer to the driver than she wanted to be and didn't have enough room to get where she wanted to be without bucking and rolling on the seat. And that kind of movement made young Samir anxious.

"What are you doing?" He screamed at her if she even tried to stretch a little. If he'd been smart, he would have just shoved her in the trunk. But maybe the joker hadn't the time.

Michael's stomach growled. Too bad hunger wasn't taking a break for the situation. And she was thirsty, too. There were a lot of things to consider, but she focused on her water bottle, last seen on the passenger seat. And the untouched half of sandwich she hadn't eaten at her desk many hours ago. Black forest ham and brie, with a slathering of mango chutney. Just before she left, Mary Lou had hinted that her lover would like it, so she'd given it away. Still hoping in vain that something more exciting would come up. Call her a dreamer.

The thought of her lost opportunity with Pete snapped Michael out of it. She moved to get a look at the clock on the dashboard, kicked with her legs to push herself up.

"Stop that!" Samir screamed. "What do you think you're doing?"

"Just want to know what time it is," she said. A reasonable question, she thought. She was sitting up now, feet on the floor, still wearing shoes.

"Doesn't matter to you," he said.

"Yes, it does. Where are we?" she asked.

"Fuck if I know," he muttered.

The space was so tight she could almost hear his heart beating fast. He wasn't any happier than she was. Interesting. He didn't know where the farm was. He had slowed the car to a crawl, was looking around, trying to figure it out. But she remembered the way. The directions were in her BlackBerry, the GPS system in the car, and in her head. She was always careful about these things, liked her backups. All he had to do was turn one of them on. He knew where she lived and worked, but he didn't know anything else. She guessed he was a lowly minion, errand boy, killer, and nothing more.

Gravel under the tires crunched on the unpaved road. Samir took a turn. The car skidded sideways in a muddy place and almost went into the ditch. With no seat belt on and nothing to hold onto, Michael fell over. Samir swore and pulled the car out of it but didn't speed up. Deep rain ditches on either side of the road and the sharp turns were intimidating him. Michael righted herself so she could look out.

Samir stopped the car at the first turn-off, the one that led to the abandoned mine. The road went down a steep hill to some boarded-up buildings. But this was only one of many places where the road went down before it went up again. There were other turn-offs further on, too, farm roads that led into the vineyards. She'd mapped it all out for DHS. He didn't know whether to make the turn or not.

"Want me to drive? I know the way," she offered.

Samir made a disgusted noise.

"I was here over the weekend. Call Frank and ask him. I know all about this place."

He shook his head. He wasn't calling Hamid.

"You're lost. You don't know anything about Frank's operation, do you?" Disappointment sounded in her voice.

The car started up with a jerk, knocking her against the backseat. Then stopped again, flinging her forward into the seat in front of her. Her head pounded.

"You're dead now," he muttered, like an angry kid. "You're dead!"

Fine by me, time for my exit, she thought. If he opened the back door on his side, he'd have to reach way in to get her out. She'd kick like crazy. Or...he could shoot her where she was. Would make a mess, but he could do it. If he came around to the passenger side, she might have a minute or so to roll to the floor, wiggle around to open her secret compartment, reach for the clippers, cut the plastic restraints and finally shoot him with her back-up gun. All that would take more than a minute, however. No way she'd be able to accomplish it before he opened the door. She needed him out of the car to get the compartment open. It didn't make any noise, but the space was tight. She usually accessed it by leaning in from outside the car.

After some moments, the car started inching forward again. Samir wasn't going to kill her in the car. He had other plans. She flashed to Farber, who'd been shot with his own gun. It was possible that Samir didn't have a gun. Then what weapon did he have?

"I know about the drugs," she said after a few minutes. She almost felt sorry for him. Poor guy was lost with a hostage he hated, and couldn't take her out because he was committed to torturing her if he ever found his destination.

"You're pissing me off!"

"I offered to drive. I'm telling you what I know. Come on, prove you're not just a lackey. Tell me something I don't know."

"I'm not going to tell you about the business, so forget it," he said. Then, abruptly he took the second turn-off, the one that would land them in the middle of the vineyard.

"I'm a lieutenant, not a lackey. And this is bigger than you think," he muttered.

That didn't help much. What kind of bigger? She looked out at the road and the fading light and wondered how long it would take Samir to figure out that he was stuck in a field. She couldn't wait much longer. It was just about time to make her move.

61

A Bell 407 was waiting on the hospital pad where the Medvacs came in. It was red. Life Flights was detailed on the side, which meant it was private. Pam stood near it, dressed for work. Blue pants, flak jacket with FBI on the front and back. Her favorite FBI baseball hat that had seen a lot of bad weather. Hair in a no-nonsense pony tail. Pete's face cracked with a smile to see her there. The rain had let up for the moment. Fog was lifting. One hospital worker followed him and Felix out, hoping for a smoke. When he saw the bird and the FBI jacket, he turned around and went back inside. You weren't supposed to smoke up there, and you weren't supposed to ask questions about what was going on, either.

Sometimes the weather threw curves. The building was high on the hill and tall enough to be shrouded in the clouds often. Sometimes dangerous gusts of wind whipped across the roof, preventing any attempts at lift off. Right then it was quiet. The Bell wasn't tied down. It was ready to get out fast, before the weather changed again. Pete hurried toward it. Felix was one step ahead. He got to Pam first and shook her hand.

"Hey, gorgeous," he said. Felix was in uniform, wearing a vest. Pete was not in uniform, but also wearing a vest. They might have county people waiting for them, but there was no way to know what they'd be walking into. Could be one person, could be a crowd. They both carried large PPD bags loaded with equipment.

"Felix, how's it going?" Pam replied. Her eyebrow arched at her brother. "Pete."

Pete wanted to grab her for a hug, but didn't. This was business. His eyes traveled to the hefty blonde in the red flight suit that matched the color of her bird. She stepped into the circle for introductions and he could see she was beautiful.

"Jenny Leight, my brother Pete. Felix Torres. Both PPD." As if it wasn't clear from the gear.

Jenny shook their hands in turn. Bone crunching grip. She made strong eye contact, checking them out. "Pleasure."

"Thanks for doing this," Pete said. He glanced at the Bell and wondered if it was hers. "Single pilot?"

"She's Air Force. Combat trained," Pam said.

Jenny smiled. "It's all right, Pammy. I can take the question. We do a minimum crew of three on a rescue. We're configured for single pilot and five passengers today. We can take up to seven without the equipment. We have PA speaker and NVG if we need it. Pam can take over if I have a heart attack," she tagged on at the end.

"Good to know," Pete said, about Pam taking over. He knew she was a licensed pilot. The night vision system might come in handy, too. He and Felix had some extra fire power—assault rifles, flares, water, basic first aid, plenty of communication. He didn't know what Pam would be carrying. His hope was they would have to deal with only one person.

"Smoothest, quietest ride in its class. Great hover and maneuverability, it's perfect for extreme environments." Jenny was still bragging on her aircraft.

"I knew that," Pete said.

"We could probably do a roll-over if you'd like." She was a talker.

"Maybe some other time." Felix rolled his eyes.

"Let's move," Pam said. "Still going to Archery Summit?"

Pete nodded. "Last check they were close."

"Okay. Jenny's a wine buff. She knows where it is."

They climbed in. The pilot's seat was on the right of the aircraft. Pam closed the bifold door and took the left side. The two men stowed their bags with the rescue stretcher, litter rig, rope bags and rescue kit. They were all set.

"Buckle up," Jenny said. You didn't have to yell in this bird.

Pete and Felix fastened their harnesses and locked eyes as Jenny fired up the Rolls Royce engine. The rotors turned slowly, then faster. The engine sounded good. The two women were concentrating on the panel and controls. A few drops of rain hit the window as they lifted off without a problem.

Fifteen minutes later they passed the lights shining up from the winery parking lot and kept going.

"We have a signal from the Acura in a field up here. Let's take a look," Jenny said.

Pam turned to Pete. "Can you do a vertical?"

"Huh?"

"If we can't find a place to land, we'll hover. Can you go down?" she asked.

Pete glanced at the tech rescue packs and back at his sister. You needed experts to assemble the harness and pulleys. You didn't just get in a swing and go down. He'd seen rescue teams in action. It was complicated. No way he was going to attempt.

"All right. I'll do it," she said, rolling her eyes.

He shook his head. Hell no, that was the stupidest thing he'd ever heard. He wasn't letting his sister hang from a bird with a dangerous suspect on the ground.

"We'll check it out first. The car may be abandoned," he said. "Then we'll decide."

62

The track Samir had followed ended among the vines. It stopped before the end of the row in a strange place where there was hardly enough space for a farm truck to turn around. Samir almost drove into a fully leafed, staked grapevine. He braked with a jerk, knocking Michael around some more. She didn't swear. He did.

"Shit!" For a few moments he sat there cursing. "Fuck. Fuck!"

Dumb criminal, Michael thought again. You have to plan for this kind of thing, and he just hadn't been on top of any part of this except the part where he hit her on the head. He was lucky no one looked in the car and noticed a bound and battered women in the back seat. His luck stopped when she woke up, and he didn't know where he was going. Some men just couldn't multitask. Michael could teach him a few things about organization.

Right now all he had to do was turn around, go four-tenths of a mile, and turn left to snake higher. But Samir didn't make the move. Maybe he was daunted by looming evening without familiar twinkling lights to comfort him. This was country. No house was in view. The established wineries were several miles back. The fucker was alone and apparently not quite so confident now.

"Let me out for a minute. I need to pee," Michael said quickly. She'd gotten herself propped against the passenger side back door where she was able to reach the lock and pop the door open. She'd thought about it all the way down the road. At some point the car would stop and she'd have to get going. But if she opened the door now, she'd just fall out onto her head. And that part of her body had already suffered enough punishment for one day.

"Fuck," Samir said again.

"Oh, fuck yourself," Michael wanted to say. But her head hurt too much to argue.

He turned around to look at her. From where he sat he

couldn't see her feet on the seat facing his direction. She was still wearing her favorite heels, navy, with white piping around the top and sides. It had to be some kind of record for keeping her shoes on. Her limit was usually five minutes. These platforms with spike heels and closed toes were too pointy for Portland. They were copies of much more expensive designer do-me shoes, the kind women wear when they don't plan to walk anywhere. Samir shook his head about letting her out. Maybe he remembered them.

"Hold it for the shower," he said.

"I can't hold it. I have to go," she whined.

"It's your car. You want to piss in it, go ahead. Doesn't matter what you do now."

"I'll be quick. You can watch," she offered. What the hell, it worked with some people.

"I'll watch when we get there," he said.

No, you won't, she thought. He could have made the three-point turn and gotten out of there, but her request seemed to trigger a need of his own. He got out and stretched, leaving the motor running and the door open.

She'd asked to pee; now he was going to take the opportunity instead. Fine with her. He walked away a few feet and didn't look back. He wasn't going to do it with her watching. He was too modest to unzip even with his back to her. He stepped behind a curtain of pinot, and she waited.

It was quiet in the vineyard, darkening now and chilly as the day was finally ending. Michael listened for the splash of a tiny waterfall and then lowered herself down to the button on her hiding place. She was on her back, feeling her way, looking at the ceiling of her car when she heard something else: the distinct hum of a helicopter. She was sure of it. Someone was coming, after all. And then, over the buzzing bee, came the sound of a man pissing long and loud on a grapevine. Samir was out of sight. Michael was busy with her hands. Then he was back.

"Hey, what are you doing there?" he barked.

"Nothing."

"The hell." He leaned in the driver's side and flipped on the interior lights. "Jesus. What's that?"

"Nothing," she said.

But he didn't believe her. He was coming around to look anyway. Michael made the roll. She pulled herself up and swung her legs around. She was facing him when Samir opened the door.

"What's that?"

"You're too late. They found us," Michael said as the copter noise increased.

Samir backed out to look up as a helicopter made a low pass over them and dipped away. Michael waited, hoping she'd get lucky and he'd run away.

But he made another poor choice. He leaned in again, curious about the button under the seat.

"Get back," he ordered.

"There's nothing in there but trouble," she told him. "We're friends. I wouldn't lie to you." She said this without irony, but it made him mad.

"Get back," he shouted.

Okay, she'd warned him. She pulled as far away as she could, leaning toward the open front door and the good supply of sweet, wet air. Above them the roar returned as the bird circled back.

"Run, Samir. Run while you have the chance," she said.

"Fuck you."

He moved closer, and that's when she saw the brass knuckles on his left hand. He must have hit her with those when she went down. He was a lefty. He pulled a push dagger from a holster on his belt and gripped it between the fingers of his right hand. No, he was a righty. Samir was no longer thinking about delayed gratification of torturing her later. He wanted to hurt her now and had the means in both hands.

She made a move as if to push the button with her heel.

"Bitch!"

He struck with the knife, missed her leg, and slashed the leather seat. Then he leaned in and punched the button fast, the wrong one. The hidden door popped open and sprayed: mace in the face. Two shots, one after another. He screamed.

Samir's hands went to his eyes. The knife in his right hand slashed his cheek. He screamed again. Michael kicked him in the balls. His hands dropped to his groin. She kicked him in the face, caught him with a heel and pushed hard, freed her foot and kicked again. He struggled to get out but was trapped in the car. The door half closed on him. He collapsed forward on the seat. Blood pooled around him.

The helicopter hovered overhead.

"Police. Drop your weapons and back away from the vehicle," came the command from the PA system.

That was asking a lot, Michael thought. Her head hurt and her eyes stung from the mace. She coughed a few times, too. Nothing from Samir. She figured if he was dead, it would play better if they found her with the plastic cuffs still on.

63

The bird moved in a slow tight circle for several minutes while commands were issued over the roar of the engine. Michael imagined what they'd be seeing from the air. A car with the lights on, parked in the middle of nowhere with exhaust steaming out, and the driver's door open. They'd see a male half in and half out of the passenger side back door. Legs and feet on the ground, head and torso hidden inside the car; he wasn't moving. And there would be no sign of Michael. She was not exactly hiding, but now that the incident was over she didn't need to get out and send up flares. They knew her location. If they thought she was dead right now, they'd have a pleasant surprise. She just didn't have the tools to get out easily. She was still opposed to falling out and landing on her head.

When nothing happened on the ground, the bird swung away and disappeared. Michael knew they'd be back, but still it seemed like seven hours before a deputy's car roared down the track and ground to a stop, not too close. By this time it was full dark outside the car.

"Mike."

She heard Pete's voice calling, and it was a sweeter sound than any she'd ever heard in her life. He'd come. He might be late for the performance, but still he'd come for the show. Maybe they'd get that dinner, after all.

"Get me out of here," she said. Calm as she could. Then, because she wanted to be professional, she added; "I didn't shoot him."

She'd stayed put in the back seat for this moment, just in case it was he who found her. Her hands were pulled tight behind her back. Her shoes were still on, but she knew they were evidence. She crossed her legs. Her head was against the back seat, eyes closed against the mess on the seat beside her. She'd talked to Samir the whole time she waited for help, but he hadn't responded. Her heel had caught deep in one of his eyes. She was pretty sure he was gone. All she could think about was that he had a knife, and she was unarmed. They'd see that. And she hadn't shot him. She had a little sensitivity about that.

A female looked through the window and swore. "Oh, Jesus. Michael, are you all right?"

"Yeah." She said the right words. "I'm not harmed. I just can't open the door."

The next thing she knew she was out of the car, on her lethal feet, smelling the fragrant, misty night air, shivering a little as she flexed her cramped back and shoulder blades. Pete cut the cuffs with a pair of clippers.

"Thanks." Her muscles stung, tingled, screamed as she raised her hands over her head and stretched. Okay. That was better. He'd rescued her, sort of. She wanted to hug him, but looked around to get her bearings instead. Red lights flashed from several sheriff's department units. And then she got a closer look at the woman who'd asked if she was all right. Was that Pam, from the supremely uncaring FBI?

"Pam?" she said, incredulous.

"Sorry it took so long." Pam gave her a hug; she wasn't so shy about PDA. "I'm sorry. For a lot of things."

"It's all right." Michael found herself hugging back. "Thanks for coming," she said.

"Pete called me," Pam said. "He was on it from the start."

"My hero," Michael murmured, daring to look at him for the first time.

He wasn't so shy about PDA either. He hugged her tight. "You okay?" he said in her ear.

"Yeah, I'm okay. But I think there's brain matter on my car seat." She didn't want to go soft, not right then. They stood there for a beat too long, holding on. Michael hadn't been imagining it; the chemistry was definitely there. And he was a more reliable guy than his brother. Felix came up and patted her on the back.

Felix here, too? "Thanks," Michael told him. "Thanks for coming."

He laughed. "Good to see you, too."

One of the deputies came over. He was a young guy and

looked a little spooked. "He's gone. Want to take a look?"

Pete held Michael at arm's length. They locked eyes. No question about it. Something beyond the present situation was there between them. Just for a little while it might be nice, she thought.

"Felix and I are going to take a look. I'll be right back. You okay for a few minutes?" he asked.

She nodded. "I couldn't get any information from him except he's the one who killed Farber. Hamid was on the phone with him ordering him to burn me up in the barn tonight. We have him on that. Abduction with conspiracy to commit murder."

Pam looked impressed. "You did just fine."

"Yeah, good work," Pete said. "Anything you need right now?"

Michael leaned in close until they were heart to heart again. She knew she didn't smell so great, but it felt really good. He held his arm around her protectively as she whispered in his ear. "There's a compartment under the seat he was trying to get into. There's a lot of stuff in there that could raise questions if there were an inquiry in this jurisdiction. Could make trouble for me and my agency down the road. Will you close the door for me?"

"No kidding." He touched the back of her head where she had the mother of all bumps. "We'll see to that head injury in just a minute."

Then he and Felix joined the locals to look at the dead man. Pam and Michael followed and watched. Michael wondered how this story would be told. Self defense in a car-jacking? She was pretty sure Samir still had knuckle dusters on one hand. The nasty little push knife had fallen to the floor in the fight. Self defense was a legitimate defense, but she didn't want to have to make it again, especially as a civilian. There'd be a hearing. She'd have to tell about the golf course incident, Samir's delivery to her house. The whole bank thing. It wasn't just a simple car-jacking. There was a wider conspiracy. She watched Pam's face as she took in the scene and tried to figure out what happened. Then realization dawned. Pam looked down at Michael's bloody shoes and up at her face. Really?

Michael nodded, just a little sheepish. The heel did it.

"Looks like a gang hit to me," Pete was telling the deputies. "Knife slashed him and went right into his eye. Pull him out, will you? We have to get going."

The two deputies lifted the body out of the car and laid it on the ground. Pete flicked the knife out, too. It landed close to the remains. Then he went in and took a look at the compartment. Guns, files, computer, and the unmistakable odor of mace. He shut the door and turned to Pam.

"Car needs a wash," Pete told her, deadpan.

"Okay, I'll drive it," she said.

It was Michael's turn to be impressed. Local law enforcement was relegated to clean up while the visiting team collected all the evidence. Looked like they were catching the bus back home for the next game. Pete put his arm around her and motioned for Felix. They took one unit and left the other unit and two deputies behind. It seemed agreed on ahead of time. Neither deputy said a thing to stop them. The bird was gone. Pam put the Acura in reverse, and the four of them disappeared as if they'd never been there.

64

Frank Hamid had a martini in his hand at Pacific Fresh. He and his guests were just about to sit for their first course when some men in suits came in to talk with him. He was gone before anyone knew he was leaving. He didn't have time to say good-bye or leave instructions with anyone. He was discreetly escorted into a car and taken to a secure location where life as he had known it ended. His cell phones and communication with the outside world were the first things to go. So he did not know that Samir had not been able to burn down the buildings at the farm. He couldn't even call his lawyer. He was in a different system now. His pilots and flight attendant were picked up, and some other known associates. But George and Ali were not among them.

George and Ali knew nothing about what was going on. They arrived at the lodge at nine. At midnight they left the camp with a detonator, homemade bomb, and accelerant that would add kick to the explosion made by the six tanks of anhydrous ammonia. George had convinced his brothers that he had no other choice but to blow up the police station. This action had to be taken immediately, and no one gave him an argument. George then drove the van down to Route 90 and rented a room in a motel on the Washington State side of the river where Ali spent the night obsessively fiddling around with wires and electronics.

That's how George and Ali avoided being caught in the raid when the lodge was hit by Special Forces at five in the morning. Three bedraggled young men jumped to defend the place in their underwear. Only Paul Othman ran away. He didn't get very far. And the word was out again that George and Ali were still in the wind.

About an hour later, a patrol officer nearing the end of his tour spotted George's Toyota in a panel truck rental lot within the Portland city limits. The owner was awakened at home and asked to meet two officers at his business as soon as possible. He was there in fifteen minutes, eager to help. He explained that he was just the owner and didn't process rentals himself, but he was able to locate the receipt for the truck rented by Ali Satan. He remarked that the name was unfortunate and wanted to know what Ali had done.

"Just wanted for questioning is all we know," the officer told him.

The owner handed over the receipt with the license plate number of the truck. "Anything else I can do?" he asked.

Yeah, there was. The officers wanted to know if the trucks had any kind of locators. The owner admitted that he'd had problems with stolen trucks recently because of the economy, so now all of them were equipped with chips in case they weren't returned. A signal was picked up for Ali's rental on Route 90 north of Carson at 7:00 a.m.

By 7:20, helicopters were buzzing like bees overhead. One had been in the air on morning traffic watch. Two others were law enforcement, booming commands above the roar of the engines. For someone who had stayed out of the spotlight for so long, George was as bewildered by the attention as he was frightened by the caravan of police cruisers following him with their sirens screaming and red lights flashing.

"Oh, shit." Ali bounced in his seat like a kid at the circus. As if he thought the whole thing was way cool.

"Shut up," George barked. Traffic was heavy, and he needed to concentrate.

"George Hamid, in the white truck. Pull over. Pull over." The command came from above.

"The fuck?" How did they know it was him? Didn't matter, he wasn't pulling over. He thought he could get around this and escape. His brain didn't compute. It told him he could do it. A tanker on his right prevented him from pulling around the car in front of him, though. He couldn't outrace the tanker.

"George Hamid, pull over."

The van weaved in morning traffic. Cars were trying to get

out of the way, but nobody slowed down. It was as if all the morning commuters had agreed to stay in the race for the city to see who'd beat the van chased by the police, and get there first.

For George, time slowed down and speeded up at the same time. The command kept coming from above, and on the highway the traffic clogged as they neared the I5 bridge. George saw that he was getting boxed in. There was no opening to squeeze through. There was a click. It seemed audible but could have come from either his head or Ali's. George turned and saw that Ali had stopped bouncing. His body was completely still for the first time in nearly a year. He'd stopped fiddling with the detonator and held it in his hand with a fixed expression. In a split second George could see him making that shift in his head from wanting a fix to wanting it over. He'd hoped for that click to occur as Ali drove the into the Central Station garage alone. Instead, it was happening now. As the traffic slowed, Ali made his decision.

"Fuck it," he said.

"Nooooo!" George screamed and lost control of the wheel as Ali hit the detonator. The van blew just as it slammed into the tanker. Everything around it crashed and burned.

When the blast occurred, Pete and Michael were about a mile back in the truck, responding to the call they'd received in Pete's cabin where they had spent the night. They felt the ground shake and saw fire shoot up into the sky. The pile-up and fire that resulted involved thirty-seven vehicles. Fifty-two people died. Hazmat teams converged within the hour and wouldn't let rescue teams in to help the wounded until radiation levels had been assessed and other tests for deadly toxins had been made.

In catastrophes, cops and first responders are trained to get to the scene anyway they can, and as fast as possible. Pete was no exception. He didn't wait for the traffic to lock or the hazmat people to arrive. While the shock waves were still reverberating in the morning mist, he slammed his bubble light on the roof, hit the siren, maneuvered the truck into the breakdown lane, and sped toward the blaze to help any way he could. He handed Michael his cell phone and told her what to say.

EPILOGUE

It's a well-known fact that people disappear in Oregon. Also that people are found whose real stories can never be told. Matt Brand and Cheli Abrio's remains were found at Blackberry Farm the next day. Autopsies performed several weeks later revealed their horrifying cause of death, but no one ever learned what they had been doing there. Two Yamhill County deputy sheriffs, who said they had been called to the scene by an anonymous tip, found the body of Taboule restaurant manager, Samir Yassim, in a vineyard nearby. Although many officers in the PPD had been involved in the search for abducted Treasury CI Michael Tamlin, no hint of her ordeal or involvement in his death was ever leaked to the press. Even Mary Lou Loughlin never knew what really happened.

Months later, the media was still carrying stories about the twisted lives, misguided loyalties, and deadly jealousy of suicide bombers George Hamid and Ali Satan, who were responsible for what came to be known as the I5 bombing. The police did not know what their target had been, but they believed the two young men were most likely the perpetrators of two of the Blackberry Farm homicides.

As the weeks passed, article after article came out about Frank Hamid's operations, some true and some false. Raids uncovered two hastily-abandoned camps in Washington State. Hamid never revealed why the camps had been evacuated so suddenly, who the inhabitants had been, or where they had gone. But his Pearl District warehouse held a treasure trove of information that helped to answer some of those questions. The warehouse was where false documents were assembled and travel plans for incoming individuals were made. All of it was left behind. Another raid discovered the training camp where the four young anarchists had been making bombs. But those stories were not for publication.

And others were. Sometimes ambitious reporters take a wrong turn and get rewarded for it. Articles about Hamid's drug and bomb-making activities and his support for the terrorist cause won a Pulitzer Prize for their author, but were completely untrue.

Unfortunately for Hamid, a host of circumstantial evidence and his complete lack of credibility overrode all his protestation of innocence concerning the Blackberry Farm and Lodge operations. No one believed that he knew nothing about the activities of his nephew and the other young men in his employ, or the four bomb makers who were living at his lodge at the time of their arrest. The evidence of major marijuana cultivation on all his properties was too incriminating. His insistence that he had done nothing wrong with his hedge fund or trips abroad--that he was merely a business-man doing things the American way--did not get him out on bail while prosecutors prepared the many cases.

New World Hedge Fund, along with all the investors and charities it supported, was the first thing to go down. Searches were instituted for all the people Hamid brought into the coun-try. Many of them were caught trying to flee. Some were still being sought.

At Pac GreenBank, the president, general counsel, and several other employees were fired and subsequently indicted on a number of Patriot Act, fraud, and money laundering charges that would put them away, if convicted, for the rest of their lives. Ashland Upjohn proclaimed his innocence of all wrongdoing, blaming any irregularities at the bank on a criminally negligent compliance de-partment headed by the late Allan Farber. Clifton Caulahan ar-gued that he'd been kept in the dark by his lead counsel.

Michael never got her car back or returned to work for the bank. Before twenty-four hours had passed, when the I5 was still a smoldering mess, she got a call from Max.

"I hear you need some new stilettos," he said.

"Hi, Max. How's by you?" she replied. Cool, and yet excited. He'd called himself. No intermediary.

"There's a sale at Neiman's. I hear they've got the kind you're looking for." He laughed softly.

"Are you offering me a raise and a medal?" she asked.

"No. You're lucky we're talking," he said.

"Any perks at all?" she asked.

"I'll forego the public humiliation. How's that?" Max laughed again.

"Wait a minute. You guys had no idea what was going on out here. You wanted me in Portland. Who knows what would have happened without my help in this case. I'd like a medal."

"Not everybody is so appreciative. Just get out of there as quietly as possible. Don't talk to anybody. I don't know, maybe we can cover your costs home."

"Portland PD mashed my car into a brick."

"I'm sorry to hear that. We're not buying you a new one. Are you okay?" he added after a moment.

"Yeah. Yeah, I'm okay."

"Good," he said. "Good."

An outsider wouldn't have guessed they liked each other, or that anything important had been said. Michael didn't have anything to add. Lot of things she didn't know about what went down, but she figured she'd be fully briefed soon enough. She had a few dollars in the bank. She guessed she could buy a new car. The economy was so bad the car dealers would probably fight over her. What else was there?

"You did well, Michael. Your job and your apartment are still here. Next time you'll have more support."

She let him wait. Maybe ten seconds. Pete was a nice guy and a great lover, but relocating without a much better reason than that didn't seem like such a good idea anymore.

"Okay. Give me a week. I have a few things to take care of."

She wanted to spend some time with Pete, talk to Christine Farber and Charlie Dorn, say goodbye to Mary Lou Loughlin, and tell them all she was there for them if they ever needed her in the months ahead. Then, after she hung up with Max, she steeled herself to finally call her mother and tell her the wedding was off.

Leslie Glass is the author of 15 novels, including the New York Times best-selling suspense series featuring NYPD Detective Sergeant April Woo. She is currently producing feature films and is the host of the Ezine ILoveQuitters.com. Leslie lives in Sarasota, Florida, New York City, and at authorleslieglass.com.

Breinigsville, PA USA
14 July 2010
241747BV00001B/216/P